I0623002

Aurora Rising

By

ALYSIA S. KNIGHT

Aurora Rising
By Alysia S. Knight
Published by Heart Dreams Press
Copyright © 2015 Alysia S. Knight
Cover design: by Kelli Ann Morgan @
www.inspirecreativeservices.com

All rights reserved. No part of this book may reproduced in any format or in any medium without written permission. Alysia@alysiasknight.com
The views expressed within this work are the sole responsibility of the author and do not represent Heart Dreams Press or any of its affiliates.

This is a work of fiction. Names, characters, place and events are product of the author's imagination. Any similarities to actual persons, living or dead, business establishments or events are purely coincidental.

All rights reserved.

ISBN:1-942000-15-4
ISBN-13:978-1-942000-15-0

Also available from Alysia S. Knight

☙❧

Past To Die For

Temperature Rising

Kare for Me

Blind Witness

Beauty and the Chief

Trail to Her Heart

His Governess

Her Brand of Trouble

The Ruins – Out of Time

My Spy

Whistleblower

Where There's a Will

☙❧

To my family and friends,
for all the love and support you have given me.
Thank you.

Alysia S. Knight

In a world where everyone has psychic talents, every child is tested at puberty, carefully screened to help guide them into the field that would coincide with their natural strength and interest. Degrees of talents normally range from low to average, but every once in a while one will spike off the charts, these special few usually become Guardians, protectors of the people.

For nearly a century, Guardians have protected from natural disasters, accidents and when evil arises. Now the Guardians face their strongest foe, a Guardian strength talent who is gathering a force of other strong, corrupt talents to help him wipe out the governing council and the Guardians so they can take over the world, turning it into a place where the strongest talents rule and the weaker would be subjected to serve them.

ALYSIA S. KNIGHT

Chapter One

"There's the transport." The loud cheer echoed over the throaty rumble of engines across the tarmac.

Rori stepped to the huge hangar doors in time to see the enormous slope-transport carrying sixty-two Ag-techs lumber into view around the last curve of the steep-sided canyon that led to the mountain terraces. Mud squished from tires taller than a man.

The collective sigh from the people gathered in the bay did nothing to alleviate Rori's anxiety. If anything it rose as she strode across the rain drenched pavement through the open doors. Alarm skittered across her nerves though she picked up the tendrils of relief coming from the people on the transport. She tried to believe it was their nervousness which had her worried but couldn't.

Her gaze shot to the waterlogged mountain side. The week-long rain had finally stopped but moisture hung heavy in the air and dripped from the thick foliage. For once the jungle's beauty did not reach her. She pushed out with her abilities, silly because she could not pick up emotions from the hillside. Still, within her, something didn't feel right.

Rori sensed the ground shift. Her gaze dropped back to the transport, its movement slow, laborious. She looked back to the hillside. She had no talent for elements, but again, she seemed to feel the ground groan as it pulled apart.

"Sound the alarm." Her voice was hushed, but she knew Matti could hear her, just as she knew he'd followed her out.

"What?" The comm-specialist turned his attention from the transport to her.

The noise of the vehicle drowned out all sound but inside her head. Rori tuned to the sucking noise of mud and rock.

"Sound the alarm." This time she yelled it over her shoulder as she broke into a run. Rori barely covered twenty meters before she caught the first rumbling movement. She willed her mind to hold back the hillside. Aware again it wasn't her talent but she couldn't get the image of sixty-two men and women, all friends, out of her mind. She forced the will from within her mind outward to hold back the now visible landslide.

Gasps of terror broke behind her, mingling with the shrill sound of the alarm. Inside Rori felt something rip free much like the landslide. Energy built within her, rolling forward, gaining as it went, directed through her outstretched hand forming a barrier between the mountain and the transport.

Rori cried out as a kilo-ton of rocks, mud and trees slammed against the mental-shield. Her knees buckled out from under her. She dropped to the ground, but she didn't break her focus.

Around her, she was aware of people screaming. Rescue teams gathered. Matti called her name. She ignored him.

"Raebent hues," Kinton, the rescue captain and her supervisor, cursed. "Rori's holding that thing up."

"Rori can't shield," someone objected. "And nobody can do that."

"Well, she is. And she's drawing energy in from all around her to do it. Get some med-techs and high energy talents to her now. We've got to keep her up or those people aren't going to make it."

Pain arced across Rori's forehead. She yearned to pull away from it, but Kinton's words echoed in her mind. *'Those people aren't going to make it.'* Rori felt the terror of the people on the transport, locked onto it and pushed more of her life force out. Still the slide pressed down, overflowing the sides of the shield.

Brown ooze slid over the back section of the transport. The wheels spun in the mud. The mammoth machine skidded to the side.

Rori groaned, feeling her hold weaken. The landslide crept its way down the hill. Tears filled her eyes blurring everything as she tried to keep the mountain back. Inside she fought for more energy. She felt the thread of power start to unravel in her mind. She pictured Ambery and Huson who lived next to her with their little two-year-old daughter. They were both on the transport.

Clawing deep down, Rori pulled more energy. Rising up on her knees, she reached out with her other hand toward the transport and willed it to her. Wheels spun without traction. Two-thirds of the vehicle was now covered in the mud. Rori wanted to cry but her mouth was too dry. Everything drained out of her. Pain crushed down, bowing her back.

Her vision began to fade when she felt the first tendrils of power enter her body, then around her she felt energy begin to pour in. She drank it in greedily, letting it course through her body and refocused it outward as more filled her. In her mind, she could almost make out the rope of power connecting her to the transport and pulled on it with all her might. The machine slogged forward.

At the end of the tarmac, teams of men with tow cables ran forward, hooking the huge loaders and tractors to the nose of the transport. As soon as the men were clear the heavy machinery pulled. Centimeter by centimeter, the vehicle edged forward and then with a loud slurping noise, it pulled free.

The cheer went up but Rori didn't notice as the shield collapsed. The landslide crushed its way down filling the mouth of the canyon where the transport had been a moment earlier.

ભૂૹ

Jattin Straye sank wearily into his large desk chair and took a moment to close his eyes and give thanks. It had taken all night for him and every other high level and several mid-level talents, working to capacity, siphoning off access energy, but Rori's levels were back to the normal range, at least normal for an extremely high level talent.

She was resting peacefully under heavy sedation. Chief Medic Therodor decided not to wake her until her mind had a chance to heal completely. Jattin knew by completely, they meant backing down to her previous levels. He also knew it wasn't going to happen. Aurora was at her normal level.

He opened his eyes and looked at the picture on his desk. Rori was ten, a thin, gangly girl always on the go. He remembered well that summer. He'd taken a leave from being head of The Guardians to try to repair the rift between him and his son, Roake, and his wife, Belise. It hadn't worked that way.

There was an immediate kinship between him and Rori that went past grandfather and granddaughter. It was the meeting of two high level talents, though Rori was too young to have developed her talent yet. Looking back, he knew it was a mistake to mention having Rori tested and trained. His son had blown up, yelling that the Guardians were all that was important to him, and he wasn't going to have that for Rori.

Jattin had to admit, for a long time it was true. After his wife died, it was what kept him going. He didn't know how to explain to his son the need to keep everyone else safe, so they didn't have to go through the terrible loss as he had or the guilt of not being there to save his wife. Well, that was in the past.

He leaned forward and called up a comm-link. After a second, a familiar face appeared. "Jattin." The thin chiseled face of his old friend, Manning Hiymm, grinned at him. "I thought life in an Ag-complex was supposed to be relaxing. You look worn out. Age catching up?"

"It was a long night."

"Problems?" The face turned serious.

"Nothing for you to worry about, it's all handled now. What I'm calling for is I have a new Guardian for you."

"Right." Manning grinned, then as if picking up that he was serious, Manning leaned toward the screen. "Jattin?"

"I'm serious," Jattin assured him.

Pleasure lit the face of the man who had replaced him as commander of the Guardians. "Name?" He placed his hands over the keyboard.

"Aurora Straye," Jattin announced and waited for the reaction. It wasn't long in coming.

"Aurora, Rori? Your Rori?"

"Yes."

"But you said Rori was a class four seeker and a class two empath. That's not nearly high enough to be a Guardian even if she is your granddaughter."

"You better watch this," Jattin said simply as he called up the recording. "Luckily, this was captured by a surveillance recording yesterday afternoon." Jattin stopped talking as the image of the transport appeared in the mouth of the canyon. There was no need to explain as the mudslide rushed toward the vehicle and crashed into an invisible barrier.

"That's impossible." The hushed words came over the link.

"Keep watching," Jattin returned unnecessarily as the transport seemed to be drawn forward, its wheels spinning uselessly, unable to get traction.

"That's impossible." The words repeated twice more before Jattin ended the recording. "You're saying your granddaughter did that? How many helped her?"

"She did it on her own for the first couple minutes until they could get other talents there to feed energy to her. Still she did it on her own."

"I can't believe that. I've never seen anyone do that. Why didn't you call me sooner?"

"I had to wait until they got her stable."

"Stable." Manning cut in. "She burned out?" Disappointment echoed in his voice.

Jattin knew it was because burnouts often never fully recovered all their abilities. "No, she was running hot. Anyone who could, has been tapping her all night. Her levels are now stable just extremely high. They're not going down." There was certainty in his voice.

"So what are we looking at?"

"I honestly can't tell you because she hasn't regained consciousness yet. And true, what she did on the tarmac was empathy pumped with an adrenaline reaction. But where her levels are, she's a great promise as a Guardian, even if it only ends up her empathy's that high. She could calm a crowd or ease masses in a disaster."

"That much pain is hard on a person."

"Yes. But the main problem will be training. She hasn't had extensive talent training, just as a basic search and rescuer. But think of the possibility as a locator, if her seeker talent is strengthened or if she can shield." Excitement pushed back the weariness in him. "I always knew Rori was stronger than testing showed."

"You sure it isn't wishful thinking?" Manning interjected in. "It may be her levels will drop back off."

"They won't. I've been thinking about this all night, and I think I figured it out." He looked to the picture on his desk. It was the key. "I came to visit when Rori was ten."

"I remember. The only vacation you ever took while

Guardian Commander."

Jattin nodded. "I wanted to make amends with my son. To say our relationship was strained is putting it mildly. But Rori and I bonded immediately. We spent a lot of time together. I swear I started to pick up fissures of strong talent in her, though she was too young for it to be showing up. I made the mistake of mentioning it to her parents. Roake and Belise went ballistic. Roake blamed the Guardians for the split with his mother, and in some respects it was true. But Marella was an Ag-tech and wanted to pursue that. I couldn't hold her back."

"And he couldn't forgive you any more than you can forgive yourself for not being able to save her," Manning finished. "Jattin, I'm aware of what happened, but what does that have to do with this?"

"I think Rori knew of the fight, either heard or sensed it. Knew it was centered on her and being a fledgling empath, and being raised with both parents showing distain for strong talents, she either consciously or subconsciously hid or tamped down her talent to ease her parents and the rift between us."

"What you're suggesting, I've never heard of before." Manning was quiet a minute. "But, it does make sense, if she was strong enough."

"As you said, if she was strong enough. When she was faced with the disaster yesterday, it tore through the, for want of a better word, shield she'd built around her talent, and all that repressed energy burst out," Jattin said, satisfied in his logic.

"So what do you think we are truly looking at?"

"As I said before, her empathy to comfort is high. I think that fed her seeker ability. She senses distress. But I also think she will have shield ability. It too may be linked to empathy and a need to protect. On a Guardian team, it would be incredibly useful. She'd have to be trained though." Frustration heightened Jattin's voice before he could temper it.

"You will always be a Guardian Commander." His friend chuckled, his own pleasure at the possibility of a new Guardian rising.

"It's such a waste though. I knew I sensed her right all those years ago. She should've been raised and trained properly to it. At least, she's been rescue trained instead of as an Ag-tech. That would have been a total waste."

"She's had rescue training?" Manning asked to clarify.

"Yes, top level certification. The youngest Rescue-tech they've ever had, and their chief is good, a solid mid-range talent, who's an excellent instructor."

"Interesting," Manning paused obviously thinking. He was still thoughtful when he started speaking again. "I have a young team that went through training together, and because they worked so well, they were kept together instead of splitting them with the other teams. They've only been operating just over a year but have a good success rate. Their leader is a very strong multi-talent. He may be the strongest ever. You might remember him since you oversaw his initial training."

"Keyen," Jattin stated firmly.

"Yes."

"But they had a full team?"

"No. Chall couldn't take the stress. She lost it a couple times and had to be pulled right after they started. I know you had concerns about her years ago. Another team member also couldn't take it and quit a couple months ago."

"It's tough and not for everyone, even if they are strong talents." Jattin nodded, feeling a touch of sorrow for the loss.

"It's not a total loss. Chall is teaching now with the younger levels and is doing quite excellent. It fits her better."

"I can see that for her. She just couldn't handle panic

situations well, no matter how she tried."

"Yes. Now, let's get back to Rori." Manning's anxiousness came through in his voice. "Do you think she will be willing? You mentioned her parents' disapproval of Guardians. Will that hold her back?"

"No. Rori is a protector. She won't be able to ignore the need," Jattin said with certainty.

"Then when do you think we can expect her?"

"A week, two at the latest."

Chapter Two

Rori watched out the window as the airglider descended to the docking terminal. The city of Rae-Isis stretched out as far as she could see. It took her breath though she'd been there twice before. Still, it was hard to imagine anything of its size. The majority of the population of Raeland lived around the city.

On her first visit, she had been a young child, clinging to her father's hand, gawking at everything, amazed at the height and number of the buildings. Neither of her parents liked cities. She'd felt their unease, and it had made her terrified until her grandfather had taken her up in his personal Air-rave, then she could hardly take in enough of it. It was fascinating, especially the huge bay extending out into the ocean.

On her second visit, when her grandfather was retiring and being honored for his service, he'd walked her to the beach that bordered one side of the Guardian Complex. He confided to her that he loved to relax there, and for the week, she'd joined him on his morning runs on the sand. Well, she'd get plenty of time to run there now.

She eyed the Guardian Complex barely visible in the distance. It looked like a huge shining sail against the azure background of the ocean. That would be her home for who knew how long.

Rori steeled her nerves then felt them jump as the glider dipped to their port. Buildings grew in size and the reality of her situation rose up to meet her. This was her new life. The light bump at the docking bay forced it home. Swallowing hard, Rori stood, retrieved her shoulder bag, slung it across her body and waited for her turn to disembark. People crammed the platform everywhere she looked. She stared, immensely overwhelmed.

"You agreed to this," she said aloud to herself. Drawing in a deep breath, she blew it out. How was she supposed to find who was to meet her? The only person she knew in the city was Manning Hiymm, who was an old friend of her grandfather's, his replacement, and her new boss. But the message she'd received with travel arrangements said Hiymm was unable to meet her but someone would be there.

Unease crackled over her nerves. Rori placed a hand to her forehead to steady herself. Since waking five days earlier, she'd been aware of so much more around her. It was like a veil had dropped and her senses were highly tuned. She felt different but right. Her grandfather assured her she'd get used to it. She knew it was true, but for now, she fought to control the sensations that battered her continually.

Rori shifted her gaze to the side, picking two men out of the crowd walking her direction. They were an odd pair. One was tall. His narrow frame was dressed to perfection in a tidy suit. The other looked like a walking block with a small head perched on top of his huge frame. His clothes were the type Ag-techs wore with numerous pockets.

Though neither were looking at her, she knew she was their prey.

Her hand froze midway up to flag them as the wave of malevolence hit her. Without thinking, Rori shifted to the side, slouching down among a group of people. She moved with them. She tried to tell herself she was being foolish but couldn't get past the feeling of – evil.

Reaching the end where the platform opened up into

the main terminal, Rori risked a look back. The men had stopped, looking around the area. The tall one lifted his hand and spoke into a comm-link. He spun her direction, nudging his partner with his elbow.

Knowing she'd been spotted, Rori lengthened her stride, looking around for an enforcement officer. Instead, her gaze met another pair moving toward her, this time a man and a woman, both wore black, like the archetypical bad guy.

There was a tightening around the woman's eyes, and pain slashed across Rori's mind. She staggered and pushed out subconsciously blocking the attack that she didn't even realize was one until the pain abruptly ended. Fury flashed across the woman's face. The woman's hand went to her own head, and she wobbled on the spiked heels she wore.

Around Rori the air began to feel hot. A few feet away a trash receptacle burst into flames. People started to scream, panic and run. The duos continued toward her, but Rori's attention shifted to a woman clinging to the hand of a small child as she was bumped and shoved by the crowd. The child stumbled, and the woman, trying to steady her, fell.

Rori reached her hand out to the woman as she wished the crowd to calm down. To her surprise, people slowed, and the pushing stopped. A man in a security outfit ran to put out the fire.

The four were almost on her. Rori darted to the man with the extinguisher. Snatching it out of his hands, she turned it directly into the faces of the man and woman. The woman screamed, but Rori was already swinging toward the other pair. The men pulled back, giving Rori the room she needed. Dropping the extinguisher, she took off in a sprint, weaving around people with no direction in mind.

"We'll get you." The words echoed in Rori's mind threateningly, but she didn't slow. As she ran, she slammed up a mental shield between her and the man who'd been

with the woman. It didn't take long for her to outdistance the block man, but the tall one kept up with her outside and down two streets, where her stamina training and climbing the mountainside around the settlement paid off. The distance between them spread out.

Taking the opportunity, Rori darted down a pedestrian walk packed with people. Ducking into the open doorway of a shop, she pulled back behind a rack of filmy dresses and waited. It wasn't long until she saw the man pass by. Searching, but obviously he couldn't sense her. She watched several minutes more before she let out a sigh then almost screamed when a hand landed on her arm.

"Sorry." The woman looked just as startled. "May I help you?"

Rori's knees felt weak, but she managed a reassuring smile. "Yes. Is there a comm-link I can use? Please, it's an emergency."

The woman eyed her a moment then nodded. "You can use the store's." She turned, leading Rori toward the back of the shop.

With a final look out the window, Rori followed. Calling up the link, for a moment Rori was afraid she was not going to be put through, so when the person asked who was calling she gave her grandfather's name. A voice answered almost immediately. "Jattin, is there a problem with Rori coming?" Then Manning Hiymm moved into the picture. "Rori."

"Director Hiymm, I think someone just tried to kidnap me," Rori said the words that sounded too unbelievable but true.

"What? Where are you?"

"I don't know. Not too far from the glider terminal, I think." She turned to the woman who stood not far away. "Excuse me, but can you tell me where we are?"

She repeated what the woman said.

"You're in Ray-Isis?"

"Yes, the glider was on time, but the people waiting to meet me ..." she paused, wondering what to say, how to describe them. "They were ... they were not from you." Finally she gave up and went with a simple, straightforward answer. "They felt evil. One started a fire. Another, I think she tried to disable me with her mind."

"Are you all right?" Concern was evident in the man's voice.

"Yes, I just have no idea how to get to the complex. I don't think I should trust a shuttle."

"No, don't get on a shuttle. I'll send my assistant Tasc for you. Wait for him in the shop. This is what he looks like so you can recognize him." An image filled the screen of a middle-aged man with a thin, angular face and balding head. "Stay out of sight. It shouldn't be long."

"Yes, sir." Rori disconnected and turned to find the shopkeeper was staring at her with an odd expression. At a loss how to explain, Rori said the first thing that came to her mind. "Is it all right if I wait here?"

The woman nodded and for the first time Rori noticed the aqua streak in her short, blonde hair.

"Would you like to look around?" the woman suggested, off-handedly.

Figuring it was the least she could do, Rori nodded and moved around the shop while keeping a discreet eye out the window. The place was filled with clothes made in lightweight materials and bright colors, totally different from her usual serviceable attire. Much to her surprise, Rori found several things that appealed to her. Especially a flowing mid-calf dress, that was about the same color of the woman's streak. When the clerk commented on how it matched her eyes, Rori took it as a hint and, since it wasn't too expensive, decided to buy it though she had no idea where she would ever wear it.

A few minutes later, Eton Tasc walked in. "Aurora Straye," the man greeted her formally. He was middle aged and shorter than her. What hair he had was cropped close to his head accentuating his sharp, bird-like nose.

"Yes, sir," Rori returned just as stiffly.

Tasc wasn't a man who inspired a relaxed, casual response. He was all business from his quiet confidence to his precise, quick movements. "If you'll follow me, you were not expected today."

The man turned and was already on his way out the door before Rori could question him. What did he mean she was not expected today? All the travel arrangements she'd been sent were for today. Rori hurried after him. Out on the sidewalk a man the size of a walking wall, wearing a uniform, fell in step behind her. Rori scanned the street but didn't see any sign of the attackers or anyone paying too much attention to her.

Deciding to experiment, she pushed out with her senses, trying to pick up any animosity in the crowd directed at her. For a second there was nothing, and then she was flooded with emotions from happy and relief, to anxiety and pain. She stumbled a step catching the wall to steady herself as she tamped down on her senses.

The emotions dried up immediately. Carefully, she tried again, this time focusing on one person, a man hurrying the opposite direction. She was about to give up and pull back when the emotions came through as clear as if they were her own. Excitement, anticipation, nervousness, and pleasure mixed with thrill and love. Rori caught her breath. The man broke into a run, disappearing around the corner. She wished him good luck knowing his wife was having a baby and that she was in labor now.

She turned her attention back to her own surroundings in time to notice they had reached the end of the pedestrian mall. Directly in front of them, in a no parking zone, sat a small multi-transport with a logo on the side that Rori recognized as the Guardians. Another man, not much smaller than the barrier, leaned against it.

Briskly, Tasc went around to the front side seat while the man against the transport straightened and released the latch for her to enter. Rori was forced to slide over to make room for the man following behind.

"Thank you, miss." The silence was broken as the man took the seat next to her.

As the other man settled in, Tasc addressed him in what Rori realized was Tasc's normal, efficient, demeanor. "Take us to the complex then come back and retrieve her belongings. If you'll give them your marker." He glanced back over his shoulder to make certain she complied.

Rori handed over the small, silver ident-marker and settled back for the ride. She turned her attention outside the window. Rae-Isis was remarkably clean and organized, laid out in a grid pattern with wide lanes that made travel easy. Shops along the way boasted a bright array of things to keep her attention until she caught sight of the Guardian Tower ahead.

They were close enough now to tell what gave an illusion of striping on the building was really balconies looking out at the ocean from the living quarters of the staff housed there. One of those would be hers, and from her grandfather living there, she knew it would be on the upper floors, closer to the main control room and Guardian docking bay for their personal air-riders or hoversleds.

That was going to be her home. The thought went through her mind for the thousandth time since she had regained consciousness. Her breath caught. It was going to be so different from her small home in the jungle settlement. She blew out the breath she'd been holding as they pulled up to the main front entry.

"Follow me." Again in his brusque way, Tasc was out of the transport heading for the main entry. Luckily, the walking wall got out quickly despite his size.

"Thank you," Rori said to the men. She caught what she thought might have been a grin passing between them as she hurried after the assistant before she lost sight of him.

Rori reached him just as the lift doors slid open. If she expected him to say anything in the way of preparing her for what lay ahead, she was mistaken.

Unable to take the silence any longer and deciding on another experiment, she again sent her mind out trying to figure out why he was so annoyed with her. What she received was an analytical, controlled competence. She probed deeper and found a layer of annoyance then realized it was not focused at her but at himself for not being prepared for her arrival. His mind was distracted, shuffling possibilities around, looking for an acceptable answer. She released the mind touch and pulled back.

"I want to thank you, Mr. Tasc, for coming to get me. I do appreciate your efforts."

The man looked at her in surprise. "You're welcome. Please, do not be distressed by the mix up on your arrival. I assure you we will work out suitable arrangements for you to stay tonight. Your new quarters will be ready tomorrow."

"I'm not concerned. Whatever you arrange will be fine, I don't need much." Rori tried to assure him.

"Yes." Tasc looked at her and really seemed to look at her. "You know, young lady." A spark of light lit his eyes. "It is not considered polite to use your talent to probe someone."

Rori's breath caught with her embarrassment that he knew what she'd done.

His lips twitched. "Then again after reading your chart, this is all a new aspect of your talent for you isn't it?"

"Yes." Rori felt herself start to blush even more.

"It's all right." The man actually grinned. "You need to explore and develop. You haven't had much time yet." There now was compassion in the man's voice. "Have you been able to identify any other emerging talents?"

"I'm not sure." Rori fumbled over the words.

Tasc's brow furrowed slightly and she knew he was studying her. After a second, he actually smiled. "Do not be concerned. You are a multi-talent like your grandfather, though much stronger. You will do well."

"Mr. Tasc?"

"Just Tasc is fine. Yes?"

"What is your talent, if I may ask?"

"Probably close to what you've surmised. My talents led me to organization. I see patterns, but I also can read talents in other people. Much like you were doing with emotions. I can usually figure out what they are. Place or sort them, if you will. You, though, are hard to read because you are so strong and varied. Your talents are muddy, overshadowing and layered. I'm guessing that is because they have been repressed and have not had the chance to develop individually yet. Dr. Narrasa should be able to tell you. He is over the physical and mental care of the Guardians. He is a strong reader besides a healer. It will be hard to catalog your talents, though, until you start to use them. I can tell you that. Also you will be a great asset to the Guardians."

Rori was shocked at all that came out of the man who had remained so brisk and quiet until then. "Thank you." Her insides quivered and she hoped what he said was true. She hated to admit but it worried her. Within her, things felt so strange but right.

Guardians usually went into training in their mid-teens and graduated out into full service at nineteen or twenty. And although she started rescue training at fifteen when she showed she was a searcher, finding a young girl lost in the jungle when no one else could, she was now nineteen years old. It sounded like she was being placed with an already existing team, so it would be basically on-the-job training. The thought terrified her.

"Through the doors. He's waiting for you." Tasc broke

into her thoughts nodding to the door, once more back to his abrupt manner.

Rori didn't need to send out her talent to know his mind was already focused on organizing things as needed. She forced herself to the door which slid open on cue. She'd liked Manning Hiymm when she'd met him years earlier. Still, she was nervous. He was turned away, talking to someone on the comm-link when she approached his desk. Unconsciously, Rori took a rigid stance, her head held high, body stiff. She caught a glimpse of a man in a security uniform before she heard the director say, "I'll get back to you later for more information." The screen went blank.

"Rori." The wiry man turned to her. "Relax." He stood, coming around his desk, reaching out to grasp her in an informal greeting. "How is your grandfather?"

"Fine, sir." Rori was aware Hiymm talked to her grandfather regularly and it was a ploy to get her to relax. Fortunately, it worked. When she settled into the chair, she felt much better. The man chatted amicably about old times with her grandfather for several minutes before he turned serious.

"Rori, I need you to tell me everything about your trip here. We'll start with why you came today instead of tomorrow."

At his question, Rori became certain something was wrong with her showing up today and not just that her quarters were not prepared as Tasc wanted. "I received instruction two days ago there was a change in plans, that you wanted me here earlier, and I received a new set of travel plans."

The man's brow crinkled. "Do you remember where the plans were sent from?"

"Here, sir." She pulled her personal planner from her packet, pulled up the information and turned it so the man could read the file she'd loaded there.

His mouth tightened as he studied it then reached for the device. "May I transfer this to my computer?"

"Certainly." She handed it over. "Sir, then I'm not wrong in that there was no change in my travel plans?"

He eyed her thoughtfully for only a second before he spoke. "No, you were to be here tomorrow. So the questions are, who was able to get into our system and send the change from here? Who was at the docking station and why were they after you?"

Chapter Three

Though Rori expected the answer, it still hit her like a blow to the stomach. Air rushed out of her. She felt oddly sick. Someone had really tried to kidnap her.

Steadying herself, Rori met Manning Hiymm's gaze and repeated everything that had happened. She felt tension and anger build in the director as she presened her report and sought to ease it. "But who knew I was coming? And better yet, why me? I'm not part of the Guardians yet. I'm not known here. Maybe it was a mistaken identity?" Even as she suggested it, she knew it wasn't true. She had been the target.

Hiymm's head was shaking to confirm her thoughts. "I'm afraid that is not it. I guess you should have been informed before you made your decision and headed here."

Rori felt a weight surface, settling heavy on the man.

Hiymm sighed deeply. "There have been several attacks on the governing council and on Guardians. Nothing as obvious as this, in fact, the first few were brushed off as coincidence, though talents seemed to be involved. You are certain they were strong talents?" He almost looked like he hoped she'd deny it, but she couldn't.

"I have no way to measure them, but what they did and how I felt when the woman went after my mind to put me out, yes, I'm sure they were strong. They were very confident they could take me." The last words hit home, the blow of the possibility was followed by Hiymm's words.

"Now there is no doubt. With what you felt and I saw on the security recording from the port." A grim resignation settled over the man. "It was an organized talent-attack. What I can't figure out was how they knew about you. There are not many people who are aware of you, and that you were on your way here. I'm sorry, Rori. I know this is a lot, especially when you've just arrived."

"This is why I'm going straight to a team?" she ventured a guess.

"Partly, we have four teams of Guardians. Two here in the city and two more stationed out at widespread points, so we can cover the greatest area more effectively."

Rori nodded. She knew this from her grandfather. Just as she knew that until eleven months before there had only been three teams, until they graduated the fourth and elected to keep them together. "And what if I don't fit in or my talent doesn't hold?" The latter was the question that plagued her for days now even though her grandfather had waved the concern aside, telling her not to worry when she broached the subject with him.

"If you don't fit with the team we'll transfer you to another. Your personality scans have linked you quite favorably to this team though. As for your talent not holding, we'll face that if it occurs. Your grandfather is not concerned with that at all, and I've never know him to be wrong on picking talents. He's the best. He thought he had picked up your talent before you were of age. Did he ever tell you that?"

She felt a pang of regret and shook her head, more to clear it than to answer.

"We should know more after our people run a complete charting on you. I've talked to them and moved it up to tomorrow morning since you're already here. For tonight, I suggest you relax and get some rest. So," he rose from the chair, "let's go see what Tasc has been able to arrange for you."

"I'm afraid I've thrown him off."

Hiymm turned her toward the door. "Don't worry about it. He thrives on challenges like this. It's unfortunate we didn't have a unit ready in the Guardians grouping but since we had no new guardians coming up they hadn't worried about having a room prepped." Hiymm Manning looked at his assistant as he stepped through the doorway. "Found anything yet?"

"All the visiting dignitary suites are full because of the conference that is coming up soon. I have one unit available two levels down, but it's not a high-security floor. That may be a possibility and we'll just add an extra guard for the night."

"Guard? Do you think that's necessary?" Rori couldn't help ask, shocked at the idea.

Tasc turned to her. "After what happened at the transport dock, I think it would be best not to take chances. Do you concur?" He shifted his attention to Hiymm.

"Yes. See what you can find. If there's nothing else, go with that. I'm going to take Rori on a tour to get her acquainted with the layout here."

The assistant nodded. "I will have everything arranged on your return."

"You really don't have to take the time to do this," Rori said as they exited the office. "I know you're busy and weren't expecting me."

The director motioned with his hand as if waving her concerns away.

"I'm happy to take the time. It will give me time to ply you with tales of your grandfather and reminisce about old times. I will not get to have dinner with you this evening and introduce you to my wife as I had hoped because of the upcoming conference Tasc mentioned. I am afraid I will be tied up with that for the next while. It is expected that I attend all functions. I don't know why, but it is. Now, did your grandfather ever tell you how we met?" He started off the long series of stories as he showed her around the building.

Rori found the stories fascinating but doubted she'd be able to find many of the places they visited again. Luckily, when they returned to his office Tasc took over showing her where she'd being staying that night. He also loaded a layout of the building and surrounding area on her personal organizer.

"The central dining room will be serving now," Tasc informed her from the doorway of the room. "You'll probably want to head down there soon. Your belongings were left in the bedroom. In the morning, if you will leave them there, they will be shifted to your permanent quarters during the day. Is there anything else you need?"

"No, thank you. I apologize for being such a problem for you today."

"It is not your fault. The most disturbing thing is who could have messed with your schedule. I assure you I will not let it go until we get answers. Just try to get some rest. Tomorrow will be a busy day for you. The testing will take most of the day. If it can be completed in time, we will introduce you to your team captain, and hopeful have you begin training with him."

Rori nodded, trying to take it all in.

"Good evening, Aurora." The man inclined his head at her and the door slid closed behind him.

Rori stared at the closed door for a moment before she turned to study her accommodations. The room was large and furnished nicely but there was a barren quality about it. She imagined her own private suite would be similar and, if so, she was going to have to get some things to give it life. The balcony drew her attention and she moved out onto it.

Her breath caught at the view. Blue-green water stretched out forever, more beautiful than she remembered. A few water-craft dotted the surface. The sun was lowering to the water, giving the sky a warm glow. It was later than she figured. No wonder, when Tasc mentioned eating, her stomach reacted with interest. She really was hungry. With one last look out over the ocean, she went inside. Washing up quickly, she headed right back out the door to eat.

"Hi." The young cheerful voice surprised her.

Rori turned to see a lean, white-blond haired boy, who she guessed was about eight, standing by the door next to hers. "Hi." She smiled back.

"Did you just move in?" The boy's curiosity bubbled up.

"I'm just staying here for the night."

"I live here. My dad works upstairs monitoring problems. He's one of the people who decide when the Guardians need to be sent out."

Rori felt the wave of pride come through the boy so strong she didn't need to use her talent. "That's an important job."

The boy nodded, obviously pleased at her comment. "Have you met the Guardians?"

"Not yet."

"I know them all. One day I hope I'm strong enough to be one. My dad's a strong talent, but not Guardian level. His is more an administrative type."

Rori felt the corner of her lip twitch and had to fight to keep from laughing. There were no secrets with children. "That is just as important as a Guardian or any rescue team. They couldn't do their jobs if they didn't have someone feeding them the details."

"I know." The boy again looked satisfied at her comment.

"Tad, what are you doing?" A female voice came from inside the apartment.

The boy looked back inside. "Waiting for you and just talking."

"Talking?" A second later, a petite woman in her early thirties appeared in the doorway. "Oh, hello."

"Hello," Rori greeted back.

"I didn't know anyone had moved in there. I'm sorry if he's bothering you. He's not at all shy as you can see." She smiled fondly at her son.

"I'm just staying here tonight and he's no bother. I'm Rori Straye, nice to meet you, Tad." She held out her hand to the boy.

"I'm Dena Tern. If you need anything, just let me know," the woman said.

"Thank you."

"We're going down to eat at the dining room tonight," Tad burst out.

"That's where I'm headed. Maybe you can show me so I don't get lost."

"I know the way," he assured her, puffing out his small chest.

"I thought you might."

"Are you alone?" Tad's mother asked. "Would you like to join us?"

"I'd love to. I just got in today and haven't met anyone yet."

"Well, just stick with Tad. He knows everyone." The woman shook her head. "I don't know how he does it. I'm with him all the time and I don't know half the people he does."

Tad took Rori's hand as they walked. The central dining room was a large room broken into smaller areas by an array of plants and a waterfall that bisected it.

"Wow, this is nice," Rori commented as they stepped in.

"Yeah, the food is really wonderful too." Dena led the way to the buffet. "Tad loves to come down here. So we come down at least twice a week. Once on our own when his father's on duty and another time with his father. I have to admit I like the freedom of coming here and not cooking all the time. It really is handy."

They were waiting in line when Tad tugged on her arm, all excited, motioning to the exit. "Look over there. There's Keyen. He's one of the team leaders of the Guardians."

Rori tried to see but only caught a glimpse of a tall, dark-haired man as he disappeared out the portal. She wished she could've gotten a better look. It would've at least been nice to know what they looked like.

"Keyen's the best and he's my friend. You'll like him. He's a real strong talent. They say one of the strongest ever."

"Enough." Dena laid her hand on his shoulder. "We have a touch of hero worship here if you can't tell."

"No problem," Rori assured her, trying to quell some of the unease she felt at her coming role as a Guardian. She was glad when they reached the food, and she could focus her attention on the selection.

Over dinner, they talked about random subjects then headed back to their rooms where they said goodnight as it was time for Tad to get ready for bed. Rori settled down on the balcony to look out over the water and read for a while before she decided to turn in. Though it was still early, she was exhausted due to the events of the day and fell right to sleep.

Rori jerked awake with the wail of alarms. Scrambling off the bed, she got her feet under her only to have them knocked out from under her as the whole floor lurched beneath her. Dropping to her knees saved her from the shower of debris as the outer wall on the other side of the bed collapsed. The rumble of the explosion drowned out the siren for seconds that seemed to go on forever.

When Rori pushed up, she looked out at the night sky through torn metal and crumbled debris. The balcony she'd sat on was no longer there. Shock and terror filled her. Bright lights slashed in through the opening, blinding her for a second before she got her arm up to shade her eyes. A second later, the light swung away followed by a series of flashes that burst across the sky.

Someone was firing a weapon. Common sense told her to stay back, but unable to stop herself, she moved toward the gaping hole.

The cool breeze off the ocean flattened her thin sleep-shirt to her body. She ignored it like she did the electricity sparking from torn wiring. Her attention was ensnared by a figure on the hoversled hanging in the air not far from the opening. The sled darted closer, and for a fraction of a second Rori was compelled to reach for it before another blast forced it away. Still Rori was drawn toward the opening again until fear and panic burst over her nerves.

She stumbled after breaking the mental hold then stepped to the edge again, this time focused on the destruction of what had been the apartment next to hers. Though heavily damaged, it was the boy clinging to the exposed cables dangling seven stories above the ground that gripped her.

A chunk of facing broke free hurtling toward Tad. Instinctively, Rori threw up a shield around the boy, knocking it away. Tad jerked from the unexpected impact and slid farther down the cable.

"Tad, hold on," Rori yelled. "I'll get you, just hold on."

Forgetting the hoversled and the gun blasts keeping it back, Rori climbed out on a beam, using torn sections of flooring and whatever she could reach to hold onto as she worked her way to the boy.

"Rori," he cried out seeing her, and she felt a wave of his fear and tamped it down in an effort to keep her mind clear as she reached for another handhold.

"Hold on. I'm on my way." She sent out as much reassurance as she could. Moving to the side, her foot came down on a piece of metal which sliced deep. She jerked in pain and her feet slipped out from under her. For a moment, she hung as precariously as Tad from a section of cable. It took two tries to get her feet back under her. Letting out a sigh, she continued until she reached a beam that extended out over the boy.

Shimmying out on the metal, she reached down only to be several inches short.

"Rori." Panic filled the boy's voice.

"It's okay. I'll get you. Look at me, Tad. I won't let you fall."

"I'm falling," Tad cried.

Quickly surveying her surroundings, Rori braced her feet under a piece of piping. Tucking her nightshirt into her bottoms to keep it out of her way, she scooted to the edge of the beam. When it was at the back of her knees, she uncurled her body, until she was hanging upside down. She reached out for Tad.

"Rori!" he screamed again as he lost his grip.

Chapter Four

Rori felt the jerk as she caught him under his arms. "It's all right, I have you," she assured and then gasped as the pipe her feet were locked under shifted. Her heart jumped and breath held as she feared it would give out.

"Tad, I'm going to lift you up against me. When you can, I want you to wrap your arms around me. All right?" she said quietly, trying to keep the boy calm, while pushing out with her talent.

"Yes," the boy's voice quivered.

"You're doing well. Up you go." Rori strained to lift his weight toward her. Arms curls were never what she considered something she was good at. The odd thought passed through her mind, but she shoved it away as she felt the pipe give again. She glanced toward the building debating if she could toss Tad to safety but knew she was too far out and at the wrong angle to make the attempt.

Across her senses she felt power tingle and the pipe became steady. She didn't know what to think of it and didn't have time to contemplate when Tad's little arms reached out, locking around her chest.

"That's it." She shifted her hold so her arms were locked around his legs. "Now, I want you to climb up my body to the beam. Slow and easy. I still have hold of you." Tad's little body squirmed against her. Rori felt her nightshirt slide down her body, catching at her waist.

Tad reached toward the beam and Rori felt him lifted from her. "I have him." The baritone voice showed no signs of strain. Rori tried to look up but only managed to catch a brief look of the man moving back along the beam with Tad locked in his arms.

Tightening her stomach muscles, she curled up until she could get a grip on the beam. After a moment of tricky maneuvering, she squirmed around until she was lying along the beam. She gulped several deep breaths of air, then looked at the ground far below and gulped once more. Closing her eyes, she steadied herself a second before opening them again.

On her hands and knees she moved back toward the building, aware now of the rough metal against her skin and the pain in her foot. With relief she made it to the ruined side of the building. More cautiously than before, she searched for a handhold to pull herself up when a hand appeared in front of her face.

"Here." The same voice of the man who had taken Tad called to her. Rori raised her gaze to the form standing on a section of flooring just above her. Extending her hand up, his hand locked around hers, pulling her up as easily as he had Tad until she was standing next to him.

Forced to tilt her head up as he towered over her by at least a head, she felt oddly lightheaded, and it had nothing to do with shock or fear of what she'd just experienced, but from the man who still held her hand caught securely in his. All her senses jumped and for a moment she was afraid she really was going to burn out, but instead of dampening, her talent surged with energy wiping away the fatigue she'd felt seconds earlier.

She felt a loss when he abruptly released her hand almost like it had burned him. When he rubbed his palm against his pant leg, she wondered if maybe she was running hot and had singed him. The scope of her talent was too new to her to be sure.

"I ought to yell at you for being incredibly foolish, but since there was no way a rescue could have gotten to Tad, well done. That was amazingly brave."

Rori followed his gaze to where Tad was locked in his mother's arms as she cried and kissed him. For a brief instant, Dena lifted her head meeting Rori's gaze. "Thank you." The mother mouthed the words before pressing her face into the boy's hair with more kisses. Rori took a moment of pleasure in the warmth of love and gratitude she felt flowing off the pair to steady her nerves before she turned back to the man.

Taking time to get a good look, she realized he wasn't much older than her. Muscles rippled over his bare chest as he folded his arms across it, studying her with the same intensity she studied him.

Again her breath caught. He was handsome. His dark hair was cut short. His intense eyes were such a light brown they almost looked like molten gold, even washed out in the emergency lights. She shook her head to clear away the odd thoughts. Still, her eyes drifted down the tawny skin of his chest. The muscles were well developed from exercise and work, with a good dose of heredity thrown in. He'd pulled on pants and athletic shoes before he'd come to help.

A cool breeze brushed her heated skin, and she became aware she was standing there in just her nightwear that hardly covered her body. "Oh." She wrapped her arms around herself, realizing the room was also filled with other people, most dressed in security or rescue gear though there were several others who had obviously been pulled from their beds.

A smile broke over the man's chiseled features and his eyebrows cocked up. He started to make a comment as Rori shifted, putting weight on her injured foot. There was no stopping her outcry and whatever he was going to say died on his lips as his attention dropped down the length of her legs to where the blood seeped on the ground.

"You're hurt."

Before she could react, he swept her off the ground

into his arms. Heat from his skin was blessedly warm to her, but she didn't get time to enjoy it as he was already striding across the ruined room into the hall where more people lingered.

"Quade, we need a medic." He walked up to a man with a medical insignia on his sleeve. The medic motioned to stretchers waiting along the wall. Gently she was lowered to it. The minute she was down, the medic lifted her foot to look at it then motioned to someone else, and she was being whisked away, barely able to catch a last glimpse of the man.

⊂⊃

The minute Keyen released her he wanted the woman back in his arms. He watched the med-techs take her away and wished he could go after her, but he was needed. Forcing himself, he turned and reentered the apartment.

He stopped and studied the damage. The outer wall of the two apartments had been sheared away. Luckily, the blast hadn't gone deeper. Then again, studying the area, it hadn't been designed to. It was a controlled blast from a well-placed explosive device. What he couldn't understand is why.

He looked around at what was left of Tad's small bedroom and into the bedroom on the other side. Except for the missing outside wall and part of the wall between the bedrooms, the room was almost entirely intact. According to the information he'd pulled up, the residence was supposed to be empty. Keyen eyed the blankets on the bed that looked to be messed up by someone sleeping in it, not the explosion.

One of the visiting dignitaries, the thought crossed his mind, but he didn't have time to continue with it as the security chief called him out of his contemplation.

"Keyen, can you give us a hand here?"

Keyen eyed the bed a second longer before he turned to Macey, the building specialist. "What do you need?" He moved to the men standing close to the opening.

"See that chunk of loose material. We were wondering if you could steady it while we bring the lift closer, then free it so we don't have to worry about it breaking off and falling.

Keyen nodded. "Ready?"

"Yeah, March is standing by." Macey motioned to the large hover lift.

"Okay." Keyen stepped a little closer to the edge and concentrated on the slab of concrete which hung precariously by a single cable that ran through it. At a meter wide and several long, Keyen knew it easily weighed ten times his weight but it didn't matter to his mind. Keeping the movements gradual, Keyen raised the piece with his mind as though it was attached to a crane. Getting it level, he held it in position while the driver of the hover lift moved expertly under it. Once in position, Keyen lowered the section of debris carefully letting the lift adjust to the weight. Two men on the back of the lift hurried to secure the piece as Keyen released it from his mind.

"You want me to break the cable?" Keyen asked the building specialist.

"If you can that'd be great."

Keyen concentrated again, this time focusing in on the braided cable. Using the thought of what could have happened to little Tad to fuel his mental torch, he directed intense heat on the spot, pulling it from deep within him. A second later, the end of the cable snapped releasing the chunk.

"Wow." One of the men beside him exclaimed.

Keyen turned, experiencing a second of lightheadedness, he pushed it way and smiled. He understood the reaction. As far as he knew, he was the only one who could do that. There were pyro-talents, able to make fire, but even they had limitations. Being able to melt through something like that was a whole different thing and took a lot of power and control.

"Thanks," Macey reached out to shake his hand. "You saved us the rest of the night trying to get that secure, plus a considerable amount of risk."

"That's what I'm here for."

"Still...."

Keyen accepted the thanks with a nod. "Anything else you need?"

Macey surveyed the rough edges. "Everything else looks good. We'll wait for morning to handle the rest of the clean up and start reconstruction."

"All right." Keyen turned his attention to the security chief. "Caph, have you been able to figure out what happened here?"

"It wasn't hard. There were at least two attackers on sleds. The first one came in, without setting off alarms," he added pointedly. "He got close to the building then sent the explosive device over to the balcony. Telekinetically, I would say."

"A talent."

"That's what it looks like on the monitor that caught it." When the explosion went off, we stayed focused on that person, afraid he might plant more, but the person just kept moving around."

"Keeping your attention." Keyen understood where he was going.

"Yes, it was just lucky we saw the other sled. Jayes stopped in to see if one of the others could change shifts with him so we had an extra person in the control center. He hopped right on a monitor to check the damage and saw the other sled maneuvering toward the opening. He opened fire on it, driving it back, but it came in again. Jayes said it was like they were after something. He kept up firing and it peeled off and the other with it. Unfortunately, we couldn't track them."

Keyen studied the hole in the wall. "So what were they

after?" he said more to himself but Caph answered.

"I don't know, unless they thought it would be easier to get in down here than up on one of the secured floors but that doesn't make sense because this was hardly subtle."

"You're right. They wanted something here. And as much effort as they put into the attack, it seems unlikely they hit the wrong place." Keyen was still thinking to himself.

"Maybe a visiting dignitary?" Caph suggested.

"They're in the visitor area." Keyen waved it away.

"I think someone was here. Tasc ordered up a guard on this floor for the night."

That got Keyen's attention. He turned to face the man straight on. "You're sure?"

"Yes. He called me directly. He said it was just for the night and only people living on this level and with a top security level clearance were allowed. You think it's related?"

"It's a big coincidence. I'll get a hold of Tasc and Manning in the morning."

"Actually, you're supposed to meet with Manning at nine o'clock in the morning. He gave me the message because you were out helping get the boy and he didn't want to distract you just then by opening up your link."

Keyen nodded, his attention returning to the other room and the messed bed. He wondered who'd been there and where they were now.

∞

Rori relaxed back on the exam table waiting for the medic. Her foot throbbed but it was bearable. Still it helped to focus on something to keep her thoughts from going back to what happened. She was relieved to find out that despite the amount of destruction, the cut on her foot was the most severe injury. Even Tad had come through it with only a couple scrapes and bruises.

With that knowledge, what bothered her most was the

knowledge it again had been all about her. She could still feel the beckoning impulse drawing her to the edge. What she didn't know was why her; she knew the prompter had been a man; was drawing her to the edge. Was it so he could kidnap her or push her over to her death? Either scenario chilled her. Rori thought of asking for a blanket, though she knew it wouldn't thaw the fear. Instead, she shifted her focus to the man who had helped with Tad.

She rubbed her hand over her thigh as just the thought of him touching it had tingles going up through it. Total foolishness, she didn't even know who he was. She guessed rescue team or security. He wasn't built like the walking wall, but he was strong enough. He'd known the med-tech by name which didn't mean anything.

Either way, it didn't matter. She wasn't there for a relationship, wasn't ready for one. And it was definitely not the time for a life mate. Still, there was something about him that called to her more than the mental compulsion from the man on the hoversled had.

"Well, let's see what we have since I'm already here." A woman wearing a med-techs white smock hustled into the room. Her once dark hair was highly salted with white. There was a soothing quality that radiated out from her in strong waves that Rori figured was as natural as breathing.

The medic lifted her leg studying her foot. "Nasty little gash, isn't it? Don't worry, I can have that feeling better in no time." A warm feeling spread through Rori before the woman even finished speaking, and she knew the woman was helping it heal. Rori focused on the waves of energy she felt, never before had she been able to pick out another's talent except to feel a slight tingling, quite often when talent, certain kinds of talent specifically, were being used.

Abruptly, the woman's gaze shifted her gaze to Rori's face. "I don't know you." There was surety in the woman's words but a crease line formed between the medic's eyes as she looked at her.

"I just arrived." Rori found herself stumbling over the words, wondering if she had overstepped the bounds of courtesy.

"You're a healer?" The woman looked questioningly.

"An empath," Rori stuttered, surprised.

The medic studied her a minute more than nodded. "You're very strong," she said sagely.

"I don't know." Again Rori stumbled over the words, wondering why she felt so self-conscious when she usually was quite self-assured. She just didn't know what to make of the woman, but it was like she disturbed something sleeping deep within her.

"You're the special test in the morning."

Her announcement caught Rori by surprise. "I don't know. I am to have some testing in the morning." Rori remembered what Hiymm Manning had said.

"Well, what a welcoming."

This time Rori didn't need her talent to feel the warm comforting impulse the woman sent out. "You look familiar to me. Are you sure we haven't met?"

"I don't think so." Rori felt steadier now.

"What is your name?"

"Rori, Aurora Straye."

"Jattin's granddaughter," the woman said firmly. "You don't look anything like him, except the eyes. You have his eyes and something inside. I am also an empath besides being a healer. You say you're an empath but not a healer?"

"Yes, I've never shown any ability to heal, just comfort."

The woman nodded accepting her answer. "By the way, I'm Areathea Adue, Chief Medic for the Guardians. So you might hope not to get to know me well, but you will. I will be conducting all your physical exams and observing on your tests tomorrow with Narrasa, he's our Chief Talent Reader. It should be most interesting."

The whole time Areathea talked a soothing calm flowed around her. "Well, let's finish healing this so you can walk on it tomorrow. If I know Hiymm, and I do, even after the night you've had, he'll still be anxious to put you through all the hoops as fast as he can. I believe he has special things planned for you. So let's fine tune this so you don't have any discomfort."

The communications link in the medic's pocket sounded. "If I'm not missing my guess, that's Hiymm now checking up on you." She answered the device. "Yes, I have her." There was a pause. "She's fine, just a cut on her foot. I'm seeing to it personally. She will be as good as new tomorrow. Yes. All right, I'll take care of it. You can tell Jattin I'm taking good care of his granddaughter."

A second later, she closed the link, looking down at Rori.

"Well, from the sounds of it, your room is pretty much destroyed, so if it's all right with you, you'll bed down here for the rest of the night in one of the recovery rooms? Don't worry, we're on a high security floor, and your stuff will be retrieved and waiting when you wake up."

"That's fine," Rori managed to say.

"Good. Then let's finish healing your foot before we get any other interruptions."

Rori felt the sensation stir her awareness and, without thinking, followed it back. She could almost see the healing waves as they ran over her foot, delving in, pulling together layer after layer of torn skin, working their way back out.

When finished, Areathea shifted to meet her look. "Well, that was interesting," she said cryptically. "Now let's see you to a room so you can get some sleep."

"I doubt—"

Areathea raised her hand, cutting off Rori. "Don't worry I'll take care of that."

Rori felt the nudges of relaxation the medic had been giving off increase, along with the urge to sleep. Rori covered her mouth as a yawn slipped free.

"That's good. Now come this way."

Rori slid off the table barely noticing there was no pain at all from her foot when it connected with the floor.

"We were very lucky." Areathea talked as she guided her out into the hall. "I heard a boy almost fell. I know the boy. He's the son of one of the system techs. Cute little guy, he knows just where I keep my treats when he comes to see me."

Rori's thoughts went to Tad and was hardly aware of entering the room and lying down. "I'll see you in the morning. Well done. Thank you." Areathea pulled the blankets up around her. "Sleep." The word took her the rest of the way under.

Chapter Five

An older man hurried in through the open doorway. "All right now, let's see what we have." Thin hair rimmed his head with a dull brown ring. Annoyance radiated from him that Rori had trouble reading. He looked at the computer link and snorted. "They have you classed as a level four searcher and two empathic."

"Yes," Rori answered, feeling the nervousness she'd been experiencing since she'd awaken rise.

He rolled his eyes. "And what do they expect me to find." He stopped, looked at her and froze. After a moment, he blinked. A thoughtful look crossed his face. "Well," he drew the word out. "I think we can safely say you're a lot higher than that." Curiosity from him filled the air. "Let's get started. You've done this before, but this time it will be more detailed."

He touched the controls and the door slid closed. "Oh, I guess I should introduce myself I'm Med Narrasa, if you hadn't guessed, and you are," he paused obviously stopping to read it on the screen. "Aurora Straye." He glanced back again. "Any connection to Jattin Straye?"

"He's my grandfather."

"Really, then how did they ever misdiagnosis you so badly?" Now there was a demanding quality in his voice.

Rori wasn't sure how to answer. "It's complicated."

"Well, we'll look into that later. Now, this room is set to amplify your talents, making them easier to read, categorize and evaluate. When the lights go out, I want you to focus on the red light. Ignore everything around you, just listen to my voice and follow my instructions." He hardly finished speaking when the lights went out, leaving the room pitch black.

A small glow appeared on the edge of her peripheral vision. Rori knew it was from Narrasa's computer screen. Before she could look toward it, a bright red light appeared above her, circled by several rows of small yellow lights that seemed to pull her attention in.

"All right, Aurora, I want you to focus. Don't hold back. I want you to open your mind fully, then your talent."

Rori pushed out with her mind and felt like the air stirred around her—like it was charged with electricity.

"Good, but let it flow. You're fighting it. You don't have to worry about keeping it in check. There's no chance of hurting anything in here. This room is designed to absorb the talent, not letting it out. Not even the strongest talent, no matter the type can escape. It's the same technology used in dampening restraints and holding cells for talented prisoners but on a more complex scale. It doesn't dampen, just keeps the talents focused in the machine." The words came out of the darkness and she tried to follow them.

"Good, relax, let it flow. We're going to try something easy. Find me with your mind."

Rori reached out, feeling for the impulse that she had picked up from the man. She felt him there. She locked on then things shifted, and she knew it was the machine causing the distortion. Still, she had no problem following it back to him and felt a wave of satisfaction from him.

"Good. We are going to move on. I'm going to show you some images. Let your natural impulses flow from what you see.

The red light faded and pictures came in rapid succession, beautiful and peaceful intermingled with accidents and destruction. She cringed and held onto the image of the mudslide bearing down on the transport. Inside, every cell in her body tightened before the image switched to a soft beautiful sunset, then the images faded and the red light reappeared.

"Aurora, I want you to think back to last night. I heard you helped save the little boy."

The picture of Tad came so vividly to her mind Rori almost slid off the table. The small body hung out over the abyss and the chunk of debris coming toward him. She started to reach out though she knew it was just a memory and Tad was safe.

"That's good." The words seemed to come from far off, and Tad faded from her mind. She was staring again into the red light, then it too faded and the main lights came on brightening gradually, letting her eyes adjust. Still Rori closed them, taking long deep breaths. She was exhausted.

"Interesting."

She heard the word muttered by Narrasa and opened her eyes to see him still concentrating on the computer screen. She waited several minutes but he just kept muttering to himself as if she wasn't there. Finally, she gave up waiting. "Med Narrasa?"

"Hmm." He looked up. "Oh, Aurora, I'm sorry. I forgot you were still here. You must be starving. Areathea had some food brought up. You can eat and rest while I go over this one more time."

ೞ೮

"Keyen, come in." Manning Hiymm greeted him at the opening, ushering him in, in his normal, affable manner. Hiymm's small frame barely came to Keyen's shoulder, but there was no doubting the strong talent. It radiated off the sharp featured man.

Keyen waited until they were both seated. "Director, I'm certain it was a strong talent involved in the attack last night. I checked over the security recording this morning. A talent placed the explosive on the balcony. He was powerful, with a great amount of control, sailing it over easily. True, it wasn't very big, but there wasn't even a bobble, and he was still controlling his hoversled." Keyen was ready for a denial that didn't come.

"I concur. I just viewed the recording and talked to Caph."

Keyen thought of the messed bed inside the room where the bomb had been set. He also thought of the woman who had rescued Tad. He had trouble not thinking about her. He'd felt a connection to her that didn't seem to fade, and he didn't even know her name.

This morning he'd called to the medic facility, but Med Areathea was busy and he couldn't get any answers. So he'd gone down to security and viewed the recording. He'd seen the woman come to the opening, amid the destruction. He clenched his fist at the thought of her standing there, the wind whipping at her, then her perilous climb to reach Tad. One misstep and she could've fallen to her death.

"Sir, I was wondering if you could tell me about the woman in that room?"

"That's what we're getting to. To start, there is something else you should be made aware of. Yesterday there was another attack involving high level talents. A pyro and a hypno for certain and possibly two others, we are not sure what they were."

Keyen felt his stomach muscles tighten. "You're saying there are four high level talents that have gone rogue." He couldn't keep back his shock.

"Not just turned rogue, but apparently have created an assault squad." A flash of anger crossed the man's face before his calm demeanor could tamp it down.

"But how can that be?" Keyen's thoughts shifted from the woman to the absurdity of the possibility. "High levels are brought in for training and screened very carefully."

"Yes, and believe me, we're trying to figure it out. So far, we just don't understand how we've missed them. There are no records of these talents, but given these two latest incidents and what Ty's team encountered thirteen days ago, there's no denying the facts."

Keyen understood what Hiymm was getting at. He'd talked with Ty after his team returned from a rescue, where Ty was certain at least three talents were responsible for a power grid exploding and injuring several people, causing a lot of damage. His thoughts were so locked on what had happened that he almost missed what Director Hiymm said next.

"I want you to warn your team to take extra precautions when you go out on calls. Though that, and the attack last night, was not why I wanted to see you today. What I wanted to talk to you about is that I am adding a new member to your team."

Keyen stared back in shock. "A new member?" They were pretty set in their group. They got along well. Sure they missed Carin, but he really couldn't picture anyone from the other team members being shifted in. Well, maybe Roedy but he knew he was happy where he was. Then the thought hit him. "You're switching me out as team leader?"

"No, I'm afraid you're there to stay. Like I told you when I placed you there, you're a natural leader. Others look to you. No, you're getting a brand new guardian."

"New, sir? No one is ready to move up. I know we're pressed, but I've spend time in the training arena with them."

Hiymm raised his hand, forestalling him. "I'm aware of that, and you're right, there are none ready. Rori is new to the Guardian program. You're going to be training her as you go."

"What?" Keyen came out of his seat, agitation coursing through his body.

Hiymm waited patiently until he settled back down.

"You heard me right. And I don't think it's as bad as you think. I believe Rori will be an asset to the team. She is rescue trained and a strong talent. Narrasa is testing her now."

"She hasn't been tested?" It was all Keyen could do to remain in his seat once more. He couldn't believe the director was putting an untested, untrained talent on a Guardian team; his team. His refusal must have been written on his face because the director reacted before he could form an objection.

"I know it sounds odd. But as I started to say, Rori is rescue trained. She has been working at an Ag unit for three years and helped out for a couple before that. Due to some unusual circumstances, she was misread and her true potential has just come to light. Narrasa will have his full evaluation soon, and we will know what we're looking at or what to expect. Until then I can tell you, she is a strong empath, which will be useful to your team as you don't have anyone with empathic abilities. Also, I am quite certain she can also shield." He leaned back, interlocking his fingers on the desk in front of him.

"I wanted to give you a heads up, so you can prepare your team and also let you know I'd like you personally to train and mentor her. I'm aware it will take a lot of extra time to bring her up to level, and I'm afraid we might not have a lot of time."

Keyen couldn't believe what he was saying, but trusting him he could do nothing but nod as his mind switched back to the attack. "You think the rogue talents have teamed up to commit criminal attacks?"

"I'm afraid it's more than that. Something bad is brewing, Keyen. I just don't know what to make of it, but the signs are there. You know one of the members of the governing council was killed in an accident recently. I'm beginning to think it wasn't an accident. I'm rechecking it, but I do know for certain about last night, and as I said yesterday there was another attack. I believe it was an attempt to kidnap Rori before she reached here."

"Rori." He picked up the name Hiymm had mentioned earlier. "The new Guardian?" He felt a stirring in him.

"Yes. The thing is, very few people knew of her and that she was on her way here. But someone managed to gain access to our system and change her arrival plans. There were four people waiting to pick her up, at least two were talents, but I'm guessing they all were. I want you to watch this recording." Hiymm activated the monitor and the transport dock came into view. Hiymm then focused in tighter.

"The man and woman?" Keyen studied the images. A fire erupted in a garbage can. "He's a pyro."

"Yes," Hiymm affirmed.

"What's she doing?" Keyen glanced quickly to Hiymm and back to the screen.

"Rori said it felt like she was being urged to sleep or she was trying to put her out."

"She actually felt it?" Keyen reacted in surprise.

"Yes, she felt it and blocked it."

Keyen could tell by the reaction of the woman on the screen just when it happened. Keyen didn't know which was more amazing. To detect and block a mental attack like that or that the woman thought she might have been strong enough to put someone out. He'd never heard of anyone being able to do that, comfort, calm and urge to sleep but to totally takeover and knock out someone. It made him uneasy to think of it but he'd bet anything that was what the woman was actually trying to do.

Keyen switched his attention to the edge of the screen to where the pair were focused, but before he had a chance to see who was there, the image on the screen changed and he was looking at two men on the dock. Hiymm enlarged the image.

"These two were also involved. Rori felt power," he

paused a beat, "and evil coming off them. That was what alarmed her originally. The tall one chased her, but she lost him and called me."

Keyen leaned forward, studying the two men. "He might be the telekinetic from last night who planted the bomb."

"I concur. I am having images of all of them sent out to the other teams. I want everyone to be able to identify them on sight." Before the director could say anything more his communicator chimed and he turned his attention to it. "Oh, good. Narrasa is done and Rori is on her way up. So let's switch back to her. Her name is Aurora Straye. You know her grandfather."

Keyen's mind had already gone to the man that had mentored him when he first came into the program. Jattin really had become like a father to him since his entire family had been killed when their apartment building collapsed in an earthquake that had brought out his talent. It was hard to believe it had been almost ten years ago. He'd just turned thirteen, all long limbs and gangly, with too much anger and new talent to be easy to handle. But Jattin had the understanding and patience to do it.

Keyen remembered Jattin telling him about losing his wife. Not being there to save her. Well, Keyen had been there. He'd moved debris with his hands and mind until he passed out due to his own injuries. He'd been credited with saving dozens but his mother, father and brother had not been among them. The pain still lingered deep within him. Jattin had told him it always would, that you couldn't save everyone no matter how hard you tried, you just had to use your talents as best you could.

The image of the large, burly man came to him, and he tried to picture what his granddaughter would look like. Keyen managed not to grimace at the female version of Jattin, and hoped for the girl's sake all she favored in Jattin was a strong talent and that she looked like one of her other ancestors. The comm sounded announcing her arrival, and Keyen stood turning to the portal as Hiymm moved to greet the newest member of his team.

The woman who stepped into the room was younger than he expected, looked nothing like her grandfather and was not a total stranger. Slightly over medium height, her body was lean, athletic but nicely curved. Rich brown hair hung halfway down her back in a thick braid. She greeted Hiymm with a friendly smile that changed to an 'oh' as she caught sight of him.

She looked back to Hiymm. "I'm sorry, I was told to come in. I didn't know you were busy." Her eyes came back to him, and Keyen realized she did have something of her grandfather, though on her face, shadowed with dark eyelashes, her eyes looked like deep, clear emeralds.

"It's all right, I wanted you to meet. We were just discussing you." Hiymm caught her hand drawing her into the room. "Rori, I want you to meet Keyen Saegun, blue team leader. Keyen, Aurora Straye, your new team member."

Keyen watched as the information settled in her. Her eyes widened slightly and intensified as she studied him. He wondered what she thought. He doubted it was what he was thinking. Though there were no rules about dating team members, it was probably because it hadn't come up before, and it probably wasn't a good idea. Keyen reined in his thoughts before they could get any more out of hand.

"Aurora." He stepped forward extending his hand, while letting her name slide from his lips. She flushed slightly and he wondered if maybe she felt the same connection he did.

When his hand closed around her smaller, feminine one, the same jolt that hit him the night before struck him again, and he knew it was going to get complicated between them. "I believe we've met." Though now she was dressed in lightweight pants with multi-pockets and a plain shirt, he pictured her, as he had done several times since seeing her the night before, dressed in the brief sleep outfit. "How is your foot?"

Her blush deepened. "Fine, thank you. It's all healed due to Medic Areathea."

"You've met?" Hiymm cut in.

"Yes, last night after she rescued Tad." Keyen took his eyes off her briefly.

"That didn't show up on the recording." Hiymm looked between them.

Keyen nodded. "There was some debris hanging in the way." He knew, he'd looked at the recording himself to see her.

Hiymm joined in the nod. "Why don't we sit down so we can go over Narrasa's report?"

Rori started to move and found her hand still caught in Keyen's. She stared at it in surprise. Funny, it felt so natural to have it there. His eyes followed hers down, and he released her hand, leaving her missing the touch.

"Let's see what Narrasa found." Hiymm was already speaking before she settled in her chair. He brought up the report on the computer. "Well, I can't say this is surprising. You're a full level empath with reading abilities. You are also a top level tracker and strong shielder. He thinks possibly the strongest we've ever had, but you will have to be trained up to see. It seems he had a great deal of trouble reading you. He says it's like your talent shifted and evolved as he tried to probe it. I've never known Narrasa to have trouble reading anyone, but he says here you may have other talents that he couldn't detect. You are definitely an extremely, strong multi-level talent. Your numbers almost equal Keyen's here, and he's the top of the charts."

Rori wasn't sure what to say. She was so used to being lower mid-level that she still almost believed that it was all a mistake but evidently not. Still, to think she was that high level was strange to her.

"So," Hiymm continued, "what will happen next is I am putting you in Keyen's hands. He will oversee your training. He is quite qualified, and since you are on his team, it will give you more time to get used to each other."

Rori felt the air leave her lungs. "I'm going right out on a team without any training?"

"Yes, I've thought very seriously about this and feel it's for the best. Especially after everything that has happened since your arrival. Your quarters are finished. They are right next to Keyen's so he can show you where. Your belongings have already been move there. The voice commands have been set for you."

Rori glanced to the man sitting next to her, her team captain. He was watching her. His light brown eyes were intense. Her heart kicked up a beat and she fought to steady it. Now was not the time to develop a crush on a man, especially her team captain. She hauled in her runaway thoughts.

"Areathea already gave you a physical and says you're good to go. Though, she does want you in her lab at the end of the day to put in your IPI."

"My what?"

"Your IPI, I forgot, we added that after your grandfather left so you wouldn't know about them. It stands for an Intergrated Personal Intel. It is a tiny implant that monitors your vitals, and has a direct link to us. We can track your whereabouts and it has a built-in computer that is voice activated or touch controlled. The monitor projected with the mind and operated by hand movements, beside vocal commands. She prefers to put it in right before you go to sleep. It lets your mind integrate with it while you're asleep."

Rori looked to Keyen who nodded and she felt a wave of reassurance come from him. "It's painless, quite easy to use and amazingly helpful," he assured her.

"Okay." She looked back at the director. "If you say

so."

"Good. I will get back to you with the time, but why don't you plan right after dinner. For now, I will leave you to Keyen to start your training. I will warn you, he can be a hard taskmaster. He learned under your grandfather, but don't think he will be soft on you because of that. He takes the safety of his team very seriously. That's why he wants you to be the best you can be. Any questions?"

Rori shook her head, not sure what she could say. It was all happening so fast.

Chapter Six

Rori wiped the sweat off her forehead. She knew she was in good shape, but the run Keyen had just taken her on, had just about done her in. She gulped in air and sent mental thanks for Med Areathea's healing abilities. Rori could just imagine running with an injured foot, and she had no doubt Keyen would still have made her run. And to think, she thought she was attracted to him. She glanced over at him, pleased to see he was as winded as she was. Still, the man was sadistic.

Leaving Manning Hiymm's office he'd shown her where her quarters were. Giving her just enough time to get changed into some exercise clothes, they started their workout, which meant running until she dropped.

Rori liked to run, she really did, but if she could, she'd hit him right then. She wondered if she could do it with her mind. Before she could make an attempt, he spoke.

"You did great. I didn't expect that. Wow."

She looked over, and he flashed her a crooked smile. A burst of adrenaline zinged through her. "Question?" she managed to get out, "do you always try to kill off your new team members?"

His smile changed to a wicked grin and faint laugh lines appeared at the corners of his eyes. "Only the ones that seem to try to out-do me, are you always this competitive?"

"Competitive? I was just trying to keep up."

"In other words, you don't give up easily. That's good to know. Good to have at your back when in trouble. I just wish you'd told me before we about killed each other." He rolled his eyes in mock tease. "All right, let's see how you are at flexibility and balance."

"Do we get a break first?" She interpreted the look on his face and answered. "I guess not."

"I just want to see what you can do. I saw you out there rescuing Tad, so I know you can handle heights, but there can be a lot more than that going on. Tomorrow we'll start with simulations, for today, just stamina, strength, and flexibility."

She nodded. "What about intelligence?"

"I'm afraid I can't teach much of that. I have to work with what you've got, but I can improve the other."

Rori gave him a wry look but he just smiled back at her before leading her to the middle of the track where an obstacle course was set. "This is pretty basic. You go from here to there." Keyen pointed to the other end. You have to go over, under, or around. For today, there will be no victim markers. We'll just see how you handle it."

Rori glanced around the course and nodded. "All right." She took a start stance then looked back at him when he started to move off. "Are you running against me?"

"No, I'm going to observe from up there." He pointed to some walkways above them that extended out over the course. He quickly made his way up. "Go," he called down without any further warning.

Rori took off, hurdling the first two obstacles. Catching the edge of the next, she pressed up until she could swing her legs over. She dropped to the other side, started forward then almost went down as the floor tilted and shifted under her feet. Rori gasped out as her shoulder connected with one of the forms. She used it to catch her balance as the floor shifted again.

Staggering forward, she let her hand trace along the structure, following it around several bends until it dead-ended. Not letting it stop her, she caught a piece of piping, using it to pull herself up until she was able to reach a ledge. Crossing it, she found another handhold. Rori climbed to the top of the structure.

Rori felt the stir of talent across her mind and turned just in time to see a brick sail through the air toward her. She threw up her arms to block it at the same time she subconsciously pushed out with her mind. The brick dropped away before it connected with her. When it bounced several times, she realized it wasn't real but a formed of a soft material.

"Nice," Keyen said above her. "You can shield."

Another brick hit her from behind almost knocking her from the wall. "But you need to work on keeping your attention on your surroundings." There was laughter in his voice, and Rori sent a glare in his direction, then dodged again as she caught a movement out of the corner of her eye.

"You're telekinetic," she gasped out and took off along the top of the wall, dodging and trying to consciously block the objects sent at her. Several made it past her shield before she successfully managed to stop one.

"Good," Keyen said, but she didn't stop. Reaching the edge, she dropped down, barely missing the next object Keyen sent at her. Scrambling under an overhang gave her some protection but he was waiting. When she emerged, she ducked the first foam brick and dodged the second but the next hit her.

"Shield!" Keyen ordered.

"I don't know how!" She jumped to the side to miss the next.

"You did it before."

Rori took shelter around a wall section. "I barely saw it coming toward me. I thought it would hurt. I didn't think about it. It just happened."

"Well think. Picture it out in your mind."

"It's invisible." She ducked to the side to avoid another object he sent at her.

"It's still there."

Rori studied the course for the next cover and made a dash for it. She almost reached it when a blast of air caught her, sending her to her knees.

"The air's invisible but I can still move it," Keyen said pointedly.

"But it's still there," Rori yelled back, her frustration rising. Getting to her feet she turned to glare at him a second before leaping between two sections to miss the next block.

"So is what you do to shield."

Rori ignored him, making a run for the end of the course, slowing to hurdle and dodge several obstacles. She was almost to the end of the course when a large piece hit her square in the back, sending her sprawling across the finish line. Though the ground was cushioned, it knocked the air from her and felt like it jarred every bone in her body loose. It took all the strength she had to roll over on her back. Draping one arm over her eyes, she fought for breath.

Rori didn't know how much time passed before she became aware of someone standing over her. Shifting her arm away, she looked up at Keyen, who scowled down.

"What?" she demanded defensively.

"You need to shield."

"I told you, I don't know how." She wished she had something to throw at him for a change. "Besides, you didn't say you'd be throwing things at me. It was an obstacle course."

"And they were some of the obstacles." He tilted his head back and sighed with his own frustration before dropping to the mat beside her.

She sat up.

"I'm sorry. I forget that you're new at this. You handled the first so easily, naturally. I guess I'd better back up. Okay, try to think of what you felt when you made the shield before."

She wrapped her arms over her bent knees and looked over at him. "That's the thing. I've only done it a couple times and didn't think of anything."

He looked thoughtful. "When else have you shielded?"

Rori shrugged and dropped her chin to her arms, not sure what to say because she wasn't certain.

"When I watched the recording of Tad hanging from the beam, it looked like a piece of debris was knocked away from hitting him."

"I don't know. I remember seeing the piece break free, coming at him. I felt a need to protect him and a surge of power but–"

"Okay, when else?"

Rori paused, not sure how to explain it. She really didn't remember it but couldn't doubt it happened. Finally, she started. "Right before I came here, there was a landslide. An Ag-transport was just making it out of the canyon. I don't remember, but I guess I held it back."

"The landslide or the transport?" Incredulity was evident on his face.

"The landslide. I drained power off everyone around me. When it was free I passed out. I was running so hot that it took everyone at the station to absorb the … after burn." Rori glanced at him to see how he took it, but instead of looking at her like she was a freak, he just nodded.

"It was kind of like that when my talent came out, though probably not that strong." He looked at her with understanding.

"My grandfather thinks my talent was always there. I had just dampened it so long that, when it burst out, it was like a flood tide of its own."

"It makes sense. That's why you were just being tested."

It wasn't a question, but she nodded. "I had been tested before but ..." Rori let it fall.

"But you had dampened your talent. So now that it's free, how do you feel about it?"

No one had asked her that question yet, and her first instinct was to brush it away, but for some reason she couldn't. Rori looked at the man that sat beside her and wondered what drew her to him. She wanted to tell him—for him to understand. And though she acknowledged there never could be anything between them, still he was her team captain. She'd have to turn to him for instruction. Maybe he would—could understand. "Nervous, I know what they're expecting of me, and I just don't know if I can do it."

"I understand. If it helps we all feel that way. It is a lot to bear."

"It's not just that." She took a deep breath. "I don't know what I can do." Rori looked to him. "What if I try something and it goes wrong? I could hurt someone." It was out. The fear that had wedged itself in her since she'd recognized the power surging through her. She'd looked at the exhausted faces of the med-techs around her and knew right away she'd caused that drain. She'd tried to pull in the energy but couldn't force it back down. The best she could do was to contain it.

Rori was surprised when a smile lit his face.

"What?" Her heart sank a little. She'd really hoped he would understand.

"You're a high empath. Your reaction is totally understandable. You need to help, protect. You have an inner core that demands it of you. I think we have just found the key to your talent. You are a natural guardian, a protector. I don't think you'll have a problem shielding when the time comes, though we will have to get tricky on bringing it out in practice."

He tapped a finger against his chin. "Your grandfather told me something once. I think I'd better tell you now. It might even be more applicable to you than it was to me." He took a deep breath and turned to her. "The greatest challenge you face when battling, is you won't want to cause harm to anyone. You will have to come to accept that sometimes you might have to hurt one to save the many. You won't be able to save everyone. And there are some that won't want to be saved."

She nodded, accepting what he was saying.

"No, Rori." He stopped her, holding up his hand. "It's not that easy. Believe me, there will come a day when you may have to use your talent to hurt someone, maybe purposely destroy someone. As an empath, in rescue it gives you extra strength. Then, I don't think you have to worry as much about hurting someone. But at the other times, when we have to bring someone down, and it will happen, not often, but it will happen," he stressed. "You cannot let it destroy you."

Rori wanted to ask him why he was telling her this now, but even as the thought crossed her mind she knew. At any time they could get called out, and they wouldn't know what they were facing until it happened. There might not be time later.

"Now, besides being nervous about doing harm, how do you feel about your new talent?" There was a knowing look that passed over him as his lips twitched up slightly.

She found herself starting to smile in return. Inside her, another piece seemed to settle in. "Good, like it was always a part of me."

"I think Jattin was right. It was always there, you just had to accept it and for some reason you didn't, and," he held up his hand, "I'm not going to probe why not. We have other work to do. Using your talent to shield should be similar to my lifting things. Mass isn't as important as length of time and amount of control. That's not saying when something is big or really heavy it doesn't take more power, it's just not as much comparative to the length of time and the amount of control. Something that is small but has to have precise control takes more effort or energy than chucking a piece of rock if it doesn't matter where it goes.

"You were a seeker before. When someone was lost, you'd pick up on them, go that direction then pick up again until you honed in on them because you couldn't keep up a link the whole time." Keyen stopped, reading the look on her face. "Obviously, bad example. When you locked on someone you remained with them." It was not a question as he read it on her expression.

"I ... Yes. No one ever told me that wasn't normally how it was done."

"I've never known a seeker who could sustain a link for an entire search."

Rori looked embarrassed. "I was only fifteen on the first search I helped with. They hadn't been able to find her. When I sensed her, I was afraid I might not be able to locate her again, so I stayed with her. She was so scared."

He shook his head in amazement. "And no one realized. You must have quite a good recovery rate."

"One hundred percent on alive and conscious. Unconscious, I drop a little. Body recovery I'm not good at."

"There are no emotions for you to tap into," Keyen acknowledged. "Okay, so this gives me a base to work with on helping you train. But for now, it's time to eat and then I am to deliver you back to Areathea for the IPI."

"I'm not sure about that," Rori said hesitantly.

"There is nothing to be worried about. It's painless and will in no way affect your talent. You'll find it very easy to use and useful in emergency situations. Just think of it as your own personal information link that you can access at any time, but no one else can see. You can be trying to handle an emergency and pull up relevant information or ask another team member or the control center a question, and no one else will know you're talking to someone."

"When do I get to meet the others on the team?" Rori stretched, looking at him.

"In the morning. We've had a couple days down time, so they went to visit their families."

"Why didn't you go?"

"I don't have a family," he said it so plainly, and his face showed no emotion but the pain deep within him blasted her.

"I'm sorry." Rori felt the need to reach for him but held back, his body demeanor said he didn't want her sympathy.

"It was a long time ago."

His attempt to brush it away got to her. She laid a hand on his arm. "It doesn't make me any less sorry."

"Are you reading me?" Anger flared in him.

"No, I wouldn't do that. I don't need to. It has to be hard not to have anyone."

"I have the Guardians, all the people here. They are my family."

Rori knew what he said was true. Keyen had made the team and everyone around him his family. They were in him, a part of him. Still, she hurt for him and the loss he suffered.

"Are you trying to comfort me now?" The demand in his voice wasn't so sharp.

"What? No!" Rori started to object then realized that was exactly what she was doing. A groan escaped her as she buried her face in her hands. "I wasn't, I didn't mean to. It just came out."

Keyen took her hands, drawing them away from her face. "It's all right. It's part of who you are." The understanding was back in his voice.

"I never have liked anger and hurt. Even as a child,"

she tried to explain, needing him to understand.

"You could sense the discord."

"Yes."

"And you naturally try to fix it." Keyen brushed back a lock of her hair which had come free from its tie.

"I really didn't know."

"It's all right, though I can see it might be tough trying to stay angry at you. Come on, we'd better get cleaned up."

Rori hated to have the time end. It felt good to sit and talk with him. She felt lighter inside since she'd gotten some of her concerns out. Still, there was much to think about, so much to figure out. She was afraid she hadn't even come close to terms with her talent. Rori almost wondered if she wanted to. The possibilities were intimidating at the least, terrifying at the most. The question was still there. Could she really do what they expected of her?

Rori became aware of a hand in front of her face and realized Keyen was waiting for her. Reaching up, she caught the hand then almost dropped it as fire seemed to ignite within her. Her gaze shot to Keyen's, the same fire seemed to blaze there. She wanted to let go, but a glint of challenge sparked in the amber fire in his eyes, and Rori couldn't back away from it. With a grin, he pulled her to her feet. As soon as she was up, she released his hand. When she looked back at him again, everything was back to normal but for her pounding heart.

Twenty-five minutes later, showered and changed, Keyen and Rori entered the dining room where she'd eaten the night before. It seemed impossible it was only the night before, so much had happened.

"We commonly eat here," Keyen told her. "It's fast and good. We have an advantage. We never have to wait in lines because we never know when we'll be called away. You learn fast not to eat too much. There's nothing worse than just finishing a large meal then finding yourself in a situation where you have to maneuver in a tricky area when you feel like you can hardly waddle. Most of us eat three moderately light meals with two large snacks a day."

"That makes sense."

"Believe me it does. It's also not fun being empty and on a drawn out rescue. A lot of times, there's no time for a break to eat until it's done."

"How often do we get sent out?" Rori focused on Keyen, shifting her attention away from the crowded room as she got the uncomfortable feeling people were watching them.

"It depends. Sometimes we'll go a couple days without a mission then we'll have them back to back, and you go a couple days with almost no sleep. That's why they try not to give us assignments that can be handled easily by a regular rescue team."

Rori glanced around the room, a tingling sensation ran up and down her spine. "Keyen," she whispered. "Do people always stare at you."

A smile crested his lips. "Not me, you."

"What? Why? They don't even know me." She gaped.

"Exactly. Most everyone here knows all the Guardians and the trainees. They don't recognize you though, and you're dressed as a Guardian." Rori glanced down at the outfit she wore. It had been one of many that had been left for her. It was not so different from her rescue uniform. Trim fitting with numerous pockets in which, out of habit, she'd already packed the normal basics. The gray-blue material was sturdy but soft, comfortable with plenty of give for freedom of movement. Rori honed in on the small emblems on her sleeve and over her pocket. She knew it was the insignia of the Guardians. She just hadn't thought much about it until then.

"You're going to create quite a stir for a while until everyone gets used to seeing you," Keyen explained, picking up a plate.

"I think I'll go back to my room. Can I order something from there?"

He laughed and took her arm before she could turn away. "Come on, oh brave Guardian, let's get this over with."

"I don't like attention." Rori felt like pleading for escape as she was buffeted by the curiosity of the people in the room.

"Well, you better get over that."

"Rori, Rori!" A child's high pitched voice drew her attention. The small figure darted around people like a miniature missile toward her

"And here comes your first admirer."

Rori heard Keyen say in her ear as she watched Tad cut through the room. She barely leaned down and got her arms out in time to catch the boy as he thrust himself at her. His arms went around her neck squeezing her tight.

"You didn't let me fall. You saved me."

She hugged him a moment than eased him away. "I see you're all right today."

His head bobbed up and down. "You saved me. I was going to fall. My room collapsed. It was scary but you rescued me."

There was no keeping back her smile. He was so delightful she forgot about everyone watching.

Tad leaned back in her arms and looked at her, his eyes going wide. "You're a Guardian." His voice was full of awe. His face alight with amazement.

"Yes. I am." Rori felt the words as she said them. Holding the boy she could still easily picture hanging out on debris, now safe in her arms. Rori knew whatever she faced, she was where she was meant to be.

A second later, Dena reached them followed by a medium height man with the same whitish hair and eyes as his son.

"Tad." There was gentle admonishment in Dena's

voice.

"It's all right. He was just saying hello." Rori turned to her with a smile.

"Thank you. And for last night, thank you. I never told you but I can never thank you enough." Tears came to the mother's eyes.

"You just did. I'm happy I was there to help."

Dena smiled. "Oh, you haven't met my husband, Harvus."

Rori turned to him. "Hello."

"Welcome and thank you." The man opened his arms and Tad went to him. "You're the new Guardian?" The man looked to her and then to Keyen who nodded and added a greeting.

"Yes, I just arrived here. I've been at an Ag-unit."

"I will say welcome again and thank you for my son. I'm on the tech-team so will see you in the future. For now, we'll let you get to your dinner." After a brief good-bye, the man led his family away with Tad waving over his father's shoulder.

Rori was still watching them walk away when Keyen leaned close to her ear. "And when you're bone-deep tired, in pain, and you wonder why you are doing this, if it could possibly be worth it, just remember this and the answer will always be…"

"Yes," she finished for him.

A few minutes later they sat down to eat. Rori was again conscious of the attention she was getting. Knowing it wasn't going to change, she decided to experiment with it. Opening up her mind, she reached out, immediately the feelings intensified. She could almost hear their words. "Who is she? She's dressed like a Guardian. Never seen her before." There were even a few telltale flashes of envy. She glanced at Keyen.

"Do you know several women in the room have a…" she paused to come up with the right term, "have an ardent desire for you?"

"Really." He glanced around quickly then back to her. "Which ones?" He grinned back teasingly before shifting to serious. "You'll learn fast that there are those who will seek you out because you're a Guardian, some pressured from their families because they want such a strong talent in their family."

Rori knew what he was saying was true, even though her parents were only mid-range talents. She knew from her grandfather many people sought out higher talents. Her mother's parents had been ecstatic that her father was from a high talent. It was common that offspring from strong talents were usually at least mid-talents, though it all just came back to genetics and luck.

"You want me to point them out?" she returned teasingly.

"No, I like the company I'm with tonight."

Rori felt a wave of heat. Silence dropped over them. Keyen finally broke it. "I take it you're readings people?"

She nodded.

"Tell me."

"It kind of feels overwhelming but I can handle it. Mostly what I'm getting is curiosity, but I knew that all ready. It's just a whole lot stronger now that I'm focusing on it."

"You ready to try an experiment then?"

"You mean on these people, the whole room?" She couldn't hold back her disbelief in what he suggested.

"Why not? There probably won't be a better chance, and it's a whole lot better than a dry run on panicked people."

Rori understood what he was saying. Still, she'd never knowingly tried anything like that on one person, and Keyen was suggesting a crowd. She looked around the room and back to him. Unconsciously, she leaned forward and whispered. "Do you really think I dare?"

"Why not? Make it simple. Just press out with the will to ease their curiosity in you. That will do nothing to hurt them."

Rori felt her stomach tighten with nervousness, and gazed around the room again before she nodded. "Okay." Taking a steadying breath, she cleared her thoughts before concentrating on damping the curiosity bouncing at her from all directions. She firmed in her mind what she wanted then pushed out gently. Almost immediately the waves of energy eased, but they didn't stop. It was more like they were buffeted, but the feelings definitely decreased.

"Well?"

Rori raised her gaze to Keyen's expectant look and took a deep breath. "I don't know what's scarier, the attention or that it actually worked."

"Rori."

She shook her head, a feeling of tightness settled in her. "I actually manipulated these people."

"I wouldn't say manipulated." He tried to comfort her.

"Oh, really, what would you say?" she challenged. She could see him thinking of an answer for her but there was none.

Still, he tried. "You're not controlling them. You just siphoned off or dampened what they were feeling. You didn't change it did you? They are still curious about you, aren't they?"

Rori nodded, letting the words sink in, mostly because she wanted to.

"You can't take over anyone's mind." Keyen voiced the fear that had started to settle in her. "No one can."

"I don't know if I want this." The words escaped her.

Keyen's hand reached out and settled over hers bringing with it a charge of reassurance. "Rori, I might not have known you long, but I know one thing. You can't use your talents against people, so it makes what you can do all right. You're an empath. Your need to help will make it impossible to harm. Do you understand? It's part of the make-up of your talent and who you are."

Rori understood all he was saying and knew from being a lower level empath it was true, but still, she couldn't look around the room without a fissure of fear at what she was able to do.

"Come on, don't think about it. It's time to head up and meet Areathea."

Rori stood with him, no longer worried about the implant as her thoughts remained locked on the ability to sway so many people's emotions.

Two hours later, the door to her room slid closed behind her, and Rori let out a sigh. She didn't have to be told the room was shielded for talents. Immediately, the 'buzz' she realized were tendrils of emotions she was picking up from other people, ended.

Funny, as soon as it was gone, she knew what it was. It had always been there, even before her talent was boosted, just stronger now and undeniable. She wondered if that was the reason she had always partially distanced herself from people. She wasn't quite a loner, not in the least. She just never seemed to be able to develop a close, intimate bond with anyone. The moment the thought went through her head, the image of Keyen came to her mind.

"No," she denied aloud, pushing it away. Unfortunately, she couldn't forget the wave of connection she'd felt when he'd touched her hand or the look in his eyes before he turned from her at the door.

ೞೲ

Keyen lay back in his bed and thought of the woman on the other side of the wall. Aurora, Rori, she was such an enigma to him yet so familiar. She was so strong but untrained. Well, not totally untrained, just not sure what she could really do. She had calmed the curiosity in the room full of people. When he had suggested it, he hadn't really thought she could do it. It was just a test, practice to build her power and control. But she'd done it so easily.

Rori had a right to be disconcerted. It had shocked him too, and he was used to the amazing things Guardians could do. Still, he'd never seen anything like that and from a novice. It was a little unnerving.

Though, for him, the most unsettling was not her empathic abilities or shielding, it was when he touched her. That was the real problem. It was like the dormant fire that burned within him burst to life.

He was used to an inner fire. Part of his talent lay in it. What he wasn't used to was having it fueled by another person. He didn't know quite what to think of it and didn't want it to end. Now ignited, he doubted he could handle it being snuffed out. But, if it continued, he might have to talk to Areathea or one of the other med-techs or maybe even Hiymm. Though, there was nothing they could do about it because he was sure he and Rori should be kept together. He let the certainty of the thought settle into his mind.

∞

Rori didn't answer her door the next morning when he stopped on the way down to breakfast. Keyen didn't see her in the dining room either. Thinking he'd told her the team would meet in the training room, he went there next, coming through a side door. Keyen heard the voices of his teammates across the room and waited, listening.

"It can't be true." Sansa's voice carried her normal cool tone.

"I'm serious. I heard there's a new Guardian. There was a 'young' woman with Keyen in the dining room last night, and she was wearing a Guardian uniform." Cassie sounded like her bubbly self.

"What'd she look like?" The male voice rumbled.

"Tankin!"

"Well, a guy wants to know these things."

Keyen could picture Tankin in his mind wiggling his

73

eyebrows in exaggeration. The man was huge as a mountain but had a playful heart he used to put people at ease.

"You know Tankin has a point," Cassie put in. "It could've been Keyen was just on a date. Men are known to do that, women, too. Just because our love lives are almost nil—"

"Speak for yourself." Tankin and Bass, Cassie's twin, echoed themselves and Keyen heard a hand slap.

"All I'm saying is maybe Keyen found someone to date, which I think is wonderful. He's too solitary," Cassie said defensively.

"He has us." Sansa's cool tone almost crackled.

Keyen decided it was time to interrupt the conversation and started forward.

"I think it would be great if Keyen found someone. Still, it doesn't explain why she was wearing a Guardian uniform," Cassie continued.

"Maybe they just mistook it for one," Tankin pointed out.

"How was the break?" Keyen broke in.

"Hey, hi." The greetings were stacked on each other as his friends turned to him.

"Keyen, what's this we heard about a new Guardian?" Tankin spoke up.

He started to nod, figuring to get right to it. "We have a new team member."

Even though they'd been discussing it, there was still a look of shock on all of their faces because none had really believed it true.

"Who? They say it's a woman and there's no woman on any of the teams that fit the description," Cassie questioned.

"She's new."

"What do you mean new?" Sansa cut in. "There's no one new near ready to move up."

There were nods around the group.

"Rori's new to the program. She's a high level empath with shield abilities." Keyen could see the question rising on all their faces, but it was Bass that got it out first.

"How can she be high level and new to the program?"

"She was misdiagnosed because her talent was late showing itself. But, she is very strong. She'll just have to be trained up some."

"What do you mean 'trained up'? Are you saying she's not trained?" Sansa's voice iced even more.

"Rori, was a member of a rescue team. She just never had…," he paused for the word, "an opportunity to work her talents to their full extent."

"You said she can shield," Tankin said in his easy way of accepting things. "That'll be handy. We can use that."

"Yeah, but he also said an empath," Sansa returned.

"So?" Bass looked to her.

"Don't you get it? We'll be trapped with a human lie detector."

Chapter Seven

Rori hurried down the hall. She was late. She wanted to be in the workout room already but right after she woke up, she discovered a message waiting for her on her IPI from Med Areathea wanting to check it out. It only took a minute for the medic to proclaim everything looked perfect with the integration. She then spent almost two hours with an Intel-tech going over all the options and training her to use it until she was confident and could operate it without much conscious thought.

"A human lie detector. Great help that will be." The voice reached her as she stepped into the exercise room.

Rori froze. Pain arched through her.

"She's not a lie detector." Rori recognized Keyen's voice as he defended her. "Rori can feel emotions and dampen them. Think how useful that will be when we have a dozen panicked people on our hands."

"Right, then we'll only have eleven panicked people to worry about," the first voice returned.

"You're saying she can handle more than one at a time?" Another female spoke up.

"Yes, she can," Keyen assured.

"So when do we meet her?" This was another male voice with a low, deep tone.

Rori debated on turning and leaving but before she could, she felt a tingling of awareness across her senses. Though she had never had any previous signs of mental connection, she knew Keyen was picking up her presence.

"Rori, we're over here," he called out her name before she could flee.

Rori stiffened, setting her resolve. This was her team. They would be like a family. She needed to have complete trust in them, and they would need to have faith in her to work together. Pushing the hurt from the 'human lie detector' comment away, she moved forward. They needed to get to know each other and it was best to start now.

She didn't like this feeling of not knowing where she stood on her team. Funny, she'd never questioned her spot on the rescue team before. Since she had started helping out early, by the time she was placed permanently, she already felt part of the team.

This was the first time she'd ever felt like a new person, an outsider. And what made it truly worse—she was still battling her new abilities. She could acknowledge that, not that it made it any easier. But this was her place now, so pasting a smile on her face and pulling a wave of confidence around herself, she stepped forward, moving around a few more obstacles until she came to the group.

Keyen stood across the team from her, sending off a push of assurance that was impossible to miss. Sitting on the floor, leaning against each other, looking like a pair of blonde bookends, sat one male and one female. Sitting on one of the blocks above them, interest radiated off a huge man with light caramel skin. On the floor opposite from them was an auburn haired woman, who without even hearing her voice, Rori knew was the one who'd made the lie detector comment. Skepticism and animosity drifted from her in waves.

Forcing her bravado, Rori gave a cheerful, "hello." She caught a knowing glint in Keyen's eyes as he straighten, taking the lead.

"Rori, let me introduce our team." He stressed the 'our', reinforcing it to everyone including her. She was a member of the team now.

"Bass and Cassie Morus, twins if you didn't guess, they can mind communicate with each other and are both strong telekinetics on their own, but when linked, they are phenomenal. Tankin Rees," Keyen motioned to the large man, "is a sound wave manipulator. He also has a way with the animals and can detect changes in elements."

"What can I say," Tankin spoke up jovially. "I'm a sensitive guy."

There was such spark in the giant's eyes, Rori had to fight to keep from laughing, knowing full well that was what the man was going for. She picked up a pleased awareness from the man knowing he had gotten to her.

A chill bit through her body as she turned to the woman Keyen was introducing. "Sansa Faultneer, she is a water talent."

That caught Rori's attention. She'd heard of water talents, but they were so rare she'd never met one, and the thing was, if Sansa was a Guardian, she had to be extremely strong. Maybe the chill in the air was more than just the emotions she was picking up.

"We are missing one other team member. Ultin Thurin, he's a pyro and energy talent."

"Someone talking about me?" A wiry man who was only a couple inches shorter than Keyen, came through the side door. It was his looks that caught Rori. He was one of the handsomest men she had ever seen with wavy dark hair, sharp features and piercing dark eyes. Those eyes locked on her, picking up signs of interest. "And who do we have here?"

Instinctively, Rori opened her senses to read the man. There was interest but it was all superficial. It wasn't that he wasn't sincere. He was, she knew, a consummate flirt.

"A new team member."

Being open, Rori felt a change in Keyen. She turned her attention to him. His posture had stiffened slightly.

When he saw her looking at him, he continued, "Everyone this is Aurora Straye, or Rori."

"Hi." Cassie smiled openly and greetings followed from her brother and Tankin. Sansa was the last to acknowledge her with a nod of her head, still studying her as if she was an insect.

"Aurora, beautiful name." Ultin headed toward her but stopped with Tankin's question.

"Straye?" Tankin's eyebrow arched in thought. "Any relation to Jattin Straye?"

"He's my grandfather," Rori acknowledged.

"Wow," Cassie said. "We all started under your grandfather. He used to come in and check on our studies all the time."

"He loved the Guardians. It was his life," Aurora acknowledged.

A scowl creased Sansa's brow. "I don't remember you ever coming here. How come?"

Rori fought to keep from shifting in unease. She knew there would be questions. "My parents didn't like it here. They are both Ag-techs. The city is not for them."

"Keyen said you were on a rescue team at an Ag-unit," Sansa probed.

"Yes. I'm a tracker and rescue trained."

"And an empath." Sansa's comment didn't sound very complimentary.

"An empath?" Ultin questioned.

"Yeah," Sansa answered before Rori could. "So don't try your games on her. She can read right through you."

"I don't play games. I just like all women. Is it my fault I can't pick one? Maybe the one I want doesn't want me." He scowled at Sansa and Rori knew there was some truth in his words. Ultin was interested in Sansa and the woman had absolutely no idea. Ultin turned his attention back to her as if he knew she was probing. "So you're an empath?"

"I haven't had much experience with it except using it as a tracker." Rori felt it was fair they knew her experience. "I'm very new to shielding but I will work to develop it."

Around the circle, heads nodded, accepting her answer. Rori felt more curiosity but Keyen halted any further questions.

"Okay, intros done. Let's get to work. As Rori said, she needs to practice her shielding, and we need to get her integrated in moving with us. To start, let's put Rori in the middle, Tankin, Cassie and Bass on the left of me, Rori on my direct right, then Ultin, and Sansa. Rori, this time just work on moving with us, so you know what we can do and follow our lead."

Rori felt a flittering across her senses like a bug buzzing in her ear. Her first instinct was to ignore it, but when it came again she honed in.

"Well, I think I like her," the words seemed to whisper in her mind, broken with static but discernible along with the impression of Cassie.

"I think Keyen likes her." This time she got the feel of Bass.

There was a pause. "I didn't mean like that. How do you know Keyen likes her?"

The next thought took Rori by surprise. "A man knows when another is staking his claim."

Rori's gaze darted to Keyen. He was talking to Tankin. Her heart beat hard at the possibility. When she looked back, she found Cassie studying her oddly. Unconsciously, Rori raised her hand to swipe away an annoying buzz.

"All right, positions," Keyen announced. "The program starts in twenty seconds."

The group moved into place on either side of Rori. Keyen looked at her and grinned. "Meet you on the other side." A bell chimed and they all took off, moving through the obstacle course as air bursts shot out, the floor shifted and blocks rained down.

Rori was impressed at how well they worked together. She found it easy to fall into step with them. Following Keyen's lead, she slipped over a large block just as hot air burst out from the side of her. It chilled before reaching her so it was a comfortable breeze.

Rori looked over to find Sansa looking at her with a totally blank expression. The woman turned away, but not before Rori saw a hint of a smile. Out of the corner of her eye, Rori caught the movement of a block shooting toward the woman. She didn't think other than Sansa was going to be hit. Sansa spun but was too late to dodge. Instead of hitting her, the block bounced off Rori's shield. This time when Sansa looked at her there was surprise on the woman's face.

"Nice," Keyen said before he dodged around the next wall.

Rori let the wave of knowledge at what she'd done sweep through her before she followed. They almost reached the center of the course when an alarm rang across her mind as well as the shrill sound echoing through the room.

"Come on," Keyen yelled even though it was unnecessary. Rori understood the alarm meant there was an actual emergency. She turned and ran with the group into the lift.

"Are we taking her with us?" Ultin asked, turning his gaze on Rori.

"As I said, it's on the job training," Keyen answered and there wasn't any more time for discussion as the door opened.

Rori had been in the hanger at the top of the building with Hiymm on the tour he'd given her, but it looked totally different with the hanger doors open, revealing the city that stretched out below. A half a dozen workers scurried around the bay, but the team seemed oblivious to them as they raced to the modified hoversled waiting in front of the opening. Rori could hear the whine of engines already powered up.

Keyen made a slashing movement with his hand, and Rori realized he was using the IPI and touched her wrist to activate her unit. Info scrolled in the air in front of her, and she almost tripped when she naturally ducked to avoid hitting them. The words followed the move, and after a second of disorientation, she became used to the effect.

"Tank, take the controls," Keyen commanded, going up the ramp. As everyone passed the portal, they snagged a vest from a cubby, sliding it on before dropping into their seats. "There." Keyen motioned to her taking down two vests, shoving one at her as the ramp raised, sealing off the portal behind them. "It should already be fitted to you."

Rori followed suit, pulling it on before taking her seat.

"An identical one is in your apartment and all our other transports. I planned to bring you up here to go over it later today."

Rori tried to follow his words but was distracted as the hoversled shot out of the opening.

"Time to destination, three minutes," Tankin announced.

Sansa, who had taken the front seat next to Tankin, picked up when he ended. "Energy port explosion, residential area. Outside power has been shut down, but we'll still be facing residual backup power, fires and continued explosions. Weakened structure with possible people trapped. We need to contain as fast as possible. Extreme risk." As Sansa spoke images flashed in front of Rori. She saw everything Sansa said, picking out panicked people scattered through the area.

"Med-techs and transport dispatched but won't be able to get close until we can lock down the area," Cassie informed them.

"Structure, class C, automated with three person overseers. Contact has been made with one man. The other two have not been located." Ultin took up the report.

Keyen nodded and turned to Rori. "I want you to observe and learn. This will be an extreme high risk situation, nothing like I'd pick for your first run. Then again, this is not like any normal run. Stay back and be careful. Everyone be careful." He raised his voice, stressing the words though all knew what they were facing.

Keyen turned his attention to his IPI. Rori watched as his hand darted in quick motions as he manipulated the angles and focused in. She followed suit for a moment before closing off the image of the power port to bring up a schematic listing all the contents of her vest and their locations.

Rapidly, she memorizing where stuff was. It was all logically placed and similar to her old rescue pack but extended to include extra items. One in particular was the energy pulse laser gun. Being from an outlying area, she was an excellent shot, carrying one when she went on jungle rescues, but it wasn't what she thought of as normal equipment. She knew it was there for two-legged predators instead of the wild, multi-legged types she was normally concerned with.

Hearing Tankin announce their approach, she cleared the list and viewed out the port.

Class C energy ports were considered extremely safe but quite large complexes, holding several different fuel pods and massive pipes connecting to pumping stations. The high wall that surrounded it was more for looks than anything. Now a huge section of the wall had been blown out. Fire dotted the area, some shooting flames fifty meters in the air. Energy sparked and slashed up like lightening coming from the ground.

Fortunately, people pulled back as Tankin brought the sled down in front of the section of crumbled wall. The team exited into a scene of pandemonium. People rushed them crying and wailing. Rori felt the tide of it hit her and almost folded under it.

Keyen's strong voice rose up. "Please everyone be calm and move back. We're here to help, but we need you to move back so we can. If there are any in need of med-techs, they are on the way. Please help the injured until they get here." Many people took strength in his words and calmed but many more reached to cling to them.

"Please, move back to a safe distance." Cassie took up the effort but her voice didn't have the power.

"Bass, Cassie see about getting through that rubble." The twins started to move forward but were hampered by the crowd.

People crushed in bringing fear and confusion with them. What Rori always had felt as minor need of compassion almost tore her apart. "Please," she said gently. "It will be all right. I promise. We will help."

Needing to comfort, she walked out among the crowd, brushing a hand over a tear streaked faced, taking a hand and raising it to check a cut on an arm. "It will be all right. Just keep pressure on it until the med-techs arrive. Please move back so we can secure the area for the other rescue workers." People calmed in her wake, wailing subsided to tears.

An explosion rocked the area and people pulled back. She instinctive ducked and turned back.

"Did you do that?" Ultin asked.

"What?" Rori turned.

"Sansa, the house fires," Keyen pointed, "Tank help her."

"Okay. She might be useful." Sansa moved past, a slight look of acceptance in her eyes.

Keyen looked to her. "Keep it up." He then raised his voice. "Are there any workers here from the port?"

A man staggered forward, dust and soot covered him. He held an arm tight to his body but was not seriously injured. "I am."

"Can you tell me what happened?"

"There was an explosion. I don't know what caused it. All systems were normal. I'd just run a check. Jusim was on the other side. I haven't been able to reach him. Communications are down."

"Is there anyone else in there?" Keyen asked, his attention focused on Cassie and Bass as together they levitated a chunk of wall out of the way so they could enter.

"No, just the two of us. The other man had a family union to attend today," he answered.

Keyen nodded. "Rori, check him out." Keyen glanced quickly to see that Sansa and Tank had the house fires about out, before striding to the opening in the wall. "Ultin, let's go," he called to the man, who had been checking over an older woman sitting on the ground. Ultin left the woman with an assurance she'd be all right and hurried to join Cassie, Bass, and Keyen as they climbed over the remaining debris.

The urge to go with them was so strong that Rori had to remind herself she was just to be an observer but it was hard. She was used to being in the main action. Still, in a situation like this, she was an unknown entity and that could be dangerous for the team.

She turned her attention to a man who'd been struck by a piece of flying debris and had a minor scalp wound. She concentrated on the wound and the pained expression on the man's face lessened.

Med-tech units began to arrive. In her mind, the comm-link came alive. Remembering the IPI, she brought up the screen, raising the volume.

"Whoa!" Ultin's exclamation reached her clearly. She spun in time to see electricity arc up from the ground.

"Ultin dampen that. Let's get it locked down." Keyen's voice sounded over the commotion.

"I can see the control box. Cass." Bass called to his sister.

Realizing she could bring up the images with the IPI, Rori activated it like the tech had shown her. Just on the left side of her vision, seven small screens appeared. She focused on Bass's and it enlarged. Destruction surrounded him, piping lay scattered like dropped toys, small shots of flames burned. Energy sparked up, causing her to blink, but Bass focused in on the small box on the side of the unit. When it opened Rori knew Bass had done it though he had to be at least fifty feet away. She could barely make out the row of switches that one by one clicked over. At the last switch the sparks died.

Bass turned from the control box, and she caught a brief visual of Keyen and Ultin. Both men stared at a ruptured pipe. Amazed, Rori could see the jagged split pulling back together. The strength and control it would take was unbelievable. She turned to see the flames on the three nearby houses had been extinguished. Ice crystals glistening in the sun on one of the roofs melted away as she watched.

"I have a man down." Cassie's voice reached her.

Rori brought up Cassie's screen to see the head, shoulders and arm of a man caught under a pile of debris. Rori felt fear for his life until she saw the faint movement of his hand. "He's still alive," she echoed Cassie.

"Bass, you and Cassie try reaching him from that side. Ultin and I will try from this angle," Keyen said, his next phrase was directed to Rori. "How are you doing out there?"

"Sansa and Tankin have the fires under control. Sansa is on her way to you. Med-techs have arrived. Everything has settled down." Her eyes locked on a man standing off to the side. He seemed to be studying her, totally unaffected by all that was happening around him.

"Good." Keyen's answer pulled her attention away.

The word hardly died away when a boy came running up. Panic covered him like his filthy clothes. "Help, help," he cried plowing into her arms. Rori sent out waves of comfort but they rolled off. "Tomma, Tomma's, Tomma's." Tears streamed down his face but he settled.

"Tell me." Rori felt fear grip her stomach as if she knew what he was going to say.

"We snuck in. He wanted to climb the tower." The boy took quaking breaths. "He wanted to prove he was brave enough to do it."

"Where?" Rori tried to remain calm, but as the boy pointed to the tallest tower, she felt a sense of dread. It took her a second to figure out how to use her IPI to magnify the area at the top of the tower, but when she did, she spied a small figure huddled against a section of metal. Part of the walkway had been ripped away along with a large section of the ladder. There was no way to climb up. An explosion rocked the ground near the base of the tower, and a burst of flames shot up toward the boy.

For a split second, Rori focused in on the rest of the team's efforts to reach the man. They were all tied up handling flaring hot spots released by the explosion. She could see Sansa had joined them, working to cool the area for Cassie and Bass to work.

Rori looked for Tankin. He was just inside the area, trying to secure a section of pipe that leaned against the wall, threatening to crumble it.

"Tankin, I need you," she called into her communicator. "Keyen, can you hear me?"

"Yes, what do you need?" He sounded breathless and distracted.

"We have a boy trapped on the top of the tallest tower."

"Raebent hues." Irritation clouded his voice.

Rori hurried to continue. "The ladder is down. You can't reach it from the bottom. I'm going to have Tankin take me up in the hoversled and come down from the top. I can do this," she added before he could object and prayed it was true. The flared cone over the top of the tower was going to make it tricky to get the hoversled close, and intermittent bursts of flames added to the danger.

There was another second pause before the answer came. "All right, but be careful."

Tankin had already reached her and had been monitoring the conversation. "I could go," he volunteered.

Rori shook her head. "I have no experience on the sled, and it's going to take a lot of skill to get close enough to make the jump over."

The big man looked like he wanted to object but instead nodded, and together they ran to the sled. This time as the sled lifted off, Rori locked the ramp into a partially extended position. Securing her hands in a safety strap by the portal, she studied the area as Tankin brought them over the complex.

Both groups had about reached the man. Ultin looked to be handling energy that sparked while Keyen shifted rubble. Rori guessed each piece must weigh at close to her weight but he moved them easily with his mind.

Her focus moved as Tankin brought the hoversled around so she faced the tower. Her heart lurched. The boy on the walkway couldn't be more than ten, though it was hard to tell the way he smashed himself to the building. When he saw the sled, he reached out one hand as if to grab her, his other hand locked tight to the metal work.

Rori studied the area. Tankin must have been doing the same. He called back to her, "There's no way you can make the jump. I can't get close enough, and no telling if the catwalk could take your landing. The rest could give way."

"You'll have to lower me from the top."

"You'd have to swing over under that lip," he answered back as an objection that was full of resignation. He knew as well as she did it was the only way. "There's a line and harness in the first locker on the right."

It only took Rori a few seconds to find and fit it to herself. Clipping the line into the lock bolted by the opening, she set the clamps on the line so she would free fall only a short way when she first went over the ramp.

"Ready." The word hardly made it out of her mouth when the sled jerked and tipped wildly to the side slamming her into the equipment compartments. Flames burst in the air so close she pulled back from the heat.

"Hold on," Tankin yelled unnecessarily. He fought with the controls for what felt like forever before bringing the sled under control. Finally, he got it leveled out, pulling back away from the tower. "We can't come from this side. I'm going to try from the other."

He brought them around. The railing hung precariously. Rori would have to cross four meters of the catwalk to reach the boy, but at least there were no bursts of fire they had to contend with.

"Going over the side." She swallowed hard, waited for Tankin's acknowledgement and dropped. Her body went to the end of the locked portion on the line and swung up toward the underside of the ramp. Rori was ready for the motion and had her feet spread out to take the impact. She swung back, already searching for a place to drop onto. Releasing the hand grip, she slid down the line a little farther, and then kicked her legs to get swinging so she could make it under the lip of the overhang.

Like a pendulum, she swung under the hoversled gaining the momentum she needed to cover the space. Above her with expert hands, Tankin held the sled steady. Rori counted off three more arcs. Catching her breath as she hurdled back to the tower, she released the brake on the line and dropped. With the landing space so small, there was no way to keep from hitting into the tower's side, but her calculation had been right on and the impact was nominal. She staggered. Regaining her footing, she turned to the boy.

Below her feet, she felt the metal shift under her added weight. She didn't have much time. Cautiously, she stepped forward. Metal groaned. She took another step. A ripping sound greeted her. A piece of floor grating came free, spiraling as it dropped away.

Her stomach tightened as she studied the open four foot section. It was nothing to jump but the question was would the walk on the other side take her landing or would the rest of the walkway rip free, taking the boy down with it.

It only took her a brief second to survey her surroundings, calculate the risk and come up with an option. She couldn't risk the jump. Placing her foot on the railing, she could only hope it and the rungs on the bottom of the coolant cone would hold her. She reached out barely able to wrap her hand around one bar. She hung for a moment then sighed in relief when it took her weight, and she stretched for the next rung. Releasing her first grip, she swung off the next. Her tether hampered her movement though Tankin, who was obviously monitoring her movements, eased the hoversled around with her.

Rori caught sight of the boy as she crossed the gap. Like the earlier vision of him, he sat on the catwalk, curled tightly to the tower. One arm was wrapped over his head and Rori could see his eyes were shut tight. Deciding the rungs of the cone seemed sturdy, she continued across. Grabbing a piece of sharp metal, it bit into her hand and a cry escaped her. Tomma's eyes popped open. Full of fear, they honed in on her.

"It's all right," she said, more for the boy than to answer Tankin's question that came over the link.

"Hi, you must be Tomma," Rori said casually, while pushing out waves of comfort. "My name's Rori. Seems you have yourself in a bad spot. What do you say we get down from here?"

His head bobbed up and down.

"Good. My arms are getting tired from hanging, so I'm going to climb down by you." She described her actions as she did them, moving slowly again to make sure each spot held before she rested her full weight on it.

"Are you hurt?" she asked.

He shook his head.

"Good." Rori smiled. "I have a harness here to put on you to hook you to me. Then I'm going to get you off here. You okay with that?"

The head bobbed again.

She was just reaching for him when an explosion ripped the air. Rori spun in time to see the top of the cooling tower next to them split apart. Pieces of metal flew out in all directions. In horror, she saw a huge hunk arrow toward the hoversled.

Tankin had no time to react. Rori threw up her hands as if she could block it. The debris stopped just shy of the sled and dropped to the ground, but she had no time for relief. The percussion wave hit the sled with a jolt. The line on Rori went taut, pulling her from the catwalk. Tomma, in fear of being left, sprang for her. His movement was the final shift the walkway could take. Metal screeched as it ripped free.

Rori willed herself forward. Stretching out, she seized Tomma's arm grappling for her. The weight of Tomma's body jerked her over and threatened to rip him from her hold. With her other hand, she reached down and snagged the back of Tomma's shirt as he started to slip.

Chapter Eight

Rori clung to Tomma as Tankin jockeyed the sled, bringing it under control. Over the pounding of her heart, Rori finally made out Tankin calling to find out if she was all right. "Yes, I have him." That was all she could seem to get her mind around was, somehow, she had him. "You'll have to lower us down. I can't reach the controls."

"On our way down," Tankin's reply came back to her.

They swung gently over the port back toward the original landing spot. Tomma's eyes remained shut tight as they'd been when he dived for her. When they were only a few feet off the ground and Rori was no longer worried about Tomma falling, Rori released her hold on his shirt, arched her back and gripped the line over her head, righting herself.

A second later, her feet touched the ground, and she moved out of the way for Tankin to land. Tomma was locked tight in her arms. His eyes finally open, looking up at her face.

"You know," she smiled down, "we were supposed to use the harness. It makes it much easier and then you can enjoy the view."

A smile lit the boy's face in answer. She let it melt her for a moment before she became serious. "Will you promise me you'll never do something like that again on a dare?" He nodded and she hugged him tight.

A shiver snaked down her back making her gasp. Her

lungs tightened. Rori took several steps forward unable to stop herself then pulled back. Her head rang as pressure began to build.

Her gaze locked on a man in the crowd. Tall, good-looking, dark hair and eyes, he was older, nearing middle age. His arms were crossed over his chest as he watched her then he extended one hand out. Rori started to step forward. Catching herself, she pulled back and shook her head. The compulsion hit her again.

"I saw him." Tomma's voice jerked her out of the haze her mind had started to slip into.

"What?" She looked down at the boy in her arms.

"The man, I saw him, another man and the lady before the explosion." Tomma glared into the crowd.

Rori followed the gaze and saw the man with a woman and another man moving away. Rori felt a stirring of recognition and knew the other man and woman. They were the ones from the transport dock. Forgetting the boy in her arms, she started to go after them when a hand dropped on her shoulder, making her jump. She spun and faced a massive chest. Her gaze shot up to meet Tankin's wide smile.

"That was some rescue. You all right?" A look of concern shown on his face.

Rori slumped in relief as the pressure in her mind disappeared. "Yeah. Quite a ride though."

"Hey, never let it be said I don't know how to give a lady a good ride." A playful twinkle lit his eyes.

"I will be the first one to attest to that."

"You all right?" he asked, turning his attention to Tomma who starred up at him wide eyed.

He nodded and Rori took over answering for him. "He's not going to be climbing towers again anymore, right?"

Tomma shook his head.

"Good decision." Tankin reached over and ruffled his

hair.

A med-tech appeared at her side.

"Tomma, this man wants to check that you are all right." Rori handed the boy over to him. "I'll come back and talk with you in a minute." She looked to the tech to make sure the man understood her meaning.

"I'll keep an eye on him," the man answered. "We'll be just over there."

Rori watched them walk to a rescue ground sled before turning back to Tankin. She caught sight of Cassie and Bass by the unit with the worker they had rescued. "How is it?"

"Keyen, Sansa and Ultin are sealing off the last hot spot. Sensors show no other energy leaks, containment complete. The worker they pulled out has a broken hip and several leg fractures, but he's going to make it."

Relief spread over Rori as she looked around. There were no more energy sparks or explosions. "Shall we go help tidy up a little?"

Rori moved off with Tankin, but her thoughts remained on the three people and what Tomma had said about seeing them before the explosion. It didn't take long to store the gear. When Rori saw Keyen, Sansa, and Ultin headed their way, she went to meet them.

"Everybody okay?" Keyen asked as Cassie and Bass joined them.

Affirmative answers came from all around.

"So much for you just observing." Keyen turned his attention directly on her.

Rori felt heat prick the air but just shrugged. "It was something I could do to help."

He nodded, seemingly appeased as energy crossed her senses before it backed off. "Good job, all of you. That could have been a lot worse."

"Do they know what caused it yet?" Rori asked the question plaguing her.

"Not yet," Keyen answered.

Ultin took over. "They'll have to get an investigative team in, but if you ask me, it looked like it started in several locations."

"There are no other explanations for the spread," Cassie started and Bass finished the thought. "Safeguards should have been enacted making it impossible."

"I think we should talk to Tomma, the boy we pulled off the tower," Rori spoke up.

"Why?" Sansa asked.

"He saw three people before the explosion. They were in the port. They're talents."

"How do you know that?" Sansa eyed her suspiciously.

"I saw them. I recognized two of them from before."

Keyen was the only one not studying her with an odd expression. She didn't need her talent to know they thought she was delusional, but then again, Keyen was the only one who knew of her previous experience.

"Let's go talk to the boy." He motioned for her to lead the way.

"He's fine," the med-tech said as they approached.

"Thanks," Keyen acknowledged, before turning his attention to the boy.

"Hi, Tomma, I want to introduce you to a friend of mine, Keyen," Rori said but the boy was already gaping at Keyen.

"I know you. You're the Captain of the Guardians." His voice was filled with awe.

"That's right." Keyen smiled.

"Wow." Tomma's gaze went to Rori. "Are you a guardian too? I haven't seen your picture before."

"She's the newest member. You're her first rescue with us, though she was on a different rescue team before." It was Keyen that answered for her.

Tomma's look of adoration shifted to her. Rori quickly pressed down feelings of embarrassment. "Tomma, can you tell me about the man you saw? The one you pointed out to me in the crowd."

The boy fidgeted. "He and the other man and woman were in the power port. I saw the other man first when I snuck in. I hid because I thought he was a worker, though he wasn't dressed like one. When I got to the top of the tower, I saw the one guy talking to the woman by the back wall. Then the first guy came up to them, and they went out the gate. Then everything started to explode."

"What do you mean everything? Was there more than one explosion?" Keyen squatted down to be at the same level.

Tomma was already nodding before he finished the question. "The big tank blew. It was so loud and knocked me from my feet, then there was one by the bottom of the tower. I thought it was going to collapse. The ladder fell down. I was going to die. I was going to fall. Everything was exploding then."

"You sure they left before the explosions started?" Keyen probed, aware Rori was pushing out little nudges of comfort.

The boy's head bobbed up and down.

"How did you get in?" The thought came to Rori.

"The side gate was open." He looked sheepish. "We didn't break it honest. We found it open. I knew we weren't to go inside. Gerroom said we shouldn't but I wanted to see inside and the view from the tower. Gerroom said I wouldn't dare."

Keyen laid a hand on his shoulder. "Are you going to do that again?"

"No, Sir."

"Good. I know you were high up, but can you describe the people to me?" Keyen urged.

Tomma was just finishing the descriptions when a woman pushed her way through the crowd. "Tomma!" she cried. Panic flared in her eyes.

Rori slipped in front of her, holding up a hand. "He's all right, just learned a powerful lesson today."

The hysterics faded from the woman's face, and Rori moved out of the way, letting the mother get to her son. Tears still came but they were not overwhelming. Keyen sat to the side letting the reunion take place before he drew the woman's attention. "Ma'am, I need to ask Tomma one more question. Would you mind giving your information to the tech here while I finish up? Someone will be over to talk to Tomma some more." He turned his attention back to Tomma. "Tomma, you've been doing very well. I want you to think. Were they carrying anything?"

"The younger man, I saw at first, he had a tool bag. That's why I thought he might be a worker." He thought a moment. "They didn't have anything when they went out the gate."

"You're certain?"

He nodded.

"Thanks, Tomma. You be good now and take care." Keyen patted his shoulder and stood, his gaze going to Rori. "You got that?"

Rori realized he was talking to someone on his communicator.

"All right, we'll meet in your office then." Keyen shifted his attention to her. "Let's go." They fell into step. "You've been doing that all your life haven't you?"

"What?" She glanced at him.

"Giving little nudges of comfort like you did to the woman. I bet you didn't even realize you were doing it. It's natural. That's why you had no problem doing the crowd. It isn't new to you. You're used to it. It's just stronger now, or maybe not stronger, you're just more aware."

Reaching the others, he left Rori to think about what he'd said and asked, "Ready to take off?"

"All set," Ultin returned and they headed up the ramp together.

Rori barely dropped into her seat when a food bar landed in her lap. She looked up to find Sansa standing over her already tearing off the wrapper of hers, the others doing likewise. "That'll hold you until we can get back, clean up and get to eat. We missed lunch a long time ago."

"Thanks." Rori realized she was famished. Glancing at the time display, she was stunned at how late it was.

"By the time we get cleaned up, we can catch the early dinner." Cassie leaned over.

"We have a meeting after we eat in Hiymm's office," Keyen said.

"So then we can catch the late dinner too." Tankin took the seat next to Rori as Keyen took the controls.

It was only a of couple minutes before they docked back at Guardian Central. Cassie led Rori into the woman's locker room, explaining the defect-showers they used to make sure no harmful substances ever remained on their bodies and showed her where extra uniforms were kept.

"In truly toxic situations, we spray off before we get back on the sled. That's not very often. I've only had to do it once. They're pretty careful with us even though it seems we are in a lot of high danger situations," Cassie explained as she undid her suit.

"I can tell after today." Rori smiled, amazed at how well planned everything was for them.

"Yeah. You did real good out there. I think you're going to fit in just fine."

"Thanks." Rori felt a warm comfort as she went in to clean up. She'd done well. She tilted her head up, feeling the rays work over her body like warm puffs of air massaging her.

☙

When they arrived at Hiymm's office, he directed them right into the conference room. Two women and four men were already seated in the room. Rori recognized some of the faces from pictures in her grandfather's study. They had been there when her grandfather was over them. Two had even been on a team with her grandfather. They were on the other set of Guardians stationed there.

Greetings were being exchanged and attention shifted to Rori. She smiled as Hiymm took over the introduction. "This is Aurora Straye, and yes, she is Jattin's granddaughter."

"Quite an initiation today," a man in his late forties, who wore the insignia of their team leader, said with a smile.

She returned it. "Yes. Nice to meet you Commander Orn."

"A pleasure. It looks like you will do your grandfather proud."

"Thank you. I hope so."

"Let's get on with this," Hiymm interjected before anymore could be said, motioning to the table.

"You never addressed me as commander." Keyen leaned over to her as they settled into their seats.

Rori had no time to answer as Hiymm started talking.

"The reason I called everyone in is because we now have enough evidence to make you aware of a threat against you and our society. We'd been picking up disturbing patterns for some time, but in the last couple of weeks, they have been coming to a head, made evident in the attempted kidnappings on Aurora and the attack today."

Shocked silence covered the room. Rori was aware of flittered glances her way, but most of the attention remained focused on Manning Hiymm.

The commander of the other group was the first to break the silence. "What do you mean?"

"There have been several," Hiymm paused, "occurrences on all teams where you have responded that I believe were more of a test, for a better word. And these tests are getting larger and more dangerous."

"Like today?" Tankin asked the question.

"Yes, we know for certain now from evidence at the site and what the boy you rescued saw, that multiple explosions were set. I also believe whoever is behind this is trying to keep you busy, separated and worn down."

"But why?" Orn asked.

"That we don't know for sure, but it is an organized plot, of that I am certain. These are three people the security got images of from the transport dock when they tried to abduct Aurora." On a screen behind him, the footage played. "Any of you recognize anyone?"

"No." The answer came from around the room.

"Are they talents?" the man next to Orn asked.

"Yes. And from what we've observed, quite powerful."

There was a murmur in the room but Hiymm didn't stop. "This is from the explosion two nights ago. Unfortunately, the images are not as clear. This is as good as the techs could do." Another set of images. He paused letting them study the pictures before continuing. "These are from today, taken from Rori's IPI viewer."

Rori was shocked when a scene from her mind came into view, though she realized she shouldn't be. She knew they were under full monitoring. At the sight of the man a shudder passed through her as for an instant she was taken back to the creepy compulsion she felt.

"That's the man and woman from the transport dock," Sansa pointed out with agreement coming from the people around the room.

"Yeah, he's the fire guy," Ultin added.

"Yes. We are still trying to identify them but are not having much success."

Rori knew from the shocked expression on several faces that was an unusual circumstance. Before she could think much of it, Orn leaned forward in his seat.

"I know that man." He stood, moving forward, his focus on the other man.

At Hiymm's direction, the fire talent and woman's face faded away and the image of the remaining man's image enlarged.

"I know him." Orn turned to the man who had been seated next to him. "Mit?"

"He does look familiar." Recognition showing on his face, he looked to Orn. "Drasc."

Orn turned back to the image. "Drasc Creed." The name came out like it was a bitter taste.

Hiymm nodded. "Yes, Drasc Creed."

"Who is he?" Alee, a woman on the other team asked.

Orn answered, his eyes still locked on the image. "He started the program about twenty years ago. He was on a team with Mit and me for a short time. Pretty full of himself. Pushed people around. Thought they should be subservient to him. Jattin was constantly having to rein him in." Orn stopped to think for a minute. "There was one time when we went out to rescue a small farming community. It was difficult to get there. I remember Drasc saying something like, why bother, they're not worth our time or effort, something like that. I thought Jattin was going to take him apart. He was in such a fury, energy crackled around him. Creed did other things. Not long after that he was forced to leave."

"Wow," Ultin let out.

Orn turned back to face them. "It didn't set well with Creed." Orn looked at Mit, who nodded and took over.

"I was in the equipment room when he burst through. Burst being the definitive word. He blew up several things as he passed. He slammed stuff around, then said 'who needs you' and some other unflattering words, then stormed out. Never saw him again."

Now, Hiymm came in again. "My memory of Drasc Creed is similar. We only had two teams back then. Jattin had just been moved up over the Guardian program but was still a team leader. I was on the opposite team but still

Jattin's assistant. We met all the time. It was how we kept track of everything. Jattin was very concerned about Creed. In fact, he'd approached the council about him back in his training. Creed was a rogue, but that wasn't why."

He glanced at Rori. "Your grandfather and I were rogues, but Creed's problem was he didn't care how he got things done, if people got hurt, so what. That concerned Jattin. Creed believed the end justified the means. If he thought he'd got the job done, made his mark and got recognition, all was good. And the more recognition he got, the more he wanted."

"Sounds like a god complex," Ultin put in.

"Exactly." Hiymm met them straight on. "He was always a little stuck on himself but, as time went on, it got worse. I'm not trying to make light of it. You must understand this. Attention feeds him and he is too powerful to ignore. Creed came from a wealthy family that wielded a lot of power. That's why, when Jattin first brought up his concerns, the council went against him. Creed showed so much talent, it was just another family coup and they were not going to lose that. To be honest, he was one of the strongest talents I've seen, rivaled with Jattin—maybe even Keyen."

"What was his talent?" Cassie asked curiously.

"He's telekinetic but showed signs of energy talent, being able to manipulate it. One of the first double talents we'd seen."

"So what happened to him? Why have we never heard anything about him?" Bass asked.

"Tasc is working on that. What we've found out is pretty sketchy. He disappeared for a while after he left, then his father died of heart trouble. Shortly after that, his brother died in an accident. There is evidence that Drasc took over the family holdings. He has been quite a recluse. His estates are like fortresses."

An image came up of an overhead shot of a huge estate

sitting on low cliffs over the ocean. The mammoth main house was surrounded with various sporting arenas and nearly a dozen other buildings. Everything had a grand appearance, including the massive fence that encompassed the whole property. A cove with a dock and several water crafts could be seen, plus what looked like several beach houses.

"Raebent hues." The exclamation escaped Ultin. "You weren't joking when you said fortress."

The room was silent again, a minute passed before one of the other team members spoke up. "So what do we know about the others?"

"The one's a pyro. What's the woman?" Sansa asked.

"Some kind of telepath," Hiymm answered. "She tried to knock Rori out at the transport dock or, at least, calm her to the point they'd have no problem taking her."

"What's going on here?" Orn motioned to when Rori focused on them in the crowd after rescuing Tomma.

"Rori?" Hiymm turned to her.

She had to swallow before she dared speak. "I felt a strong compulsion to go to him, Drasc Creed."

There were several intakes of breathes from people around the table. Keyen tightened beside her, his hand resting on the table clenched into a fist.

"Someone's strong enough to do that?" The question came from Cassie.

"Yes," Hiymm said plainly. "Their difficulty is Rori is equal or stronger than her."

"Or maybe they are going after her because she is more susceptible?" Keyen pointed out.

Hiymm shook his head. "I don't think so. They'd have no way to know. We didn't know until after she was here and tested that her empathy was that strong, and they were waiting at the transport dock for her before that, but that may make them want her more."

"What do you mean want her?" Sansa asked.

"It's something else I wanted to bring up. Since the attempted kidnapping using talents, we decided to check on other high talents not active in positions." Hiymm pursed his lips and a shadow seemed to fall over him. "So far, we have found three who have gone missing in the last two years. All are women and all under the age of thirty. No connection was made because they were far apart, different areas, and two were moving because of changing jobs, but we haven't been able to locate them anywhere. One of the missing is Carin Geac."

Rori didn't recognize the name, but it was obvious everyone else in the room did.

"No," Cassie and Bass's denial was joined by Keyen and Tankin.

"Can't be." Ultin got out.

"You're—" Whatever Sansa was going to say died on her lips with shock.

Hiymm just nodded. "She left on a vacation after she left the Guardians six months ago and has not returned. There has been no contact with her. She was feeling burned out and wanted to be on her own, so her family didn't think too much about it, though they've been getting very concerned."

A heaviness settled over the room.

"Okay," Orn injected after a full minute of silence. "Where did the other talents come from? High talents are logged at testing."

"That question came up earlier, and now that we know about Creed, we may have come up with a possible answer. One of Creed's companies has a research division on talents, how they are affected by chemicals and other stimulants. A couple years ago, a missive was sent to the council that they were doing testing to artificially boost mid-level talents, ones measurable but not strong enough to really use in high level positions."

"I haven't heard of this," Orn said.

"That's because there was no real investigation."

"Why not?" The woman from the other team asked.

"The man who made the claim died of a heart attack before the meeting. There was an inquiry, but the company said the man had been let go and was disgruntled."

"Convenient," Ultin added.

Rori had to agree then the thought struck her. "Drasc Creed's father died of a heart attack." The words slipped out in hushed words but everyone else heard her.

"Yes, and Drasc can control energy." Keyen followed her line of thought, looking up at Hiymm.

"I hadn't thought of that." There was no doubt he was now. "Well, I want all of you to use extreme care especially when you are sent out on rescue. Be aware of everyone around you, watch each other's back. I want you to stick together in downtime too. No one goes anywhere alone, always in a minimum of twos at all times." The director stood. "That's all for now. I will give updates when we learn something new. Dismissed." He turned and walked out of the room leaving the group talking behind him.

Anger, frustration and speculation were only some of the emotions that radiated off the two teams of Guardians, and after the already taxing day Rori had endured, it didn't take her long to be drained by them. She needed time alone. She wanted to go running down on the beach, but after what Hiymm had said, that wasn't going to be happening. Still, she had to get away.

"You want to go with us?" It took Rori several seconds to register the other team had left the room and Cassie was talking to her.

"Pardon?" She tried to come up with what they'd been talking about.

"Evening snack," Tankin gave helpfully, an excited expression returned to his face.

After the last hour of tension, it was a soothing release and she smiled. "No. Thanks. I'm kind of worn out. I think

I'll head up to bed."

The others filed out until Keyen was the only one left in the room with her. He stopped in front of her. "Are you okay?" His golden eyes took her in, and for a moment, she felt soothed then she started to feel heat rise within her.

"Yes." She stuttered over the word, feeling herself flush. "It's just … it's been a major emotional gambit for me today, after quite a week."

"Would you like me to walk with you?" He shifted a little closer.

"No, you can go join the others. I'll be okay, I promise."

His hand bumped into hers and caught giving her a light squeeze. "See you in the morning."

"Goodnight." Rori felt breathless as he walked away. It took a minute to calm her heart before she followed. A few minutes later, when the door to her chambers slid closed behind her, sealing out all the stray emotions, she sighed in relief. Instead of heading to bed, she changed into her sleepwear and settled into a stretching routine she used to relax and free up her muscles. She was just finishing up when her comm-link sounded. Her grandfather's image came into view as she activated it.

"Rori, how are you?" She had to rely on his image to read his concern but it wasn't difficult to tell.

"I'm fine."

"I just got done talking to Manning. He said you were amazing on the rescue today." There was pride in her grandfather's words.

"I don't know about amazing but it went well. I think I will fit in just fine."

"They are a good crew. I remember when each of them came for training. They were all so young. But they have developed nicely. What do you think of Keyen Saegun?"

Rori picked up a craftiness in her grandfather and wished she could read him but it was impossible through the comm. Still she studied him. "You're not trying matchmaking, are you?" Before she could stop it the image of Keyen came to her mind along with a disturbing flash over her senses.

Her grandfather laughed. "No, but I am pleased the way that boy turned out."

"He said you helped him, watched over him."

"He was so hurt when he arrived and so full of not just talent but power. Fortunately, he was such a good boy, and now he's grown and learned to handle his talent. He's a good man. I'm proud of him. I guess you can tell. He needed me, and I think I needed him because I had such limited access to you back then."

Rori understood what he was saying. Her grandfather regretted not being able to be there for most of her growing up years. "I knew you loved me," she said gently.

"You were so easy to love, and I'm not talking about your talent."

"I know, you cared even when I showed only to be lower-mid range."

"Yes, well that's past. How are you doing with the adjustment?"

"Good." She thought for a moment. "It has been better than I thought. Though, I still have trouble thinking of shielding and doing it. It comes better when I just react."

"Well, if I had to pick which way to start working with it, instinct is better. It's easier working on developing it consciously than teaching it to come naturally without thought."

"I hope so."

"It will be. Manning brought me up on what's happening. I want you to be careful. I don't like the patterns we see developing. Manning doesn't miss patterns. If he sees it, it's there, and Drasc Creed's involvement can only mean something bad. Especially if as Manning fears, he's been experimenting on talents to boost them."

"Do you think it is possible?" Rori felt a twinge of fear.

"It's always been speculated on. When I was younger, it was looked into. The problem was the only way to know was to experiment on talents. It caused quite a stir. Then, when some of the subjects who volunteered were physically damaged, a ban on all testing was decreed."

"How were they damaged?" Her fear spiked.

"Several were fried. All became unstable and a couple turned violent. They became crazed, cunning killers. I was on the team that had to go after them. We didn't take one alive, either we were forced to kill them or they killed themselves." Pain was in his words.

Rori knew how her grandfather felt about life.

"Do you think they are experimenting on talents?" she asked.

"I'm afraid with Drasc, anything is possible. He is wrapped up in himself. That's why I want you to be especially careful. He may see using or hurting you as a way to get back at me."

Chapter Nine

"Rori, duck!"

Rori dropped to the ground and rolled to the side in time to see the disk veer away as it flew over her and knew Keyen had shifted it. She came to her feet running for the control panel. She opened it and dodged to the side as another disk flew passed her. Swinging back, she flipped the series of switches shutting down the training exercise.

"Woo. Hah," Exaltation erupted from Ultin and Tankin, with cheers echoing from the others.

"Record time," Keyen said as they gathered in the middle of the training room.

After the energy port rescue, they had a computer simulation set up for them. Fortunately, there had only been two minor rescue runs, so over the week they were able to spend most of their time training, letting Rori integrate into the team. Now they moved together with ease. Shielding was coming easier for her, but she was still stronger when it was a natural reaction.

"Great day-" Keyen started but Ultin cut him off.

"No, tomorrow's a great day. Our day off." Ultin hooted, giving Tankin a hand slap.

Rori had learned that the two men had a light side, loving to joke and play, and they fed off each other. But when it came to work, they were all serious. She trusted either at her back.

"So what are you going to do for your day off?" Cassie

looked at Rori. "We're going to hit the street fair. Want to join us?"

Rori was about to answer but Keyen beat her to it. "We already have plans."

Rori jerked around to look at him, her surprise evident, but it didn't seem to bother anyone else. And any objection she might have formed disappeared when she caught the gleam in his eye. He was challenging her to object.

"Maybe we'll join you later," she said to enforce part of her will.

"Great," Sansa said. "The music in the evening should be hot."

Rori became aware of the buzzing across her senses and honed in on it without thought.

"It looks like Keyen's making his move." Rori got the sense of Cassie with the words.

"What makes you think he hasn't already?" Bass answered.

"We've been kind of busy and we all had dinner together every night. You think he's kissed her?" Cassie asked back.

"Well, yeah." Her twin exclaimed.

"He has not!" Rori burst out, feeling a wave of embarrassment at the conversation. She couldn't believe what they were saying.

"Rori, you heard that?" Cassie stared at her, shock on her face.

Rori blushed. "Everyone could, you just said it." She looked at the group and found them looking at her curiously.

"No, they couldn't," Bass said a little in awe. "We were mind talking between ourselves."

"No one has ever been able to pick us up before," Cassie finished his thought. "But you've done it before."

Rori looked from one to the other. "No," then added, "I don't know."

"Rori?" Keyen said her name and she turned to him.

There was question in his gaze and she answered it. "I don't know."

"This could be real handy if she can," Keyen pointed out.

"Rori, can you pick up what I'm thinking?" Bass leaned toward her.

She tried a second then shook her head. "No."

"How about me?" Cassie took her attention.

Rori focused on Cassie but nothing came to her mind. "No."

Cassie looked at Bass, and Rori unconsciously reached up to brush away the buzz from her temple.

It was Keyen that caught the motion. "Rori, what did you just do?"

"What?" She turned to him.

"You just brushed back a lock of hair." He reached up and did so at her temple, where she had. "I thought it was just a habit you do. I've heard some women do. But you don't do that all the time."

The buzz came back and her hand automatically came up. She halted the motion and looked at her hand. Out of the corner of her eye, she saw Bass and Cassie nod.

"What happened just now?" Keyen probed.

Rori felt a touch uneasy. "There was just a kind of a buzz, like hearing a bug by your ear."

"And you've heard it before?" Keyen took over questioning.

"Well, yes."

"Have you always heard it?" he probed, his blue eyes studying her.

She got that it was important and thought hard about it. "No, it's just been in the last couple days, and it hasn't been often."

"And when you heard Cassie and Bass, what was it like?"

"I don't know. I heard them, but it was kind of muted, like they were whispering."

Keyen looked to the twins. "Try again."

After a minute, Rori shrugged her shoulders. "Nothing."

"Maybe it has to do with emotions?" Tankin suggested. "Rori's an empath. Her skills seemed to be linked around that."

"You may be right. We'll have to check it out some more. In fact, I think we'll stop by and talk to Areathea or Narrasa before dinner."

"You do that, but for now, we're off." Ultin rubbed his hands together in anticipation.

"As off as we get," Keyen added.

"Don't put a damper on it. Think positive, a whole day free. Let's go."

"Just remember, stay together."

"Yes, papa." Ultin saluted.

Keyen just grinned, obviously used to the by-play.

As the group turned Keyen caught Rori's arm, keeping her back. He waited for the others to leave. "So what would you like to do tomorrow?"

Rori caught a small side shift movement in him and opening her senses, realized he was nervous. Keyen was afraid she'd turn him down. It made her feel good knowing it was important to him. That he wanted to be with her. For the last week, he hadn't given any hint of feeling for her, and she'd begun to wonder if all she was feeling was one-sided. Now she knew Keyen just kept things locked tight inside him and now he opened to it. She could feel his longing burning under the surface like his talent.

"I thought you had a plan," she teased.

"I have one idea but I also want to know what you'd like to do. You haven't had a lot of chances to do stuff with moving here and getting settled in. Now, with having to have a constant companion with you, it doesn't allow much free time. I thought you might like to get out."

"You're right."

"So, what have you been wanting to do?"

She felt her lips tug into a smile. "What I've really been wanting is to go for a run."

"A run." His eyebrow arched. "We run every day."

"Yes, but I want to run on the beach. My grandfather and I would do it when I came to visit him. I loved it."

He was smiling now. "I can go for that. How about a picnic breakfast after?"

"Picnic breakfast?" This time it was her turn to arch an eyebrow.

He nodded. "Though we call it our day off, you never know. We still could be called at any time. If we wait for lunch, we might not get it."

"I've never had a picnic breakfast," she said, feeling a twinge of excitement.

"Neither have I." His eyes blazed as he looked at her, and Rori felt the breath leave her. She could have sworn the air began to heat around them. Then suddenly Keyen pulled back. "Come on, let's go see if we can find Narrasa and Areathea and find out what they think you're experiencing."

Keyen stayed with Rori as they talked with Narrasa. The man ran a hand scanner over her. The muscles in the man's face twitched, then an eyebrow kicked up.

"Interesting," he finally spoke. "When we ran the diagnostic you showed no sign of telepathy, and it is not reading now either. But you are in a state of flux."

"What does that mean?" Rori asked, feeling self-conscious.

"Just what you're thinking, your talent is still evolving."

"So I may lose this ... boost to my talent?" Rori could feel Keyen's eyes go to her as she asked the question.

"No, I'm quite certain you will remain like you are

now. Maybe even grow stronger. It is hard to tell. The closest case we have to give us a guide would probably be Keyen." Narrasa motioned to him. "You both came into your talents, in Rori's case the strength of your talent, under severe trial and stress. It's hard to say if they had developed naturally if you would have been so strong. Keyen...," he looked at him. "You were so young and traumatized, and you...," he switched back to Rori. "You had suppressed your natural talent for so long and when it came out it was, for a better word, ripped from you, much like Keyen's was from him. You are both the out of norm cases and, honestly, I don't think we've yet seen all either of you can do."

Rori caught the look of surprise on Keyen.

Narrasa gave him a knowing look before turning back to her. "As for what you're experiencing, still I'm only guessing, but I think it links to your empathy. The twins' bond is an emotional link, so somehow you are tapping into that bond. It will be interesting to see if, as you develop camaraderie with your team, you develop any links with the others. We've already seen your empathy can do great things when invoked. Unless there is anything else, keep us appraised of any changes," the man said in way of dismissal.

"So it looks like Tankin had it pretty much right," Rori said as they headed out.

Keyen gave a little laugh. "You know, he usually is. Let's go eat. I'm starved, and we have a picnic to plan for tomorrow."

C38O

Rori came to a stop, trying to draw air into her lungs. "Remind me to quit trying to beat you in a race." She got the words out between gasps.

Keyen grinned at her, breathing in much the same condition. "It's never going to happen."

"Conceited."

"Just good. And I believe this means you have to set up breakfast and serve me." There was a hint of wickedness in his tone.

"Here I get invited to breakfast and have to do all the work," she grouched but there was no heat to it.

"You're the one who wanted to race." He shifted. His hand bumped hers and caught it.

Rori looked at the hold then up at him, her heart racing for a different reason. "I'm all sweaty." The words slipped out.

"I know." A low, huskiness entered his voice and he drew closer to her. Her breathing, that had just started to ease, picked up a new labored movement. His head bent toward her. Her lips parted on their own accord. She was spellbound by the intensity in his eyes. Suddenly, he dropped his shoulder. Wrapping his arms around her legs, he lifted, draping her over his shoulder.

"So let's clean off." He ran waist deep into the water and threw her into the incoming wave.

Rori was sputtering and laughing when she surfaced. She turned to splashing him, but she lost sight of him as he dove under the water. Knowing an attack was coming, she turned to swim away but a hand caught her ankle pulling her back. His arm wrapped around her thighs. Rori was hauled out of the water as Keyen rose like a serpent from the deep.

Unable to contain herself, Rori threw her arms up in the air letting out a shriek of pleasure as the water streamed down her. When she looked down, he was smiling up. She tipped back her head and laughed.

Keyen knew he'd never seen such a glorious sight. He held pure joy in his arms and it filled him, settling in his heart and he knew he'd keep it forever. He swung her around, ignoring the waves that buffeted him as her arms, still stretched to the sky, seemed to pull light down upon them. Then she smiled down and the sun took second place in radiance.

"Something tells me you liked that." Keyen didn't know how he managed to get the words out.

"Oh, yes." Her hands came down onto his shoulders.

He felt her body tighten and stretch along him. He knew she wasn't doing it as a temptation, but he was aware of the length of her against his body. Their jogging clothes offered little barrier in separating them. Heat burned in him and his gaze fell to her lips. All night he'd thought of them.

From the moment she'd answered Cassie's unspoken question, he felt he'd known what the question was. Now he had to know for sure. "When you said 'he has not' to Cassie yesterday, what was that about?"

Color rose in her cheeks. Her eyes went to his mouth and he had his answer for certain.

"I think it's time to change that." He lowered her down his body, giving her plenty of time to object.

"This probably isn't smart. We're teammates." Even as she said the words, she dipped her head to his. "Keyen," she whispered his name just as their lips touched. He felt his name on her lips and followed it in.

Keyen would be the first to admit he didn't have a lot of experience with women, but he didn't need it. Everything with Rori was right, perfect and natural. The kiss continued and he became lost in it until a large wave broke over them and almost took his feet out from under them.

Rori pulled back looking as dazed as he felt. Nothing like that had ever happened to him before. He wondered if it might be her empathy talent coming out, but looking at her, she appeared just as surprised by her response. He searched to name the reaction and came up with several. On a primitive level, he'd say he had found his mate, a spiritualist would say soul, and a romantic would call it love. He figured it was all just Aurora.

He lowered Rori the rest of the way down, so she stood

on her own. Instead of pulling away, she laid her cheek on his chest, resting there, over his heart where she belonged. Warm water lapped at them in caressing strokes instead of chilling their ardor. It took Keyen a second to realize the water was artificially heated from him and figured it was probably a good thing they were standing in water so he didn't internally self-combust.

He felt a shift in his arms and looked down in time to see Rori raise her head and meet his gaze. Water-spiked lashes framed dazed eyes. Her lips were rosy and slightly swollen, he thought with satisfaction. She obviously was as affected as he was.

Keyen lifted his hand, cupping her cheek with his palm, caressing her bottom lip with his thumb. She sucked in a breath, her eyes searching his face. He felt a tingle across his senses and knew she was reaching out with her talent.

"We shouldn't have—"

He cut her off. "I think we should."

"It's going to complicate things."

"Yes, but they got complicated the moment I met you out on that beam."

"You knew then?"

He brushed the thumb along her jaw. His eyes held hers. "Yes, just as you did." He knew she wanted to object, but it didn't come because it was the truth.

"Maybe I should've requested another team," she whispered.

"I don't think that will work. Something tells me it's not a good idea to separate us." He continued to let his fingers tenderly learn her cheek.

His touch was a bare whisper on her skin but she felt it to her soul. It seemed to touch something deep, an ancient part of her. She didn't need her talent to feel the answering awareness in him. It was like part of them had awakened and joined.

"What does this mean?" Rori thought she knew but was afraid to say it out loud.

"I think we are already a unit."

Rori felt her insides lurch. The oddity of the term hit her but yet, it fit correctly. A unit, one, she couldn't deny what he said. Still, her head shook. "You're meaning a connection between us? Have you ever heard of that kind of link before?"

"No," he said truthfully, dropping his hand down to cover hers. "And I don't know what it means. Maybe it's just me wanting you near, but I can't help but think it's more."

"So what do we do?"

"I'm not sure. I take it this has never happened to you before? I mean, it's not a side of your talent?"

Rori was already shaking her head. She closed her eyes, pulling back into herself as she did since she was a little child when the things around her hurt. She only got a second of inner-contemplation when she felt Keyen squeeze down on her hand drawing her back out.

"Rori, please don't pull away from me."

"I," she was going to deny it then realized that was indeed what she was going to do. Hide deep within herself like she had done with her talent. "I'm frightened." The words came out instead. "My world is changing so fast."

"And, I'm another change." Forced humor sounded in his voice, but she appreciated him trying to make it light.

"I think you might be the biggest of all." She pushed a grin of her own.

"If it makes it any better, I think you are what I've been missing in my life."

"Keyen it's so fast but..."

"It's there," he finished for her.

"Yes." Rori had to agree and shifted back but not out of his hold. She tilted her head up. "Maybe it would be better if we didn't spend too much time alone."

"Are you scared of me?" he challenged.

"No." Her defense was weakened and she blushed.

"Oh, scared of yourself," he teased. "But considering it's possible we just put on a show for the security people, we may want to be careful. I really don't want to broadcast a relationship between us. We'll face enough challenges being on the same team and both high talents."

"I don't think we can keep it from the team. They already suspect."

"I know. I'm not worried about them. They won't let it out. I'm referring to the media. You haven't experienced it yet because Manning and Tasc have kept news about you under wraps so far, but they like to focus on Guardians when they get something juicy. A relationship between two Guardians would flash on every media. Especially with you being brand new. They couldn't get enough of it."

Rori dropped her head to her hands and groaned.

"Hey, it's all right." He gripped her arms, urging her to look up.

"I finally find someone who feels right and it's going to be difficult."

There was a pleading look in her eyes he had no answer for because he felt the same. "You know what they say about good things come to those who wait and the best are worked for."

"You're taking this pretty easy."

He wanted to disagree, but he knew in a way, it was true. He was already used to the life of a Guardian. It was one of the reasons he had limited relationships. "I've waited a long time, and I knew you when I saw you. I just had to accept it and I found it very easy to do. I kind of like looking at you. Being around you is nice too." He grabbed her hand before she could retaliate, sending her a wicked grin, before settling to a little more serious. "Besides, I haven't been distracted with all the extra emotional upheavals you've had."

He brushed her cheek with his lips before pulling back. "But you do have a point about being alone. For now, we'd better spend most of our time together around others. So let's go have our picnic then we'll go clean up and find the others and enjoy the festival."

Together they walked out of the surf.

CRBO

The festival was like nothing Rori had ever seen before. Several streets in the city center had been blocked off. Booths of food, art items and people packed the area. In the main square, a huge stage had been set up with an enormous vision screen behind to highlight scenes of what was happening all around.

"You're looking a little wide-eyed." Tankin laughed at Rori.

"This is amazing. I think there are more people here in this street than there are in the whole community in which I lived."

Tankin laughed again. "It's still early. This evening there will probably be double, maybe triple the people."

Rori had seen pictures of festivals like this before but was having trouble believing it was real. "You're enjoying laughing at me aren't you?" She looked at the large man. Dressed in plain clothes did nothing to make him look less intimidating.

"Actually, more just remembering. I grew up in a Geo community about the same size as your Ag. When I first came here, I was just like you. I'd never seen anything like it."

"So you were fourteen when you came to Rae-Isis?"

"Fifteen. They were slow getting to my area to do the more extensive testing. They kind of figured the person who had done mine messed up. Neither of my parents are strong talents and a talent link into the ground is odd. They actually still haven't come up with the term for it because I'm the only one they've found."

"We're all just a bunch of misfits aren't we?" Ultin said over her shoulder.

"That's what makes us special." Tankin grinned. "Come on. Rori needs to try some of those skewers."

"That means he's hungry," Sansa put in. "But they are real good."

"You're from here aren't you?" Rori moved beside her as they followed Tankin and Ultin through the crowd to an area where smoke rose with an appealing smell.

"Yes, from the far side of the city. Ultin's from the outskirts on the other side. Bass and Cassie where raised in Meclan. Both their parents are pretty high level org and info techs. Their dad reminds you a lot of Tasc, just not quite so high. I got my talent from my mother. She works at a water treatment plant. Both my parents do, but my mother's a mid-range water affinitive. It can actually be traced through her line to back before people understood talents."

Rori had learned a lot about the team over the last few days. It was nice having Sansa warming up to her. Right after the rescue at the power plant the woman began to soften.

"How you doing with the crowd?" Sansa looked at her questioningly.

"Good. Most everyone's excited, so it's like a buzz of energy in the air. So, if I start getting a little carried away, bring me down."

"My pleasure, one cold breeze waiting." She laughed when Rori sent her a sour look but they both were serious.

The emotions across the crowd were so strong they seemed to shimmer around them in vibrant waves. Rori could touch them if she opened her mind but holding back was becoming easier.

"Here try this."

Rori jerked back as Ultin thrust a skewer of meat in front of her face. She accepted taking a bite just as she caught a wicked glint in Ultin's eye. Too late, rich flavor greeted her followed by a shock of hot spice. She gasped, her free hand coming up to wave in front of her face. "Oh my. Oh, I'll take the cool blast now." She gasped and tried to blow out but it did nothing to alleviate the fire in her mouth.

"Here, try this instead." Sansa handed her a small piece of fruit.

Anxiously, Rori bit into it, letting the sweet counter the spicy. Still she blew out, having to wipe tears from her eyes.

Ultin laughed.

"Hey, what are you doing to her?" Keyen demanded, coming up behind them. His shoulder bumped hers as he reached out with his opposite hand to take the skewer, bringing it to his lips. Before Rori could warn him, he took a bite but didn't seem to mind the hot flavor.

"Sorry, I didn't think it was that hot," Ultin said, his face still alight with amusement.

"You don't think anything is hot," Keyen answered back.

"Watch what you accept from this guy. He burned his taste buds out years ago." Cassie moved up beside her. "Let's try some sweet-n-mild ones. Those are more my style."

Rori accepted the new one more cautiously, though it wasn't necessary. It was incredible tasting. "How can you eat that?" She looked back at Keyen who was finishing off the one he'd taken from her.

"I got used to Ultin trying to burn off my taste buds years ago. I can hold my own against him now."

"It's a male thing." Sansa leaned over.

"Hey, I'm willing to try the other." Keyen started to reach for Rori's new skewer.

"Oh no, I like this one just fine. You get your own." She pulled her hand back glaring threateningly.

Keyen's brow arched as if he debated challenging her then he motioned to the vendor for another one. "Mmm." He let out biting into it.

"Find anything interesting?" Sansa asked Cassie who had been checking out some of the shops with Keyen and Bass in tow.

"There's a couple great stands over there I want to show Rori." Cassie pointed to the side. "They have some really nice things she might like to look at since she's just setting up her chambers."

As soon as everyone finished eating, they ambled over to where Cassie wanted to go. Rori was surprised the guys didn't complain about shopping. Hanging close, though, they opted to stay in a shop just one down.

"You'd think we couldn't take care of ourselves," Sansa remarked at their obvious movement. "We go into all sorts of dangerous situations, and they worry about us at a festival."

"Yeah," Cassie agreed. "And it's not like I'm ever out of contact." She tapped her head.

Rori understood what she meant. Even without the IPI, Cassie was still linked to Bass. It was funny the guys were so obviously keeping an eye on them. It was nice being part of a close knit group. She did feel one of them now. The warmth of it spread through her.

"Well, let's see if we can spend some of your relocation credits. See anything you like?" Cassie cut through her thoughts, and Rori started to look around.

She did find several things. There was a nice table to go in her seating area carved out of a beautiful piece of wood with an intriguing swirling grain in it. She got a soft throw blanket and a painting of a waterfall in a jungle. Her favorite find was an iridescent bowl of shifting colors. It reminded her of shifting emotions but was soothing all the same. The craftsmanship was incredible. After arranging for them to be delivered, they went to find the men, which

ALYSIA S. KNIGHT

wasn't hard as they all stepped into the street at the same time.

"All done shopping?" Keyen asked first.

"Yes. I've spent enough today," Rori answered.

"She didn't even make a dent in her budget," Cassie countered.

"That's my sister. She'd have you all set in a day. Sometimes I think that's where her true talent lies." Bass dropped his arm over Cassie's shoulder in what Rori now realized was a normal manner.

"So what's next?" she asked.

"Music," Ultin answered. "I vote for the azure stage. One of my favorite groups is supposed to be up soon."

"Fine by me." Keyen looked down at Rori for agreement.

"I'm good for it," she answered his unasked question.

"Don't worry, we're safe," Sansa said. "His taste in music is much better than his taste in food."

"I have great taste in food," Ultin retorted.

"If you're trying out to be a flame thrower," she challenged.

Ultin threw back his head and laughed. "Just because you can't handle it."

Rori became aware of curious looks as they moved through the crowd. As if noticing the same thing, Tankin spoke up. "We'd better split up a bit. We're starting to draw attention."

With a silent command, Cassie and Bass peeled off. Keyen took Rori's hand and led her off at a different angle.

"Having a good time?" Keyen lowered his head toward her.

"Yes." She met his gaze.

"Good, because I'm still kind of wishing we were on the beach." He winked and the action took her breath.

Heat radiated off Keyen a second before he backed it off. For a minute, the crowd around them was forgotten, and she was lost in his amber eyes. Her heart rate increased. Keyen's thumb brushed over the pulse point on her wrist as if to check on it. The corners of his lips rose in acknowledgement.

Then someone bumped into Rori's back, and she fell against Keyen's chest. His arms came up around her, and she found herself sheltered against his body. His head lowered and Rori responded tilting her head up. At the last second, a burst of fireworks on the stage had them breaking apart.

"Man, and I was trying to help," Tankin said.

"Thanks, we are trying to keep this to ourselves," Keyen looked back at him.

"Like that's going to happen," the big man scoffed. "Come on, we found a good spot over here, out of the way but with a prime view and sound."

"Am I going to be able to hear when we leave?" Keyen sent him a sour look.

Tankin just laughed, leading them to a small platform where equipment for videoing the crowd was placed. "What do you think? Prime, huh. Bass ran into a friend who's on staff. She said we could hang out up there with her."

"Not exactly inconspicuous, but we'll have a great view. Why not." Keyen motioned Rori to the ladder first and they climbed up to the others.

They were listening to the second band when Rori's attention slipped out to the crowd. Waves of pleasure wafted up to her. She was feeling happy and relaxed when the spike of maliciousness hit her like a knife slicing deep.

Her gasp was loud enough that everyone turned her direction.

"What is it?" Keyen reached for her, taking her arm as she swayed.

"Something's wrong," the words made it out as a whisper. "Someone … evil. Drasc! He's here."

Chapter Ten

Cassie turned toward them. "All these people." The anguish she was picking up from Rori registered on her face and was mirrored by Bass who, with the rest of the team, was already scanning the crowd.

Keyen realized even he could feel Rori's unease. "Can you find him?" He ignored the emotion.

She shook her head.

"Rori, you have to tamp down." Keyen tried to draw her attention.

"What?" She looked up, anxiety formed creases on her brow.

"You're projecting."

"I..." She stopped then started again. "He doesn't care if he kills everyone here." Even as the words made it out, the sense of fear she was sending ended and she straightened. Back in control, she continued to search the crowd as she talked. "He's planning to hurt a lot of people. He wants to. He wants to show his power." Her gaze moved toward the stage on the far side. Everyone else followed her.

Keyen scanned faces as his attention divided. "Link open, command center." The acknowledgement was hardly there before he started. "We need full deployment at the festival. Orn's team, our gear and Mass Med."

"Orn's team's already out, structure failure in Taeleese. A sled with your gear being deployed and med."

The reply came immediately followed by Manning Hiymm's voice cutting in.

"Keyen, what's happening?"

"Rori's detected Drasc Creed here at the festival."

"She's certain?" Hiymm asked but there was no doubt in his tone.

Before he could answer, Rori did. "Oh yes. The malice off him is so strong it's unmistakable. There's an unhealthy hum in the air." Her voice was steadier now but the expression on her face was no less intent.

Keyen didn't doubt her and Hiymm must not have either. "Full team deployment," Hiymm ordered.

Keyen joined in the search, feeling his own sense of frustration. Several thousand people packed the area just in front of the stage area and that wasn't counting those milling around the concessions and at the other stages. Finding Drasc would be like finding a diamond in a puddle of broken glass. But Rori was focused on the one area so that's where they would start.

Tension rose with the crescendo of the music.

"Whatever happens, it's going to be big," Rori said in a hushed voice. Before she could say more, fireworks burst up from the stage with the last beat of the music followed by a bigger explosion that rocked the ground. All the remaining fireworks in the area detonated at once.

The music ended but the noise level grew. Screams of excitement turned to fear.

The platform they were on shook and swayed, knocking Sansa, Bass, Cassie and Ultin's friend to their knees. Ultin, standing close to the edge, was thrown over. Only his quick reflexes and hours of training enabled him to catch a support rod to break his fall. Keyen caught Rori's arm as she almost followed Ultin over the side. He grabbed a piece of bolted down equipment to steady them.

"Sansa," Keyen's command was unnecessary as, even from her knees Sansa gathered her talent to dampen the air around the largest concentration of fireworks shooting sparks into the crowd.

Tankin grabbed Ultin, hauling him back up as a burst of fire blasted above Tankin's head.

"That's not me," Ultin yelled, as he dropped to the platform followed by Tankin.

Keyen pulled Rori to the ground. Another ball of fire hit the equipment above them, blowing it off the platform in a burst of flames.

"We have to get off of here." There was no need for Keyen to say they were under attack. "Tank, Bass, Cassie, go and take her with you." He motioned to the recording tech. "Rori try to cover them. Sansa stay with the fires," Keyen yelled to be heard over the screams from the crowd and then only the aid of their communicators in their IPIs let him be heard.

Keyen moved to the edge with Ultin to find where the attack was coming from. Tankin gripped the sides of the ladder and, locking his feet on the outside of it, slid down. Cassie moved the tech into position to follow him. A ball of fire shot toward them. Rori's shield intersected it a few feet from the tech and the fire burst apart, but the tech, startled by the explosion, lost her hold and fell. A scream didn't even make it out of her mouth before Tankin plucked her out of the air. Cassie went next, ignoring the blast against Rori's shield. Bass didn't hesitate following his sister down.

Keyen flinched when a fire ball exploded in the air over his head as it connected with one from Ultin.

"This guy's good," Ultin yelled.

"Can you handle him?" Keyen shouted back. Not waiting for the nod that he knew would be there if he looked. "Rori, the crowd, you've got to calm them." There was no questioning her either.

Below them screams drowned out all other sound. Panicked people pushed and shoved, trying to flee but with no conscious thought of where to go. Keyen didn't want to think of people being trampled in the confusion. He felt the soothing waves wash over as Rori sent out calmness. He didn't know how she managed.

"Sansa," Keyen barked her name and the woman went over the edge. Ultin followed without waiting.

Below them the crowd quieted.

"Go." He grabbed Rori's arm propelling her to the ladder. Rori was just going over the edge when a burst of energy scored the ground near Keyen's foot. "They've changed to pulse lasers. Everyone be careful," he yelled, wishing he had his own laser.

Another burst hit dangerously close to Rori but she retained her hold. Keyen caught a panel leaning against the platform with his mind, raising it to shield her for her continued descent. As soon as her feet touched the ground, he raised the shield, sliding down the ladder as Tankin had.

He reached the ground, catching Rori's hand to pull her out of the main throng of people fleeing the area. Though no longer panicked, the crowd was in a highly unstable emotional state that wouldn't take much to stampede them again.

"Can you keep it up?" The words hardly left Keyen's mouth when another explosion rocked the stage area. Plumes of smoke and debris shot into the air. People began to scream again, but above the roar came the grind of metal ripping apart pierced the air. In stunned shock, all eyes went to the stage in time to see the massive frame holding the screen and columns of huge speakers sway and topple.

Rori cried out and Keyen felt the air around him shift and surge, rolling out toward the stage. Rori groaned but Keyen couldn't take his eyes off the area in front as the enormous structure caught and held in the air, stretched over the crowd.

"Raebent hues." Ultin's expression of amazement came over the open comm.

"Let's go. She can't hold that forever," Keyen yelled.

Tankin voiced amazement but no one answered.

Keyen locked on the first speaker lifting it free with his mind, lowering it safely to the ground. Bass and Cassie started doing the same with another. The rest of the team helped the security people, and others who hadn't panicked, move people out from under the hanging mass. With the largest loose items free Keyen concentrated on the metal frame trying to take as much weight as he could. Again the twins joined him, and to his side he heard Rori sigh in relief.

With the area cleared, they started to lower the frame works. It was still two meters from the ground when a laser blast almost cut down Bass and Cassie. Only the energy bolt from Ultin intersecting it saved them, but with their concentration broken on one side, it slammed to the ground with earth shuddering force.

Keyen groaned at trying to hold his side, lowering it more gently to the ground. Fatigue swamped his body, but he pushed it back, doing a quick check on his team. Tankin was not in sight. Cassie and Bass were on the far side helping several injured people to shelter. Sansa struggled to handle fires that dotted the area.

Out of the corner of his eye, Keyen saw a man carrying a child go down under the feet of the crowd and locked on him with his mind, lifting him out of the crowd. The man staggered as his feet touched the ground but remained upright.

Energy bursts from pulse lasers sparked randomly in the area. Keyen became aware of people screaming and crying. He also felt the soothing touch from Rori float out over the crowd as she tried to keep their panic down so they could be evacuated to safety.

He soaked up a little comfort and followed her energy patterns back to her. He located her behind a downed section of speaker about ten meters away. A girl about sixteen clung to her. Rori motioned to the girl who shook her head. Rori said something then motioned again giving the girl a little push. This time the girl obeyed. Stumbling, she ran. Keyen didn't have to see Rori's shield to know the minute it went up, protecting the girl and a dozen others who took the opportunity to run at the same time. Blasts peppered the shield, looking like a set of miniature fireworks going off. Using the shield for his own cover, he ran to another spot giving him a better view.

Whoever they were facing had the high ground and cover of trees on the park's hillside that backed the stage. To get to them they would have to cross the open square, working their way over and around the debris. Unfortunately, barriers and buildings hemmed them in on all sides.

"Sled's here with our gear." Tankin's voice came over the comm.

Keyen gave a verbal acknowledgement, but his attention was centered on where most of the laser fire was coming from. He calculated three positions, and each spot had to have at least two to three people. When flames shot up in a column in the middle of the square, he added the pyro to the count of adversaries. Keyen ignored the flames knowing Ultin would draw the heat out of it, effectively killing it before returning to help Sansa take care of the hot spots from the initial explosion.

Keyen started to go for a different location but held up as Tankin reached him with his utility vest.

"Thought you might want this." The big man had already donned his. "This is Rori's. The sled driver is taking the others theirs. Med-techs are set up in the street around the corner. They have their hands full already but at least they seem to be out of danger there. We've got to get these guys though. Got a plan?"

"Not one I'm really happy with. But as you say, we've got to get these guys and quickly. There are just too many people here."

"And like Rori said, they don't seem to care how many get hurt."

Keyen nodded, calling up his link to the others. "Sansa, you stay back and try to get all these fires under control before something blows up big time again. Cassie and Bass, I want you two," he addressed the twins, "to try working to the position on the far left." He focused on the spot, giving them a visual. "There are at least two in there. Ultin, you and Tank take the nest high up on the right. I think that's where the pyro's located. Rori and I are taking the middle. Let's throw everything we've got at them and see what we can flush out. Just be careful. They might be using lasers now, but we know they have a whole other bag of tricks."

There was only a brief acknowledgement, and they all started working their way forward much like they did in the training room. Tankin's initial route took him to Rori to drop off her vest before curving off toward Ultin. The fire power they were facing was intense but at least they were now equally armed.

Keyen motioned for Rori to remain while he made a run for the edge of the downed platform. He hadn't even covered a third of the distance when Rori's shield intercepted a laser blast that he'd missed. He jerked but didn't break his stride knowing none of the sparks would touch him. He, nor Rori, now worried about her ability to shield. It was as natural to her as breathing.

Going down into a slide which carried him to the edge of the platform, he took a second to survey the area before signaling Rori to move to her next position. As soon as she moved, he caught the glint of a laser sighting in on her. Before the person had a chance to fire, Keyen focused, locking onto the gun, pulling it toward him. With a cry, a man came flying out from behind a tree. As the man lost his grip on the gun, he was flung a good four meters. The assailant tumbled over and over until he came to rest in a motionless heap at the bottom of the hill.

Keyen paid him no more attention. He scanned for another visual to lock on. When he couldn't pinpoint anything, he fastened on a piece of debris and sent it into some brush where he knew attackers were hiding. He felt the impact as another mind locked on the section of scaffolding. The other person was strong but not strong enough to push it away, just deflect its course so it landed harmlessly to the side.

Keyen locked onto another piece throwing it at the same location as he sighted in with his laser. He fired then jerked back as a laser blast barely missed his head. Forced down by a shower of sparks, he dove for better cover while searching for the sniper that almost took him out.

He dodged again as he caught sight of the man on the edge of a building trying to get another shot at him. Keyen dove for cover and as he came to a stop, flat on the ground, he started firing, cutting bursts along the top of the building until he saw the man pitch forward off the roof.

Keyen ignored the fall, turning his attention back to the hillside and the attackers there. He saw two fireballs intersect and knew Ultin was in battle with the other pyro. Taking a second, he pulled up the others' locations. Sansa had contained the fires and was now with Cassie and Bass working their way to the attackers on the far side.

He found Rori about twenty meters to his left. With a quick look to the hill, he made a dash in her direction, firing as he ran. Return fire peppered around his every step. Diving over what used to be a speaker, he pulled back from firing as a young man rushed him. Keyen deflected the blow then caught the young man, flipping him to the ground, controlling the motion so as not to hurt him. "I'm a Guardian," he yelled before any of the others huddled there could react and charge him. It took a second for the words to sink in. The youth he still held, finally stopped fighting.

Keyen looked around at a dozen terror-filled eyes of the group clustered between the speaker and the stage. One young woman, that reminded him of Rori, slumped against a man, clasping her arm to her side. Two other girls had their arms wrapped around another boy, helping him stand. Keyen was already cataloging what he saw.

Most of what showed was scrapes and dirt. The one girl's arm was broken but he didn't have time to handle that. Ripping open a pocket on his pants, he pulled out a pressure bandage. Stepping to the young man held by the girls, Keyen tore open the young man's blood-soaked pant leg and placed the bandage over a gash on his leg.

"You've got to get out of here." He looked back at the youth who had attacked him. "I'll cover you until you get to the canopy over there." Keyen motioned where he wanted them to go. "Then stay behind it, and you can make your way to the street. They have med stations set up there. Tell them they have a bleeder. The bandage will hold for a while though. Okay?"

Keyen waited for him to nod. "You guys will have to take him. She'll be okay." He waited with a patience he didn't feel while they shifted position. "Ready?" When they nodded he activate his link. "Rori can you see my location?"

Her acknowledgement came after a second. "I need a shield here to cover these guys to the canopy." Her confirmation came immediately. "Go. You're covered, I promise. Just stay in a tight group and keep moving as fast as you can. Go!" When he barked the last word they moved.

They hardly stepped into the opening when the first laser blast connected with the shield Rori had up. Keyen turned and returned fire. Focused on getting the group away, he almost missed when the speaker shifted his way.

Only the other telekintic's lack of strength on moving it allowed Keyen the time to block it before the speaker pinned him. Still the distraction left him vulnerable. Laser fire scorched around him filling the air with a rank stench.

He had to move. Rori was still focused on covering the slow-moving group. Raising his head for a quick survey, he barely ducked down before a blast erupted where he'd been, showering him with sparks. He was getting tired of this. He could feel the fatigue in his body and knew the others had to be wearing down too with the prolong use of their talent.

Making a dive, Keyen rolled over the speaker, running as his feet hit the ground. Behind him, the speaker sliced in two, but he reached his next cover before any weapon fire found him. Unfortunately, he found his line of sight blocked.

Taking a deep breath, he sprinted for the back of the platform that put him just below the slope of the hill. He slid under the edge as laser fire cut through a piece of support structure, crashing it down at him. He caught it with his mind, only centimeters from his face. Groaning under the strain, he shoved it off to the side.

Keyen climbed to his feet, taking another survey of the team and his surroundings. The fire power was ominous. They'd faced multiple foes before but never this many, with this caliber of talents and weapons. He knew they were still outnumbered at least three to one. The thought was hardly through his mind when Cassie's voice came over the comm.

"We're pinned down and taking heavy fire."

Keyen shifted his focus back to the twins and Sansa. Sansa fought a fire that had erupted not far from her, cutting her off from the twins who were caught behind a pile of debris with laser blasts coming at them from three angles.

Keyen followed one line back to a sniper on the hillside and focused on the man. The distance was at his far limits but Keyen fought for the hold then pulled. There was nothing smooth in the way the man was ripped from the rock outcropping. He was flung down the hill until he collided with a tree, falling into a crumpled heap on the ground.

An acknowledgement from Bass reached him followed by the twins doing a similar maneuver on another attacker.

Pulling his attention back to his own surroundings, Keyen opened fire where he knew another group was barricaded. Return fire peppered around him from two other locations forcing him down. He pressed back against the stage, trapped again.

On the stage above him, a control panel blew apart sending shards and sparks at him. With no time to prepare, Keyen was only able to catch and stop a few pieces. Luckily, his vest shielded him from the worst, but still he felt the tiny bites of pain.

Ignoring the pain, Keyen came up in time to catch the movement in the air of what looked like a small bundle floating down the hill toward him. It took only a nano-second for his mind to recognize it was a bomb similar to the one that took out Rori's apartment.

He locked on it with his mind, but before he had time to wrestle it free and send it back, it exploded. The force of the explosion tumbled him back like a rag doll. Keyen smashed into what minutes earlier had been a recording station and fell to the ground stunned.

Rori's demand to know what happened jerked him back to alertness. He stumbled his way around behind the recording console, not that it gave him much cover. Tilting his head back, he closed his eyes in an effort to clear his mind and the ringing in his ears. Behind him the console shuddered with the impacting laser blast. Keyen knew it couldn't hold up long.

"Keyen." Rori voice came over the link again.

"I'm okay." He opened a view to her to see if she could cover him but her focus was still locked on the slow moving group. Her shield was taking continual hits. If he could hold out for a minute more she could cover him.

The thought hardly crossed his mind when the stench of fried wiring and plastic reached him. He picked the closest place for cover as he worked his feet under him. He waited out the next volley of fire then ran, shooting wildly at the hill in hopes of forcing the shooters there down.

He was three meters from the vehicle he was heading for when his mind seemed to stall out on him. Pressure in his mind tightened. The world lagged down to slow motion and his body followed. A staggered step backward saved him from one laser blast.

He tried to shake the fog away, and his thought cleared enough to realize that it had to be an attack from the hypno-talent Rori had described. He fought harder, forcing one foot in front of the other. To the side of him he was aware of something exploding but focused on making the next step that would have him safe behind shelter.

The blow hit him, and he dropped. Searing pain ripped his mind from the stupor into agony. At the next gasp for breath, he slipped into unconsciousness.

Chapter Eleven

Rori sighed with relief when the group finally made it behind the shelter. Fatigue permeated her body. Not even when Keyen was in one of his masochistic training moods had she felt so taxed. She wanted to think that it was because it was all so new to her that she felt so fatigued but couldn't as she could feel the weariness in the whole team.

She hadn't even realized she was so attuned to their individual strains of emotions, but she didn't doubt she was correctly identifying each of them, just as she was aware of the unwholesome evil in Drasc.

As soon as she thought of Drasc, she could almost taste the foul bitterness of him. Keeping it in her thoughts, she turned to the hillside, locking on a spot near the top. Heavy trees and bushes obscured her view but she knew he was there, waiting back, savoring with glee like some sadistic puppet master.

Raising her laser weapon, she steadied it with her other hand and started to tighten her finger. She forced her mind from the fact that she had never fired on another human before. She held her breath and screamed in pain. Her shot went wild but she didn't notice.

"Keyen," she cried out, activating her viewer.

Nothing came over the link but she knew it wouldn't. Still, she was already headed for his position, locking into the instinct deep inside her. Lasers deflected off her shield unnoticed by her as she darted around debris in her mad dash to reach him.

"Keyen." Tears burned her eyes at the sight of him lying crumbled on the ground. Scorched material and blood covered his chest, a chunk of metal extended from the midst of it on his left shoulder.

A burst of fire jarred her out of her shocked stupor. She ran forward and grasped his legs, pulling him behind the wreckage that used to be a hoversled. He groaned at the movement, but she kept going until they were safe then dropped down beside him.

"Keyen," she yelled down at him, trying to get a response. All she got was a low moan.

Terror filled her but she pushed it aside, forcing herself to look down at his chest. She saw that the scorched material was only the outer covering of his protective vest. But the metal that looked like it had once been part of the railing on the building above them had missed the vest, piercing through him in a downward angle.

Pulling a cutting tool from a pocket, she sliced open his shirt. Unfortunately, his vest hampered her view, and there was no way to remove it with the rod sticking out a good eight centimeters.

The sled shuddered with impacts. She ignored it, activating a link. "I need help. Keyen's down."

"On my way," Tankin's answer was immediate.

"I should … have stayed … behind … shield."

His words took her by surprise. She jerked to meet his eyes. Pain filled them, and he grimaced at a slight movement.

"Stay still." She brushed a hand against his cheek, sending out waves of comfort. "Help's on the way. We'll get you out of here."

"Can't. Have to … stop them." His voice petered out.

"You're more important," she said firmly, wishing she could take away his pain.

"Giving orders." The words were slurred and ended

with a grimace of pain that she felt deep within her chest.

"Rori, how is he?" Hiymm's question grounded her.

"Not good. Do you have visuals?" she answered back.

"Yes. His vital signs are dropping. Areathea wants to know if you can do something to staunch the blood flow," Hiymm asked.

"There's no way to put a pressure bandage on it with the vest in the way. I'll need a hand to hold it steady while I cut it way. I don't know if you can tell, but the rod angles down toward his heart."

"We concur. Tankin is on his way to you. As soon as he gets there, Areathea wants you to remove the vest, put on the bandage then get him to the medics as fast as you can. Don't give him anything for the pain. They'll be ready. She's relaying instructions and they're prepping for him."

Rori acknowledged. "Tank, where are you?"

"I'm pinned down thirty meters to your right. I can't get to you."

Rori's heart sank when Tankin answered and jerked again when Keyen moaned. Edging up, she glanced over the edge of the sled and cringed at the sight. Tankin was pressed into the small space behind a drinking fountain. Laser fire rained around him. It would be suicide for him to move and a quick check showed the others were fairing no better.

"No," she cried out as a burst came dangerously close to Tankin, coinciding with a wave of pain from Keyen as he tried to move.

"Tankin, I've got a shield on you."

He was running before she even finished. Seconds later he reached them.

"Raebent hues," the curse slipped from him when he saw Keyen on the ground. "I was hoping it wasn't as bad as it looked, but it's worse."

Rori ignored him already back down by Keyen. "We need to get the vest off him. Can you hold it away from the rod and steady?"

"It won't move a millimeter." He moved into position.

Rori took a deep breath. Releasing the fastenings on the vest, she then adjusted the length of the edge on the small laser cutter they each carried. She went to work slicing apart the vest. Even with the laser, it was slow and arduous. True to his word, Tankin didn't let the vest move at all. Still, removing the vest wasn't easy. Tankin lifted Keyen slightly as Rori slid it out from under him and move the bandage into place on his back.

"Rori, Tankin," Hiymm said as they settled him back down. "Areathea say's you're going to have to remove the rod. It's too risky moving him with it in."

Rori felt a wave of panic then tamped down on it immediately to keep it from flowing over to Keyen.

Areathea voice came next. "You must be extremely careful not to do anymore damage. Tankin, focus sound waves on his chest and use it as a sonogram to guide you in easing it out."

"I understand." Tankin's deep voice had a calm Rori didn't think she could have retained.

"Rori, have the pressure bandage ready to move in place as Tankin gets it out." Rori didn't need Areathea to add more. She knew Keyen could bleed to death in seconds if they didn't staunch the flow.

Laying out what they needed, she placed her hands on Keyen to brace him then looked at Tankin. With a nod, Tankin's attention dropped to Keyen. Rori felt a stirring as Tankin pushed out his talent. After several seconds, he started to slowly draw out the metal.

Pain burned through Rori.

Keyen sucked in air but he didn't say anything. Rori pushed out with her mind to comfort him, and he relaxed with a shuddering sigh. Blood seeped around the metal. Rori didn't take her eyes from it though she wished it would stop. The instant Tankin drew the metal free. Rori pressed the bandage in place, activating the seal.

Keyen stiffened, and Rori fought to keep in a gasp of pain. Keyen slipped into unconsciousness, and Rori sighed.

Her body trembled.

"Can you shield us?" She turned her attention to Tankin as he spoke. His look held concern. "We'll never get him out of here if you can't."

"I can," her voice broke, and she couldn't say more until she forced a swallow. "Can you carry him?"

Tankin nodded.

Rori steadied Keyen's head and watched the bandages as Tankin worked his arms under Keyen, settling him close to his body in a position least likely to jar him.

Rori was unsteady as she made it to her feet. Nausea threatened and pain cut deep in her chest. She tried to ease her mind from Keyen, but she couldn't get past her fear of losing him.

Beside her, Tankin rose with much more ease though he held Keyen. He just made it to his feet when a blast hit the sled grinding across the metal toward them.

Rori's shield was already building when the attack startled her. The pain and fear she felt tumbled into the shield. Dazed, she looked at the senseless destruction, fury boiling into the mixture.

When a succession of blasts hit the shield directly in front of where Tankin was holding Keyen. Rori reacted, pushing back with her emotion fed shield, sending it toward the hillside at all the locations where the firing was coming from. Flashes of fire sparked on the hillside, followed by a series of cries. In a split second everything became eerily silent.

"What was that?" Tankin stared at her in stunned disbelief.

"I'm not sure." Rori swayed on her feet, incredibly tired. "They startled me. Keyen."

"Yeah, we've got to go. Whatever you did, good job."

Rori wasn't sure what she did and didn't care. Her entire attention rested on Keyen and the faint beat of his heart.

Rori fought to rebuild the shield but as they moved into the open no more blasts came their way. They were halfway across the space when her shield failed and Rori could not pull up the strength to recreate it. Still it wasn't needed.

"I think it's over," Tankin said.

Rori could only nod, her entire force locked on Keyen. She hadn't realized that sometime in their moving she had placed a hand on Tankin's arm to keep up. Now she caught Keyen's hand that dangled down over Tankin's arm and interlocking their fingers.

Within her mind, she felt Keyen. He seemed so far away. "Hang on, we're almost to help." His body was slipping. "No," she cried and heard someone shouting in her ears.

Rori hadn't realized they had reached the medic until Tankin started to lower Keyen's body down on a stretcher. Still, she clung to his hand.

"Keyen's life signs are falling." Areathea's voice came over the link.

"He's crashing. We're losing him," a med-tech shouted.

"No, we got you out," Rori yelled at Keyen's limp form, groping for his spirit. She felt the strain of it pulling away. She locked on to him, intertwining her life threads with his much like she had their fingers. "I won't lose you. Do you hear me? I won't lose you. Keyen, I love you."

She poured her love deep into him. His heart caught and she urged his heart to match hers, to beat with hers. Rori could feel the tear in his body and see it in her mind. The damage sickened her. She wanted to take it away. She felt his agony and pulled it into her.

Rori was unaware of dropping across his body. Around

her everything became muffled. Faintly, she heard someone say, "He's stabilizing."

"Rori's vitals are dropping."

"What's happening? Someone report." Rori recognized Areathea's demanding voice.

"Let's get her off him." Rori felt herself being lifted away and wanted to object but couldn't get the words out.

"Stop! Don't separate them!" Areathea's shriek cut through clearly.

"Her shoulder's bleeding," someone muttered.

"Whatever you do, don't break their contact or we might lose them both," Areathea's warning to the med-tech trickled through to Rori, but she ignored it, focused on her name being said in her mind.

She knew Keyen's touch. "I love you, too." She clung to the words and floated off.

Chapter Twelve

Keyen awoke totally alert. It only took him an instant of staring up at the light panel that covered the ceiling to know where he was at, and with that knowledge came the recollection of what happened.

Whispers of pain echoed through his chest. He started to raise his hand only to find it strapped down. Keyen tried to move his other arm but it too was immobilized. He wanted to move. He wanted Rori. He turned his head and froze as he saw her.

For a moment, he didn't think she was real. She was so still and pale. Her eyelashes made strikingly dark crescents on her cheeks. She looked so ethereal he felt a wave of panic before he saw her chest rise and fall, then he felt her heart beat intermingled with his.

"You're awake," Areathea said softly. "How do you feel?"

"Alive," the answer came without thought.

"Yes, well that is something. You shouldn't be, you know."

"Rori?" Keyen looked to her as Areathea continued talking.

"She will be fine. She's just sedated. It seems Rori has developed a new talent or at least a new aspect of her talent. Though it's hard to say if she will be able to do it on anyone else, and it would be best she doesn't use it until she learns to control it."

"She healed me."

"Mostly. She saved your life for certain. The damage was most extensive. By the time she and Tankin were able to get you to the med-techs, it was too late. They couldn't have done anything to save you."

"Am I medicated?" He didn't feel that way, but there was no real pain in his chest, just minor discomfort from a mostly healed wound.

"No, the remaining damage has been repaired. You now should only have a little stiffness and weakness from the blood you lost. That will pass rapidly."

"Why am I restrained?" He flexed his arm under the band, feeling the cushioned metal's hold.

"I'll release you now. We didn't want to take the chance of you two being separated until you both were stabilized, then I decided to keep you together because it seemed to expedite the healing process."

"What is wrong with Rori?" His mind locked on 'both stabilized'. "Why is she sedated?" Keyen felt a wave of panic and tightened his hand on hers, taking in the reassuring warmth of her under his touch.

Areathea drew in a deep breath. "Rori's healing ability is a bit – unconventional. At least on you it was. I've heard of people with that ability. In fact, the legends go back to old earth."

"What are you not saying?" Keyen had to fight back a sense of dread that something was seriously wrong. His attention locked on Rori, taking in her pallor and slow, gentle breaths.

Areathea moved to stand over her, laying a hand on Rori's shoulder. Keyen realized it was bare where it peeked from under the blanket. "When Rori saved you, healed you, whether intentionally or not, she … took on your injury. I guess the best way to describe it is, she shared it."

"Shared?" His concern spiked.

"Pretty much what you're thinking, she took some of

the damage from you to her when she was healing you. It was not as extensive, and the healing was accelerated. All the damage has now been repaired. She is pretty much at the same point of recovery as you are."

"Then why is she sedated?"

"She was already to the point of exhaustion from the battle. She'd put out a lot of energy. Then what she did with you drained her severely. Coupled with the injury she took on–"

"You almost lost her." Panic filled him.

"It was tricky for a while. Close for both of you."

Instinctively, Keyen reached to touch Rori's cheek, and his hand came free of the restraints as Areathea released him. He shifted up to lean over her, ignoring the slight twinge in his shoulder. Keyen brushed back a lock of her hair as he studied each soft feature of her face. "What were you thinking?" he said more to himself but Areathea answered.

"I don't think she was thinking. I think she was willing you better so strongly, her empathy, and I dare say love, took over. I don't know for sure. As I said, we've never seen anyone take on and share another's injury."

Keyen cupped Rori's face, running his thumb over one fine cheekbone. "She will be okay?" He broke his gaze long enough to look at the med-tech.

Areathea smiled reassuringly. "She's fine. All her levels are strong. I just wanted her to rest a little longer before I brought her out of it. I will suggest you two take it easy for a few days to further recuperate. Now, I'm going to step out of the room for a minute. There are fresh clothes for you to dress in. She should be waking soon."

The door slid closed behind her as Areathea went out, but for a full minute, Keyen didn't move as he continued to gaze down at the woman on the exam table next to him. His thoughts had cleared, and he now could remember back.

He knew he was going to die. He knew he wasn't

going get to have a life with Rori. It had seemed so unfair to just have found her and to lose her before they even had a chance together. He would not let anything keep him from the second chance they were getting.

There was no doubting their love. He was going to ask Rori to marry him, the sooner the better. The absurdity of it hit him. They had only known each other for a short time, and they had just proclaimed their love earlier that day. Or was it the same day? He pulled up the time on his IPI and found they had not lost only the rest of the day but most of the next.

The loss of time spurred him into action. Leaning forward, he brushed his lips lightly over Rori's. He was tempted to linger at the sweet taste of her but, with a final caress, pushed back and away. Sliding off the table, he had to steady himself before donning the new uniform waiting for him.

He knew Hiymm would be waiting for a report now that he'd been notified he was awake. He hardly finished dressing when the thought proved true, and Hiymm's voice came over his link.

"Keyen, how are you?" Anxiousness flavored the tone.

"I'm fine, sir," Keyen reassured. "I will be on my way as soon as Rori's able."

"Come now, Areathea said she wants to keep her down a little longer."

Keyen looked back at the bed torn between duty and love. But, knowing what he must do, he answered. "I'm on my way."

Unable to stop himself, he reached out, running his knuckle over the incredibly soft skin of Rori's cheek in a silent good-bye before heading out the door.

A few minutes later, Keyen reached Hiymm's office, finishing the sandwich and juice Areathea handed him as he left the recovery room.

"He's waiting for you." Tasc held out his hand for the

empty container, indicating for Keyen to go past.

"Thanks."

"It's good to see you." Tasc's voice reached him as the door slid open.

Keyen glanced back over his shoulder catching a glimpse of concern on the man's face. "Thanks," he repeated, not knowing what else to say.

Hiymm was already coming around his desk to greet him as he turned back. "Keyen." Emotion seemed to tinge the words, and Keyen wondered if he had picked up some of Rori's empathy. He didn't need to know the man's feelings as Hiymm reached out to hug him, instead of his normal handshake. "You gave us a scare." The words were definitely weighted as Hiymm patted him on the back.

"Rori…," Keyen dropped the sentence, still not sure what he was going to say, or at least how to explain what rested in his heart.

"Yes, Rori. What she did was amazing. Even in our standards. Areathea assured us she is fine, though she wants to keep her under awhile longer." Hiymm released him, moving to sit behind his desk.

"I'd like to be back when she wakes," Keyen said, aware of Tasc following him into the room.

"That's understandable. This shouldn't take long. The rest of your team has already given us a full report. And besides the recordings of your IPIs and the media, we have quite a full account."

"What were the damages?"

Hiymm sighed, and it appeared like a weight descended on his shoulders. "Seven dead, most they figure from the initial explosion, but two were just shot down, a young man and woman. They were totally innocent, just out enjoying the celebration." Anger filled his words. "A hundred and fifty-eight injuries, thirty-four of those serious enough to be retained over at med facilities. And the infuriating part is, if you hadn't have been there on hand, it would have been much worse."

"You don't think we were a catalyst?" Keyen put out the thought as it came to him.

"No," Hiymm replied and glanced toward Tasc.

The smaller man spoke up. "The investigation team has already determined the main explosives were wired into the stage and fireworks. Creed, nor any of his people, had to be there. If my estimate is right, they just stayed there for the pleasure of it."

Keyen wished he could doubt the man, but if Tasc hypothesized it, it was true. "So what do we do?"

"At the moment, not much," Hiymm looked from one to the other. "Unfortunately, there is no proof to tie Creed to it."

"You mean we're not even going to bring him in?" Keyen fought to keep his temper from rising.

"For now, no. We don't have anything concrete." Hiymm raised his hands to forestall his coming argument. "Since Rori hasn't met him face to face, and her ability hasn't been documented, we haven't been given clearance to act."

"What?"

"I don't doubt Rori, but Creed's family was very powerful. He controls all that, and there are those who want more proof. Believe me, all the teams are looking, scanning surveillance footage, and every trace left behind. So far, even the bodies of the two attackers we recovered have yielded nothing. One is still nameless. The other is supposed to be a low class telekinetic who worked manual labor."

"Low level, that doesn't seem to fit." Keyen looked back and forth between the men, both nodded.

"What was your take on the assailants?" Hiymm asked.

It didn't take Keyen much thought. "The talents all seemed to be higher level. I'd say seven to maybe nines. I don't know if all were talents, but the assault team was good. Definitely trained."

"Agreed, but for now, that is all we have that is concrete," Hiymm answered.

"I can't believe he's just going to get away after what he did to all those people." Keyen stood, pacing across the room several times before stopping to stare out the window but not seeing what lay outside.

"He's not going to get away with it." Hiymm said firmly. "It's just going to take some time."

Keyen was quiet a second before he turned back. "In the meantime, he's planning something else." Frustration burned in his voice.

Hiymm nodded in agreement. "On that we concur." He looked to Tasc and Keyen's attention followed.

"Taking in all the intel, I think this was a trial run."

"Trial for what?" Keyen asked.

"That I haven't deduced yet. I think he is still testing us, testing you. If he could've taken one of you out, it would've weakened the Guardians." Tasc's eyes had the intensity they got when he was running things over in his mind.

"How did he know we were there? Rori and I hadn't even planned on going until later."

"I don't think he knew, but he knew you would come." Tasc paused. "That would account … he wasn't ready for you yet."

This time it was Hiymm's turn to question. "What are you thinking?"

"That Creed may have been hoping to kill at least one of them, particularly Keyen. The recordings show a concentrated amount of fire directed at him."

The certainty that shown in Tasc's eyes made Keyen nervous, and the need to see Rori strengthened in him. Still, he forced his mind onto the next question. "So how much time do we have?"

"I haven't enough data to make even an educated

guess, but I will say, I don't think it will be long. The attacks have grown in frequency and severity. He's trying to train up his people and weaken us. He won't want to give us too much time to fortify ourselves against him."

"So we wait." Keyen didn't care that his frustration and disgust came through loud and clear. Enraged at the thought of the dead and injured innocent people, and Rori lying so still up in the med unit from the efforts of saving his life, fury crackled around him.

"Keyen!" Hiymm's sharp command called up his attention, giving him the attentiveness to pull in his control, though he didn't apologize to the other men. He didn't have to be an empath to know they understood and felt the same. As if to prove the point, Hiymm took up the conversation.

"Though I'm afraid there is nothing we can do outwardly to try to stop Creed for now we will be far from doing nothing. Every one of our data and stat techs are going over all the evidence and information they can find. We will figure it out."

"But will it be in time to stop the little tests of his from killing more people?" There was no keeping the snap from Keyen's voice.

Silence settled over the room as each thought of the truth in his remark. Finally Keyen broke it. "If you don't need me anymore right now, I'd like to get back to Rori. I want to be there when Areathea awakens her."

There was a slight hesitation before Hiymm nodded.

A few minutes later, Keyen walked back into the med-lab. Areathea looked up at him from her desk. "I've already started bringing her out of the sedation. She should wake up at any time."

"Thank you."

She nodded, and Keyen headed for the recovery room.

"Oh, Keyen."

He turned back. "Yes."

"Just don't raise her blood pressure too rapidly. Her

body has had enough stress, and I want to keep her calm and stable." The teasing glint in the woman's eyes nullified the comment.

"Matchmaking, Areathea?" Keyen asked with a smile of his own.

"I hardly think that is necessary. You two found each other all on your own. Congratulations."

"Thank you." Keyen grinned in acceptance, not surprised Areathea had already deduced his and Rori's relationship. He wondered how many others had. Then again maybe Rori saving his life had announced it to all. He rubbed his hand over the tender spot on his chest. Even though it had been only a short time since he woke, the area had already lost much of its soreness.

His eyes rested on Rori, and he knew nothing would ever take her from him. Stepping into the room, he felt his own pulse jump. She was so beautiful. There was a dream like quality about her, but she was real – real and a part of him, like the beat of his heart.

He'd planned on moving a chair next to the bed but at the sight of the recovery bed he'd been on still beside hers, he changed his mind. Slipping up on it, he stretched out next to her. Supporting himself on one elbow, Keyen reached out with his other hand to touch her cheek and received a small sigh for the caress. Leaning over, he brushed his lips lightly over hers. Rori made a slight shift and turned her face toward him.

Joy spread through Keyen at the motion, and he stroked again and was rewarded with another sigh.

Chapter Thirteen

Rori drifted on a cloud of warmth. There was no dream just pleasure and love. *Keyen.* The name didn't come as much to her mind as it filled her. From the instant she'd accepted him as her heart-mate, she knew that was what he was, his presence glided along her senses.

"Keyen," she echoed his name consciously, and this time, it brought back tendrils of pain and fear.

"Keyen!" she cried out, reaching for mind and body.

"Shh, I'm here." The words were within and aloud.

She opened her eyes and looked into the liquid gold of his eyes. "Keyen."

Love caressed her like the finger on her cheek.

He smiled down as he leaned over her. "How are you?"

"Tired, I have a slight headache," she answered without much thought, her eyes drinking in the pleasure of him there. She raised her hand, running a finger over the stubble on his face. She'd never seen him anything but clean shaven. She gasped as the movement brought the lingering of pain in her shoulder.

"Easy." He reacted immediately, catching her hand, wrapping his fingers around it, bringing it to his chest. His other hand cradled her cheek. "It's all right."

Rori felt waves of reassurance come off him with undercurrents of concern which stirred up traces of fear. "I almost lost you." She tightened her fingers on his.

"And I almost lost you." The pain infused in his words was so strong she understood the meaning. His words confirmed it. "They almost lost both of us. What you did, the risk was too great, but thank you."

"What I did?" Confusion filled her along with the memory of pain.

His hand on her cheek lowered to her shoulder gliding over the skin revealed above the edge of the blanket. Her heart jerked at the contact, but there was a rightness in his touch.

"You saved me – healed me."

"I can't…." She broke off at the memory of him slipping away and the knowledge of him dying. Her eyes followed the movement of his hand on her shoulder. There just above the edge of the blanket was an area of faint pink scaring. Her mind wanted to cling to the acceptable thought that she had been injured herself, but she knew it was wrong. The vision of the wound on Keyen came, and with it the lingering helplessness of wanting to take away his pain and to make him better.

"It seems you can." Keyen's husky words brought her back to the present. "You just did it in an unorthodox manner, which I'll yell at you for later because it's too dangerous, for now." He leaned down.

Rori only got a second to prepare before his lips covered hers. The kiss was deep, full of pleasure and promise.

"I thought I said something about keeping her calm." Areathea's voice came from outside the room.

"I'm just saying thank you," Keyen said loud enough to carry, raising his head, while smiling back at her.

Rori didn't miss the wickedness in his look, and her heart jumped.

"I am trying to run her vitals," Areathea called out. Then she appeared at the door. "I think I'm going to have to kick you out, so I can get a steady enough reading to release her."

"She's fine to go?" Keyen asked what Rori was going to.

"Rori is fine except you're playing havoc with her pulse."

"I can go?" Rori got out before they could keep talking around her.

Areathea turned her full attention to her. "Not quite. I want to run a couple tests first on your talent levels, and then Narrasa wants to do another talent-eval. We want to see if there are lingering signs of retention on this new talent of yours and, if so, how strong."

"There's a concern?" Keyen interrupted, obviously picking up the same unsaid comment Rori did.

"We want to know if it could become detrimental to you." Areathea kept her focus on Rori. "If it looks to be a major risk, we may want to try placing a block on it."

"A block?" Rori felt a twinge of unease.

"It's not quite what it sounds," Areathea reassured. "We cannot actually block the talent with restraints which would block all your talents. What we would do is set a monitoring alert, so when your vitals showed a major distress in using that talent and your life force dropped too low, we could decide to," she paused, "render you unconscious. But," she hurried on, "there are many things we need to plot and take into consideration before we decide on that action, and you will have the final say in it. Now, Keyen, I'm afraid you'll have to leave. I want her to eat before Narrasa gets here."

"Can't I stay?"

Compassion shone from the woman but she hid it with a playful glint in her eyes. "No, she needs to get dressed, and I think it might be possible that your presence in the room would distort the test."

Rori could sense Keyen's objection rising and squeezed with the hand he still held. "I'm afraid she's right. There is no way, with you in the room, it wouldn't skew the test. My focus would slip to you especially with what just happened and there would be overflow from you. There is also a connection that is developing between us that could muddy the testing."

"She is correct on that. The bond is quite evident and would hamper the testing. Besides, it would be a good idea if you went and got a good meal yourself. Your body is still recovering, and, after the energy output from the confrontation, needs extra fortification." The med-tech was subtly edging him to the door.

"Can I at least kiss her good-bye?" Keyen asked.

Areathea's eyebrow rose slightly, and her lips tightened in an effort to keep back a smile. "I think not." She motioned him off the table. "You've already made her heartbeat race enough today. Now, go." She made a shooing motion, driving him out the door. Rori broke out laughing at the look on his face as the door slid behind him, closing him out.

The smile slipped free as Areathea turned back to Rori. "Sometimes you just have to leave men wanting more." Areathea couldn't keep back her own laughter.

"Now that's good." Areathea smiled. "Why don't you get changed? There is a fresh uniform for you. I'll have something for you to eat when you come out. And quit worrying about Keyen. He'll be fine. I'll be waiting in the outside room."

Rori sat still a minute after the woman left, taking in everything that had happened. The main thing that burned in her mind was that Keyen was all right. Safe, whole, and there was no doubt of their love.

She felt tears rise and wiped them away. It was no time for tears. Everything was fine. She pushed off the table, going to her clothes. Dressed, except her shirt, she paused to study the scar on her shoulder. Raising her fingers, she traced the outer edge. The skin was pink and tender.

Rori shuddered. She didn't care if she carried the scar forever. It was the pain of almost losing Keyen she never wanted to face again. Still, she couldn't quite get past the lingering memory of Keyen's life force slipping through her fingers. She pushed it down and pulled on her shirt and vest.

When Rori stepped out of the room, Areathea waited for her. "What is it?" the woman asked, looking up.

"Keyen, is he all right, really?"

Reassurance flowed to her. "Yes, Keyen is totally fine. It was close, but you got to him in time. I don't know how you were able to hold him and repair so much damage while fighting through what you took onto yourself. Anyway, with what you did, it was nothing for us to finish healing him. He will be up to strength probably by tomorrow. You might take a day or so longer."

Rori reached up and touched the area on her shoulder.

"The scar will fade," Areathea answered for her.

"I'm not worried about it. It was worth it."

"Yes, I'm sure you feel that way, but I wanted you to know it will continue to heal. I'm not quite sure why we couldn't get it to heal completely." A wave of puzzlement came off the medic.

"Several of us worked on it. The only thing we can think of is that because it was your own talent induced and your body was already working on it in its own way, it was resistant to our assistance. Still we were able to help on the major damage."

"I've never heard of … taking another's injuries." Rori waited for what Areathea was going to say.

"There have been old rumors which date back even before 'talents' where people were known to have healing abilities. They were actually thought of as magic. Of course, now we know different, that it's just aspects of certain people." The woman was quiet a minute. "I will say, it will be interesting what your children will be like with the strength you and Keyen both have."

Rori felt herself blush and a thrill went through her at the idea of having Keyen's baby. She tried to temper it. "I think it is too early for that. We've only just met."

"It doesn't matter. You two are bonded more fully than any ceremony can bring. The link is there."

"When I saved him—"

"No." Areathea cut her off. "Don't even think that you forced a bond. If you want to know, I felt it strong the evening Keyen brought you here to put in your IPI that first week."

Rori stared in disbelief.

"I'm serious. It was so strong I ran a compatibility check on you two. The match is extremely high. It's almost like you were made for each other. You soothe Keyen. That has been a great concern. With as strong as his talent is, he has always had to fight to hold it in check so as not to overwhelm him, like when it first manifested itself. I don't know if you know the story but he was quit explosive. He was running hot for days. We even had to use binders to dampen him."

"We were afraid for a while he'd burn out or we would lose him. It was your grandfather who helped him get a handle on his talent. Even Jattin got singed a couple times before Keyen mastered his control. But with you, there is a shift in him. You don't dampen him. It's more like you calm the energy fluctuating in him. I don't think he even realizes it, but it's good for him. But, don't for a minute think he craves you just for the comfort you bring him because you also ignite his senses. He almost crackles with desire around you."

Rori felt herself blushing, but Areathea was already continuing.

"It's also good for you the way your empathy is growing. Keyen feeds and stabilizes it. You could say, focuses or completes it. You will need that for your children. They will be strong. I think, I can safely guarantee that. They will need your understanding and guidance."

"So you don't think the bond between us is just locked to the calming I bring to him?" Rori asked for some assurance.

"Oh no, the attraction literally hums off both of you. If it was just sexual interest, I would be worried. That's why I ran a compatibility scan. You two are perfect. It's as I said, it is like you were made for each other, true soulmates. Using all the data, the computer wouldn't have been able to find a stronger match."

Rori was aware sometimes computer matching was used, especially to check matches of high talents, so incompatibilities didn't happen. Still, it was a strange idea to her. And she wasn't quite sure what she thought of it. Before Rori could ask more, the door opened and a petite woman entered carrying a tray of food.

"Oh, Edda, thank you." Areathea turned to her.

"Rori, you sit there and eat." Areathea motioned her to a desk, and Rori was aware of the smaller woman's attention focused on her. After a second, as if realizing she still held the tray, Edda followed her over, nervousness and interest flowing from her in unmistakable currents.

"Thank you," Rori smiled reassuringly, while nudging tendrils of comfort toward the woman as she placed the tray in front of her.

"Oh, Rori, haven't you met Edda yet?" Areathea spoke, obviously picking up her action.

"No, I haven't. Hello."

The greeting the petite woman sent back was shielded by the fall of her hair over her downturned face.

"Thank you," Rori repeated.

Edda nodded, heading rapidly for the door. She paused and glanced back a second before disappearing out the door, leaving behind the lingering feelings of what felt like fear, anxiety and guilt that had Rori puzzled. She wondered if what she did saving Keyen would make everyone nervous around her, though Areathea didn't seem bothered by it.

"I forget how new you are," Areathea said, placing an odd looking instrument in the cabinet.

"Does what I did make everyone nervous?" Rori decided to broach the question.

"What? No." The woman turned to look at her, perplexed. "Oh, Edda. Don't worry about her reaction. She's always nervous. I'm afraid she won't be remaining here much longer. It is truly sad. When she came here, she showed so much promise. A strong mid-level talent but it doesn't seem to be steady and she has difficulty controlling it. We don't dare use her on anything difficult. She's just too unstable. Actually, did you happen to get a reading off her?"

"I wasn't really trying." Rori stared at the door Edda had disappeared through. "She was nervous. She was also very interested in me but trying to hide it." Rori thought about what she felt. "It was almost like she felt guilty." The words came to her again. "Was she in on trying to heal me?"

"No, why?"

"I just thought, maybe, that it might be the link. That she felt she'd failed." Rori studied the lingering sensations closer. Unstable did fit what she experienced off the woman, but a niggling feeling ran across her. Before Rori could pin it down Narrasa walked into the room.

"Areathea," the talent plotter nodded to the med-tech. "Guardian Straye." He turned his attention to Rori. "It seems like you have added to your talent. How are you feeling today?"

"Fine, sir."

He studied her and Rori felt his talent reaching out. After a moment, he turned back to Areathea. "Do you have the physical report completed for me?"

"All done," Areathea said cheerfully. "She's good. Recovery is still at a heightened rate even without continued assistance."

Narrasa looked over the screen Areathea handed him. "Excellent. Definitely talent linked. Quite amazing in its extent. Well, Aurora, if you are finished eating, why don't you come down to the lab with me?"

Looking down at the food in front of her, Rori was surprised at the amount she'd eaten, totally unaware as they'd talked. Still, she was ravenous and wanted to continue but figured she was okay to make it until after he was finished.

An hour later, the light in front of Rori faded, and she returned to awareness of the room around her. She immediately turned to the man at the control panel.

"Well, I'll say that was interesting but hardly conclusive." Narrasa looked at her then back to the console. "Your talent is still in flux. You don't have the standard patterns of a true healer, but there are strong points. They are so intertwined with your empathy that they are more like shades of the talent, though they are strong." He paused in thought as he went over something on the computer.

Rori waited until she couldn't take it any longer. "Narrasa?"

"Oh, yes. I dare say you will never be a normal healer. But, I do think it would be wise to have you train with Areathea for a while, so you can learn to handle this aspect. I will caution you not to ever go as deep as you did with Keyen, though, I don't think your body's natural defense will allow that again. Frankly, I'm perplexed as to how you superseded it this time. Your psyche is strong. You should have shut down before the harm to you reached such a dangerous level. Anyway, that is all for now. I will go over your results further and let you know if there is anything more you need to be aware of." With that, he turned away, and Rori headed for the door, knowing she'd been dismissed.

When the door slid open, it revealed Keyen leaning against the wall. She felt her heart jump. He straightened as she came to him.

"What did he say?" he asked, reaching out to catch her hand, rubbing his thumb over her knuckles.

"Basically, I'm still in flux." She emphasized the word. "I'm to work with Areathea, so I can learn to handle this in case it reoccurs."

"Do you think it might?"

She shrugged. "I don't know. I didn't even know I was doing it before. All I could think of was you."

"I guess that means I better be more careful." His voice dropped low and picked up a husky tone as he edged close. His free hand came up to slide around her, drawing her to him.

Rori felt love and desire flow around her. "You'd better," she whispered as she tilted her head up to meet his kiss. He brushed her mouth gently and was just settling in for more when voices approaching from around the corner reached them.

Keyen pulled back. Regret glowed in his eyes. "I guess we really should go get you more to eat. I know I'm starving, and Areathea said you would need to eat extra for a couple of days."

Rori nodded, feeling breathless from the light kiss. She didn't try for words. They headed down the hall just as their team came around the corner.

"Hi," Cassie greeted cheerfully. "We were told you were here and decided to come and check on you."

"Yeah, you know, we wanted to see how the man who came back from the dead was doing?" Ultin grinned.

"Wasn't that bad," Keyen answered.

"Close enough," Tankin said. "You sure had us scared."

Keyen shrugged his shoulder and tried to lightened the mood. "Well, all's fine, just a little hungry."

"You guys always seem that way." Sansa turned her attention to Rori. "How are you?"

Rori was relieved that she only picked up concern from the group. "Narrasa says I'm still in flux. He also thinks I'm intriguing, but, I feel fine, except I'm starving, too."

"I think we can do something about that. The dining hall it is." Ultin led the way. During dinner they discussed the attack, Keyen's injury, ending with Rori saving him. The evening ended with them dropping Rori off at her room early.

"It's nice to know how far you'll go for us." Sansa smiled but there was seriousness in her eyes and the sentiment filled the air from the others. "Have a good night." She leaned in to hug Rori, followed by Cassie and then the guys.

Keyen was the last to step to her. His hug was prolonged. "Sleep well." He leaned back then dipped his head to kiss her briefly.

"Hey, why don't I get one of those?" Tankin teased.

"Tank, I didn't know you cared," Keyen countered.

Rori broke from Keyen's hold and stepped to the big man, coming up on her toes to kiss him on the cheek. "Thank you," Rori whispered to him, knowing the man knew she referred to the fact that without his help, she couldn't have saved Keyen. Tankin gave her a squeeze in acknowledgment.

"Hey," Keyen objected, though there was no heat in the protest. "Are you trying to steal my woman?"

"Are you worried?" Tankin grinned wickedly.

"Not really. She's mine."

"I think we've all figured that out," Sansa said drily. "Come on. You need to let her get some rest." Sansa caught Keyen's arm, dragging him away.

He looked back to Rori.

"Yours, huh?" she challenged.

"Mine," he said firmly.

Chapter Fourteen

"Greetings, Aurora Straye," the automated voice said as she stepped into the room. "You have a request from Director Hiymm to meet him first thing in the morning. There have also been two calls from your parents and seven from your grandfather."

Rori winced but made her way to the video console as she requested an open link to her parents. It took two minutes to assure them that she was all right and handling her new life and another twelve to listen to them criticize her decision to come to Rae-Isis and join the Guardians. Finally, she was able to break the connection only to have the indicator activate for another incoming call. Her grandfather's image filled the screen.

"There you are." His voice boomed over the audio letting her know of his worry. He was never loud like that unless he was past the breaking point.

"I'm fine, grandpa,"

"I'm aware. Hiymm contacted me as soon as you regained consciousness. Do you need me there?"

Rori smiled at him. "No, I really am fine. I'm going to get some training on this, just in case it reoccurs."

"Good. What did Areathea say?"

Rori spent the next few minutes giving him all the details. His next question caught her off guard. "So how are things between you and Keyen?"

Rori fought down the blush. "He's a good team

leader."

"I know that, and you know that is not what I'm asking. I should have seen that. I don't know how I missed it. So has that boy kissed you yet?" A twinkle appeared in her grandfather's eyes.

"Grandfather!" Rori wasn't sure what shocked her more, that her grandfather would ask such a thing or that he would actually guess. Though he knew and understood her better than her own parents, it was hard to believe she was that easy to read. She was used to dampening her emotions, and now it was like everyone could see them. Her grandfather, Areathea, the team, well the team wasn't too surprising because they were together all the time, and Keyen hadn't really tried to keep it from them.

"So he has kissed you." Her grandfather chuckled, and a blush erupted on her face. "Always did like that boy."

"I heard he singed you a couple times." She tried to deflect the conversation.

Her grandfather laughed. "That he did. He has an immense amount of talent and came in to it so suddenly it was hard to handle, especially at his age. But he has a strong character and internal code. He is a fine match for you."

"Don't start that. It is way too soon," Rori interrupted.

"Are you going to deny it?"

Rori blew out a breath, knowing she couldn't. "No."

"Good. That will make things easier for you if you just accept it."

"I know. It's just hard that everyone seems to already know. Keyen and I just figured it out ourselves."

"If you're being honest you with yourself, with your talent, you probably knew the minute you met him." He waited expectantly.

"You're right, but it's just, I didn't think others would detect it. Areathea even ran a compatibility profile on us."

Jattin laughed. "Trust that woman to know. She is

extremely bright and perceptive, and though she isn't a true empath like you, she picks up the subtle currents in people."

"Yeah, but she actually ran a compatibility profile." Rori still wasn't sure how she felt about it. It wasn't that it was really an intrusion or that unusual. It was quite common with strong talents to be tested because a mismatch could be detrimental, causing discord amongst individuals. Even Guardian teams were carefully screened before members were added to prevent this. Her grandfather confided once that he and her grandmother were cautioned but had ignored it.

"So what was the outcome?"

"She says we were made for each other."

He let out a low whistle. "She would know."

"She said it was one of the reasons I was able to save Keyen; that I shouldn't be in danger from a repeat with anyone else." Rori decided to redirect the conversation even if it was back to her new side talent.

"I suspect she's right, though you have such a strong natural caring."

They chatted a minute longer then her grandfather said, "You should get some rest. Contact me if you need anything. I love you."

"Love you," she answered back, and he was gone, but the things he said lingered on, as did thoughts of what had happened. Exhausted, she made her way to bed, but as she stretched out under the blankets, her mind wouldn't stop. Again it replayed what happened at the festival.

When she got to Keyen being hurt and the pain of losing him, she pushed past it but her thoughts went directly to Areathea's conclusion that her and Keyen were made for each other and her grandfather's concurrence. She knew she couldn't deny it even if she wanted to, which she didn't. It was just all so new.

She was in love. Her eyes closed, and she locked onto

the feeling, letting the vision of Keyen form in her mind. It was surprisingly easy. Though she was surprised it was the image of the first time she saw him. Wreckage around him, his hand extended out.

Her breath caught at the recognition in herself of meeting her destiny. She shifted the image to him on the practice field then she fabricated how he'd look now. His room was just on the other side of the wall from hers. She wondered if his headboard was on the wall they shared. She could swear she felt him there.

"Rori?"

Her name came into her mind. Her breath caught. She knew she must've imagined it.

"Is that you?"

"Keyen," she whispered his name aloud and in her mind.

Pleasure filled the air around her. "I heard you. This is different. Can you hear me?" His answer again reached her mind.

"Yes." She thought back to him.

"Do you need me?" Concern tainted the air.

She felt foolish being caught thinking of him so strongly that he became aware of it. "No, I just couldn't sleep and I was thinking of all that happened."

"I'm okay."

The simple words brought tears to her eyes. "I know." Still a little jab of pain pricked her.

"I'll be right there." His words were rushed as they reached her.

She could feel him already moving. "No, we both need our sleep. Can we continue to try talking like this?"

"Sure."

She could almost see him grin as he answered her, settling back onto the bed. "It would be really useful if we can develop it. I think we should work on it every night. So what do you want to talk about?"

"Something not serious."

"Okay. Shall we talk about Ultin and Tank behind their backs?"

Rori smiled but they talked about their antics during dinner. She relaxed. It wasn't long until their conversation ended and they drifted off to sleep simultaneously.

Ϡ

A week passed with frustration escalating. Except for Rori feeling Drasc at the site, there had been no proof to place or connect him to the attack. They couldn't even bring him in. And though they made an official request for him to come, he'd ignored it.

Few calls came in requiring guardian attention, so they teamed up with Orn's team to practice. A tense feeling of anticipation permeated the group. They all knew it was the quiet before the storm, but they all felt helpless to stop the oncoming maelstrom. Two things did seem to be going smoothly. The first was Rori's training with Areathea, where, though she couldn't seem to heal, she was able to give comfort and helped accelerate healing.

The other development was the link between her and Keyen. Keeping it to themselves, they worked on it every night after they split up and went to their own rooms. While Keyen had no success creating the link with her, once she'd established it, he could communicate easily. With the lights out it forged a deeper intimacy between them as they talked, sharing private pieces of themselves.

It was the fourth day of straight practice that Rori was able to reach out with her mind to Keyen while moving through the course. The surprise of his answer distracted her so much that if Keyen wouldn't have been able to thrust up a pad in time, she would have taken a stunning hit. As it was, all she suffered was his laughter filling her mind.

"You're going to have to pay more attention to your surroundings if you're going to try to talk to me."

"Talking to you doesn't distract me. It's your

answering that does." she grouched as she flattened herself against a pillar.

"Really, you find me distracting?" he answered back easily now they'd managed to connect the link.

"Quit trying to be cute," she countered.

"But I am cute. The magazines say so all the time. I'm supposed to be a very good catch."

"Why are we talking about this now? Aren't we supposed to be making our way through this course to the rescue on the other side?"

"I just wanted you to know how fortunate you are. Besides, Ultin's the victim. It would do him good to leave him hanging for a minute."

Rori laughed feeling some of the tension she didn't realize she'd been holding, release.

"There, that's good." He came back in the way of acknowledgement. "Ready to go?"

"Ready."

"Good. Set. Mark."

Rori burst from her place, making a dash toward Ultin, trusting Keyen would intersect anything the computer sent at her. Six feet from Ultin she dropped into a slide, letting her momentum carry her right next to him. Coming up on her knees as she came to a stop, she disconnected the device.

"Took you long enough." Ultin grinned, stretching his arms over his head. "What's to eat?"

"You're right," Rori used the comm-link so everyone could hear. "We should have left him here."

Ultin just laughed, dropping his arm over her shoulder as they went to join the others.

Three days later they were halfway through a training run with Orn's team when the computer suddenly powered down and Hiymm walked out on the course to meet the teams.

"Sorry to disturb you, but I'm afraid I must end things

for today. There is a special meeting for the upcoming conference, and I want the team leaders and their seconds to attend." Hiymm looked at the two teams. "Orn, Mitt, Keyen, Tankin, if you could get changed into dress uniforms and meet me in the council hall immediately, I'd appreciate it." With that he left.

"What do you make of that?" Ultin asked, watching him leave.

Keyen looked at Orn who shook his head. "I have no idea but we'd better hurry."

Keyen took a step after the senior leader then stopped and turned back to Rori. "So much for us trying to have dinner alone tonight, I don't know how long this will take."

"Don't worry about it. We can try for tomorrow night."

Keyen hesitated then nodded. With a quick glance at the others, he dropped a kiss on her lips.

Bass let out a long whistle, and Keyen pulled back glaring at him.

"What?" Bass tried to look innocent but failed. "Someone has to watch over you two. And, don't worry about Rori. We'll take her with us. We're going to the new place one of the med-techs told us about down on the wharf. I won't even let her get anything too spicy."

Rori wasn't sure she really wanted to go, but, picking up the ease in Keyen, agreed. "Sure that sounds good." Still she caught Keyen's hand, leaning into him, dropping her voice low. "Hiymm's concerned. Something is wrong." She wished she knew more, but there were no answers for the question she saw in Keyen's eyes, or felt hanging in the air from the others in the room.

Keyen nodded. "I'd better go. I'll let you know later." He brushed another kiss against her cheek and turned. Tankin fell into step with him as they followed Orn out.

A few minutes later, they met Hiymm and Tasc in the corridor outside the council hall and strode in together. All eyes rested on the Guardians. Only the first tier of the chamber was occupied, but in two days, every one of the hundred and seventy-two seats would be filled with the regional delegates and their aids.

Keyen followed Orn's lead and took up the position right behind Hiymm with Tankin at his side. It wasn't the first time Keyen had stood in front of the council leaders but, this time, he had no idea why he was there.

"Manning, what is this?" A gray-haired man in the center seat addressed Hiymm.

"They should be here," Hiymm said directly.

"Guardians are not the security detail over the council," a portly, bald man on the side said.

"No, but they will be the ones who have to handle the trouble once it arises since you won't postpone the meetings," Hiymm said forcefully.

Several of the fifteen men and woman in the room huffed and others shifted in their seats.

"We've already discussed this," the portly man spoke again. "There is no indication the council conference is in danger."

"I disagree." Hiymm stepped forward. "There is every indication. Recent attacks that we've been experiencing raises concerns."

"What do attacks on utility facilities or on a festival have to do with a council meeting?" A woman spoke up, and though she tried to show strength, a tremor vibrated in her voice.

"Council woman Chealyn, all our strategists believe, and I concur, that these attacks are training runs and exercises to prepare for a major attack on a given location. They have also forced the redirecting of many lines of the utilities. The council building is on the track of some of those changes."

"But, not all," the portly man spoke up. "You are an alarmist. Which is understandable by what you do, but what you are suggesting is totally inconceivable. The biggest question is why would anyone attack the council?"

"That should be quite clear," Hiymm said calmly. "Eliminate the council, get rid of the Guardians, and it would be easy to take over the world."

‹∞›

The doors of the restaurant stood open, allowing the lively music out to greet people. A wooden boardwalk, built in reminiscence of eras past, wrapped around the building stretching onto the sand. Rough wooden tables, trees and shrubs filled with fragrant flowers completed the fun, casual feeling.

The only thing that saddened Rori was that Keyen wasn't there to enjoy it with her. Instead, Rori drank in the cheerful happiness radiating off others and used it to boost herself.

"This is terrific," Cassie exclaimed, catching Rori's arm, pulling her forward. "Sansa and Ultin don't know what they're missing."

"Ultin will be here soon. He just sent me a message that he talked Gennae into coming. She had just finished her shift and wanted to change first," Bass said.

"Great!" Cassie grinned from ear to ear.

"So who's he dating this week?" Rori asked, joining into the conversation.

"One of the med-techs. That's how we found out about this place," Cassie answered just as the smell of grilling meat reached them.

Rori's stomach rumbled.

"Oh, that smells wonderful," Cassie said as if reading her thoughts.

Bass fought to hold back a grin. "So you don't want to take a walk on the beach first and wait for Ultin?"

Rori and Cassie exchanged looks for only an instant before turning their attention back to Bass.

"No," they said in unison.

Though it was early in the afternoon, quite a few

groups of people were scattered around the restaurant, mostly older kids who'd just gotten out of school and young families starting their weekend early. A few minutes later, Rori, Cassie and Bass were settled at a table by the open window in the corner, with their plates piled high with grilled meat, vegetables and rice.

"Oh." Rori took a bite, savoring the combination of flavors.

"Yes," Cassie agreed, while Bass was busy shoveling mouthfuls in like a starving man.

Several minutes passed in silence while they appeased their hunger.

"I didn't realize how hungry I was." Rori sighed contently.

"Training always gets me," Bass said in way of agreement.

"Breathing makes you hungry. But, you're right, we've been really pressing it lately," Cassie said. "I wonder what's happening."

Like her twin, Rori didn't need to ask what she was referring to. Her thoughts went to Keyen. She was tempted to try to reach him but knew the distance was too far. Across the practice arena had been their maximum distance so far, which was nothing compared to Cassie and Bass, who could link over dozens of kilometers.

Rori was about to comment when three girls, about fourteen or fifteen years old, approached the table while three boys hung back. Rori picked up their timidity and smiled. Cassie and Bass followed her gaze, turning their attention to the group.

One of the girls stepped forward at a nudge from one of her friends.

Rori exchanged looks with Cassie as the girl stammered out, "You're a Guardian, aren't you?" Her attention was locked on Bass.

"Yes," he answered easily and Rori sent a wave of

reassurance.

It was like opening a flood gate. The group descended on them, chattering excitedly as they introduced themselves and asked for pictures and autographs. Rori was taken aback by the treatment, but the excitement was contagious and it didn't end when the group left.

Several other people brought their children up and asked if they could take their pictures with them. A few minutes later, Rori found herself holding an angelic red-haired girl on her hip. While all the kids watched with wide-eyed amazement as Bass floated a glass in the air and made it spin without spilling a drop of water.

Her happiness was shattered as a high powered water-glider raced up on the sand in a wave of malaise. She looked out the window as she thrust the girl into her father's arms.

"Bass, Cassie!" she cried out even before the five men and one woman climbed out. Rori recognized the woman hypno, the tall man and the block from the transport dock and fire.

Pulling her attention from the group, she looked at the parents and the others in the restaurant. "Get out of here." Raising her voice, she called to everyone. "Everyone get out of here, through the back. Go, now!"

"What is it?" Bass was on his feet next to her, watching the group make their way up the sand. She felt him and Cassie stiffen in preparation.

"They're dangerous." She didn't know what else to say, but it was enough. Bass and Cassie were ready.

"Central." Cassie activated her comm-link.

"Central here."

Rori heard the answer.

"We have six unknown…" Her words stopped in mid-sentence. Rori glanced at Cassie who stood frozen, her mouth open, as if she was trying to get the words out but nothing came.

"Cassie!" Bass shouted at her.

Sluggishly, she turned to him.

Rori pushed out a shield in front of Cassie though since she couldn't see anything, didn't know if it would do any good. Fortunately, it seemed that along with Bass's link, Cassie seemed to pull out of her stupor. "We are under attack." Cassie forced out the words.

Fire burst out from a man in the middle, striding next to the woman. Rori shifted the shield pushing the fireball back toward them and it winked out. Underneath them, the ground shook. Behind them, screams erupted from the people who hadn't left the restaurant yet, not understanding they really were in danger.

"Get out of here," Bass ordered and this time they moved, though many stumbled and fell when the ground shifted again.

"Who are they?" "What do they want?" The panicked questions were uttered behind them. Immediately, Rori knew the answer to the last question. They wanted them. They wanted her. Fear tugged at her. She pushed it down.

Another fire bolt shot out. This time, Bass and Cassie blocked it by sending a planter in its path. The thick clay exploded, sending shards and dirt in all directions, making even the rogues duck, but the attack didn't stop. Luckily, the last of the people made it through the doors that led into the kitchen and out the back.

Behind Rori, water burst from a pipe in the sink, and above all the sprinklers popped, dousing them with water. Rori flinched, barely seeing the fireball hurtling toward the front doors. She threw up a shield, but the explosion came so close that it ripped one of the doors from its hinges. Cassie tried to push it away with her mind, but her reactions were again sluggish and the edge caught her, knocking her back. Her head slammed into a pillar, and she sank to the ground.

"Cass!" Bass cried in agony and teetered, barely

catching himself by grabbing a table to keep from going down.

Emotion roared through Rori almost bringing her to her knees, but she managed to intersect the next fireball which would have hit Bass, whose attention was focused on his sister. Rori blocked the explosion and sent it back at the group that scattered in an effort to avoid the burst. Both Rori and Bass used the time it gave them to reach Cassie. They pulled up her vitals on the IPI. They were strong, but she was unconscious.

"We've got to get her out of here." Rori looked at Bass, his panic over his sister rose over hers for a friend, but he shook his head.

"I can't leave you."

Again the ground shifted underneath, feeling as if the building was being torn apart. Bass caught a piece of the ceiling that dropped toward them with his mind and flicked it to the side. "Try to give me a minute." He scooped Cassie into his arms and, keeping in a crouch, worked across the floor to the hostess podium. The stand wasn't very big but luckily when he opened the door underneath it, it was empty except for a shelf that had menus on it.

Rori forced her attention from Bass working his sister inside to the relative safety and focused on the group advancing on the building. There were only five on their feet now, as one lay unconscious on the ground, but it didn't give her much comfort.

They had to hold them off until backup came. The problem was they were over-powered with Cassie out of commission, Bass's talent, though strong, was weakened, and her talents were mostly defensive.

Rori sent her mind out to gauge feelings off them and recoiled as awful tingles races over her senses. These were all strong talents. As she read that, she also got the taste of something unsavory, unnatural. She was still fighting to recover from the feel of it when she was forced to block the next burst of flames that erupted near the front door. Almost simultaneously, the room shook around them.

Bass staggered in gaining his position by a pillar near an open window, locking onto an airscooter, he flung it at the group. He caught one man unaware, and immediately the shaking stopped.

Rori sensed as much as saw the small device float through the side window. She tried to intercept it just as everything hazed under the assault of the hypno-talent. Gathering her will, she pushed back, breaking the hold, but it was too late to do anything about the stunner.

In the split second it took to go off and the fumes to reach her, she knew that just as the Hypnos's attack was meant to distract her, the whole front attack had been a diversion to keep them busy, so that in the confusion, a telekinetic could deliver the stun bomb.

"Command…" she tried to activate the link, but whatever she was going to say was lost as she dropped to the ground. The last thing she was aware of was Bass crumpling not far away.

Chapter Fifteen

Keyen felt his chest tighten and Tankin shifted beside him. The outburst from the council members echoed off the walls. Like the councilmen, Keyen hated to think of the possibility of someone wiping them out to take over the world, but it made sense. Moreover, if Hiymm and Tasc thought it, then he was willing to accept it. There was no one better at deciphering patterns than Tasc. And a man that would attack a festival, for seemingly no reason the way Drasc had, would have no problem killing off the whole council.

"Commander, I'm sorry to interrupt, but we have a problem." The voice over the comm-link was directed to Hiymm, but it was open to Keyen, and from the reactions of Tankin, Orn and Mitt, the link was open to them also. "We received what sounded like an alert from members of Keyen's team but it was cut off."

"What do you mean cut off?" Hiymm's asked Keyen's thought.

There should have been no way to cut off contact with the IPI. The next words brought Keyen fear.

"We've lost all contact with Bass, Cassie and Aurora."

"All contact?" Aggravation filled Hiymm's voice.

"Yes, sir. We aren't receiving anything from the IPIs."

Hiymm glanced at the two team commanders. "Go."

Keyen didn't need any further prompting. Breaking into a run, he left the others to follow. "Bring up the last coordinates," he said into his link as he turned into the private underground tunnel that connected with the guardian compound.

It seemed like it took forever to reach the lifts. The high speed ride dragged on as he tried to bring up a link to Rori, Cassie or Bass, all without success. He tried to reach out with his mind though he knew it was futile. It took Rori to open the link, and they'd never been able to reach each other from any distance. Still he fought for the link, only to find none.

Ultin was already in the bay with the hoversled ready when they reached it. They barely made in into their seats when he shot out the open bay doors.

"I thought you were with them," Keyen asked as he did up his harness.

"I was picking up my date then was going to meet them. We should be there in two minutes," Ultin answered back.

Keyen called up the command center. "Can you replay the message before it was lost?" He fought to keep himself from counting seconds.

Cassie's voice reached him. "Central, we have six," then there was nothing.

"Six?" Mitt asked from the seat beside him.

Keyen was afraid he knew. Though he was trained not to jump to conclusions before he had all the facts, he'd bet his position as Guardian team lead, it was attackers just like at the festival.

Before he could answer a voice came over the comm-link. "We're picking up a reading."

Keyen felt a surge of hope, but when he tried to connect, there was no answer. "Patch me through," he requested.

"We are not receiving any response. Just a reading from Cassie's IPI, unfortunately there is no image through the viewer but vital signs are strong."

Ultin brought the sled in for a landing. It was Orn's hand on his shoulder that kept Keyen from rushing out before they surveyed the area, not that there was much to see except lingering evidences of destruction. Edges of the door and a window smoldered. Several pots lay shattered and a scooter twisted and bent. Weapons ready, they made their way up the front path.

"Mitt?" Orn said his second's name in a way of question.

"I'm picking up tendrils of strange, latent talents," Mitt, a strong talent reader, answered. "The area is cl ..." he broke off. "There's talent reading."

Keyen motioned for Tankin and Ultin to stay outside and followed Mitt, as he took the point, going into the restaurant. Around him the group checked that it was clear. There was no sign of Rori or the others. Keyen wanted to yell and demand to know where they were, but his only consolation was they weren't laying on the floor injured or dead. He wasn't sure how much comfort it was. He froze when Mitt swung back to the front of the restaurant.

"I'm picking up a reading," Mitt scanned the area, "but can't see." His eyes came to rest on the hostess podium, and he moved forward.

Keyen was shocked, as were the others, when Mitt pulled open the door and revealed Cassie crammed inside.

"Cass." Mitt was already kneeling beside her, running a scan by the time Keyen crossed the three steps to her.

"We need a med-team," Keyen said to command.

"Already on the way." A voice came back.

"How is she?" Keyen came down beside her.

"She seems to be in some kind of coma."

"No sign of the others," Orn announced what Keyen already knew.

"Keyen," Ultin called from outside.

"Go," Mitt said when he hesitated. "I have her."

Keyen was torn at leaving Cassie, but he had a

responsibility to find out what happened there and more a need to know where Rori was. Ultin was waiting for him just outside the door, behind him stood a group of young teenagers, shifting around nervously. Tears trickled down one girl's face and they all stood holding hands.

Keyen turned his attention to Ultin. "What do we have?"

"They said they'd been talking to Bass, Cassie and Rori, when all of a sudden it sounds like Rori told everyone to go through the back and get out. Before they could, things started to burst and shake. Everyone in the restaurant made it out except our team. One of the boys snuck through the shrubs to get a look. He saw this group approaching the building from the beach, then another man sent something in through a side window, and there was an explosion. After that, they just walked in and came out a minute later carry Bass and Rori. They both seemed to be unconscious. They got in a high speed watercruiser and left. The boy ran back to his friends. They were debating what to do when we showed up."

Keyen nodded, watching the med-transfer land. A group came out from it, but his attention was out over the water. Somewhere out there Rori was taken. He tried again to reach for her, though he knew it was useless. Frustration crested through him. He was afraid he knew who. The question was why was she and Bass taken?

છ૪ﻼ

The fine mist spraying up from the powerful watercruiser stirred Rori awake. Still it took a full minute for her mind to clear and remember what happened. She tried to sit up, only to realize her arms were restrained behind her back. Her view was limited to the white, padded seat just a centimeter from her nose. Shifting a little, she caught sight of the clear blue sky but nothing else. When no acknowledgement of her came, she shifted onto her back.

At first, it gave her little more information, but craning

her head to the side, she saw Bass on the seat across from her. His eyes were closed, but there was a steady rhythmic quality to his breathing that reassured her.

She twisted on the seat again. Pain arched through her shoulder. Either she'd hit it when she passed out or her captors dropped her on it. She became aware of the weak pulse of a headache above her left ear. Rori ignored it to look at her captors.

The first one she discovered, lay almost below her on the floor between her and Bass. He was unconscious or dead. He was so still she wasn't sure. She tried to reach out with her mind and find out, but nothing came. It took quite an intent study before she finally picked up the faint movement of his chest.

"She's awake."

The comment drew her attention to the front of the craft and the people clustered there. The weak pounding in her head rose to a hum. She winced as pain and nausea hit her.

"Good. We're just about at the dock."

The words reached her as she fought to quell her stomach. As soon as the group looked away, the effects eased to a faint almost whistle more than a pounding. A second later, the craft bumped lightly against the dock. The action brought a stirring from Bass.

"Get them up." A block of a man gave the order. Now that her head had cleared Rori recognized him from the transport dock the first day she arrived at Rae-Isis. "Get Pims to the med-lab," he directed two men, as a woman walked toward Bass pulling something out of her pocket.

Rori tried to reach for her as she pressed the hypodermic against Bass's neck and almost fell off the seat.

"Now, none of that." The tall skinny man grabbed her shoulder. "We don't want you to get hurt. Mr. Drasc has been waiting to meet you for a very long time. He has special plans for you and won't want you all bruised up."

The man laughed at his own reference and the block snickered behind him, making Rori's insides crawl.

The woman beside Bass shot them a disgusted look. "You two are so juvenile."

"What? You're just upset Drasc didn't think you were suitable to be his Empress." The tall man smirked.

"She's not going to be his empress. Just one of his incubators," she argued.

Rori froze and the next comment from the tall man made her sick.

"We'll see. She's awful fine and he's really intrigued with her."

"She's a freak. Just barely got her talent," the woman snapped back waspishly.

"Intel said they figured she'd been suppressing it."

The woman started to say something, but the block cut her off. "Get going. He's expecting us. Let's not keep him waiting."

Rori noticed Bass was now alert, and by his expression, he had heard what they'd said. There was no use struggling when they were pulled up from the seat and onto what ended up being an enormous dock. At least ten smaller watersliders, like the one they were brought in on were tied there and a large, stately cruiser. Rori studied them a second before focusing on the path that led up the hillside. At the top of the knoll, just visible over the thick foliage and backed by the sun, she could see the outline of a massive estate. One end of the house loomed out over the cliffs that rose from below, extending out over the water like a scavenger bird watching for prey. Rori recognized the structure from the picture she'd seen in the briefing on Drasc Creed.

A shiver went up through her. She wasn't surprised to be there. They knew he was behind what was going on. She just didn't know how Keyen was ever going to find and rescue them.

Any hopes of delaying their captors on the long hike up the hill so they could plan an escape were squelched when they were led into a passage way burrowed into the hillside. The tunnel was long with polished metal sides and two rows of lights running in parallel bands at the apex of the ceiling, which was twice as tall as Rori.

The woman took the lead with the block and the tall man flanking her and Bass. The only sound was the click of the woman's heels echoing off the walls.

Bass bumped her shoulder and Rori glanced at him. His eyes ran over her and she got the meaning, he was wondering if she was all right. She nodded and returned the gesture and received an affirmative nod from him.

They walked, what Rori figured was at least three-hundred meters into the hill before they came to a lift and were ushered in. The hum in Rori's head grew, and she couldn't hold back the wince of pain. Nausea rose within her.

It was with relief for Rori when the doors opened, and they could step out. The humming eased, though it stayed higher than it had been before. Still, it didn't keep her from studying the area.

An enormous courtyard stretched out at least the size of their practice field. A colonnade ran around all sides with huge columns extending up two floors. The courtyard looked like it was split into two areas. Half was a garden that beckoned for relaxation. The other was not much different from the training room back at Guardian headquarters.

Rori was so busy studying the surroundings, she almost missed the approach of a small rodent-like man. His eyes flicked over her. Rori tried to read him and got nothing, but the whine in her head surged to a roar.

"Mr. Creed said to put them in the room until he finishes the debriefing then he'll see them." The man turned and led the way along one of the sides. "Wasn't there supposed to be another woman?" Rori heard him ask the woman in front.

"We couldn't find her. She must have gone out with the people in the restaurant as they were escaped out the back. It doesn't matter. This is the one he really wants."

Even without being able to use her talent, Rori had no problem picking up anger off the woman and what she actually thought was jealousy.

"Testy, Faen." The man smirked.

The pounding in Rori's head flared, making her stumble. She would have fallen if it wasn't for Bass's quick reaction. Using his body, he wedged her against the column they were passing until she regained her balance.

"She's hurt?" the man snapped in what sounded like fear.

The whistle in her mind reached a crescendo, and she weaved on her feet again.

"She was not to be hurt." The rodent shuffled anxiously.

"It must be effects left from the stunner." The tall man reached to steady her.

Perspiration broke out on her brow as Rori fought down another wave of nausea. It subsided as soon as the man released her. She leaned toward Bass, finding whatever plagued her seemed to lessen close to him.

Thankfully, not much farther down the row a door was opened and they were ushered in. Once over the threshold, the door slid closed behind them. There was no need to check if it was locked.

The room looked like a holding cell. There were no windows, only two small beds pressed against the wall in each back corner. A table with two chairs sat to the side of the entrance, and surprisingly, on the wall above it was a video screen which was meant for entertainment.

Rori let out a sigh of relief as abruptly the awful whine and pounding in her head ended along with the nausea. She took a deep breath. The air had an artificial taste obviously ran through a scrubber to render any particles inactive that an elemental talent might use.

"You okay? You look–" Bass cut off.

"I don't know. I had such a headache. It must've been from the stunner," she repeated what the man had said. "It's better now."

"Since being in here?" He looked at her curiously.

She nodded.

"I think it's more likely that the talent blocking restraints are affecting you. I've heard of a few people who have problems with them." He looked around the room, thoughtful for a second before he spoke again. "It's probably has to do with your empathy. With it being such a large part of your normal emotions you are clashing with the restraints. It's not a talent you choose to use on occasions, but a part of you all the time."

She thought about it as he continued.

"This is a restraining room. So, besides deadening us in here it blocks out what's outside," he continued his line of thought.

"It makes sense. All I know is I feel better. So you're being blocked?"

"Totally, I can't even feel Cassie." There was no missing the worry in his voice.

"I'm sure they've found her by now. I could feel her vitals before. They were strong. I'm sure she'll be all right."

"I know. But like you, I'm missing part of me. I'll be okay. Actually, we've done drills where one of us put binders on and practiced without being able to reach the other. It just takes a second to adjust. I just wasn't fast enough back at the restaurant." His head hung down.

"Don't blame yourself." Rori took a step closer.

"I know." He looked up at her. "It's frustrating though to get beat."

"Considering we were cut off, without any of our gear, and you had to provide most of the protection by yourself because I'm mainly defensive, we did pretty good."

"An empath even when you're shut down." He bumped his shoulder against her, but it was his words that staggered her. "What?" He picked up her reaction.

"I think you hit on something. Before, I've always sensed something off about our attackers. It was what alarmed me when I first arrived at the transport dock. Then, remember when we talked about that enhancing drug they were experimenting with? I think that is what I'm picking up. It's warping their natural selves. They are unstable and I'm feeling it."

Bass nodded, his lips tightening and eyes going sharp as he thought about it.

Rori knew she was right and something else hit her. "There's more, I think I kind of picked it up before, but I didn't know what it was at the time. A med-tech came in when I was with Areathea after the festival. Anyway, I think I felt it in Edda, the med-tech. I didn't know at the time, but after feeling these guys, I realize why her talent is off. She's been drug enhanced."

"The leak," Bass exclaimed.

"Possibly," Rori had to agree.

"Cassie's there." Bass's voice sharpened in panic.

"Don't worry. She'll be okay. Areathea will never leave her alone. She won't let anything happen to her. And besides, Areathea already mentioned to me that she thinks Edda's talent is unstable. She would never let her work on Cassie."

Bass relaxed fractionally.

Her mind went back to what was happening with them. "I think it's more than clashing with the restraints." She looked at him, her head was clearing with the whine gone, and she could think. "What if the restraints are actually blocking my shields, which have always filtered out some of what I feel off them?"

"What do you mean?"

"Before we came here, into this room, my head was pounding, and there was some kind of whistle echoing in my mind. It was making me nauseous."

"When you almost fell?"

"Yes. I became so dizzy when that man looked at me."

"Being in here blocks our talents, but it also blocks out theirs." Bass got what she was thinking.

"And being around you doesn't bother me."

"Because I'm a natural talent," he finished for her, looking serious. "Are you going to be okay?"

"I don't know." She wondered how many drug enhanced talents were here. Just being around four of them for a short time had been taxing on her. With the size of this place and the numbers they saw at the festival, she didn't want to think about it. She figured there had to be at least a minimum of five times that many. And if they all were ever in a close proximity, she shuddered. She really didn't want to think of it.

☾☽

Keyen looked around the conference room, feeling frustrated. Cassie sat across from him looking wan. Sansa sat next to her, trying to give her comfort, but Cassie's distress had grown since waking up and not being able to reach Bass. Keyen could understand. It ate at him not having Rori.

Cassie hadn't been able to give them any leads. What she did remember was very brief. Rori's warning just before the initial attack, and then everything went blurry. Still, there was no doubt in anyone's mind who had them. The problem was getting authorization for a raid. Since it wasn't a visible emergency, and there was no direct proof, they couldn't just go in.

It seemed the council already there wanted to wait for the rest, to make the decision. The only problem, Keyen thought, was it might be too late. He agreed with Hiymm that Creed was going to attack the conference. Unfortunately, the committee members still couldn't seem to fathom the possibility just because it had never been attempted before.

Keyen stood abruptly, no longer able to stay in his seat.

"Keyen." Orn's voice sounded behind him.

Keyen spun toward him. "We need to go."

"Hiymm's trying to persuade them," Orn countered soothingly.

"You know it's not going to work." He started to pace.

"Hiymm can be pretty persuasive."

"They don't see the threat." Keyen threw back, almost at the edge of his control.

"I think they are starting to," Mitt spoke up. "You didn't see their faces before you hurried out. They were shocked. Once they get past their denial, which is what they're doing now, they'll see."

"And we'll be ready to act," Orn added, motioning to the screen where they'd been working out a plan.

The words were hardly out of Orn's mouth when Hiymm walked into the room followed by Tasc.

Keyen, with all the others, looked expectantly to him.

Hiymm shook his head, reading the question easily before it could be asked. "We are making headway," Hiymm stated. "They do concede there is a threat and have scheduled to go over it first thing when the council meets in the morning. They have also decided a Guardian team is to be on hand with the regular security force. Orn," Hiymm looked at the team leader, who nodded with reluctance.

"What about Rori and Bass?" Keyen demanded, unable to hold it back.

"I am authorizing you to plan and get in position for a rescue mission to be carried out as soon as we can get clearance, or we are given any reason to act. I want you in place by first light."

"We're going to leave them there all night?" Keyen felt a stab of pain.

"There is no other option. Right now we don't even know where they are. So even with authorization, which we don't have yet, you will have to develop a plan with just the four of your team. And you all need some rest."

Keyen wanted to argue that he was ready to go, but his gaze fell on Cassie, and though she would agree, he knew Hiymm was right. The effects of her earlier fight were very evident on her. Reluctantly, he nodded.

"Good. Orn, you stay and help with the planning. Mitt can handle the setting up of your team at the council lodge. You will need a rotation of at least two on at all times. It will be a long night and day until Keyen can return to help spell you. Unfortunately, Alpeous' team is handling a major disaster, and Wallance's is so far away and having troubles of their own to handle. So, for right now, we're on our own." With that, he turned and headed for the door. He stopped and looked back at Keyen and then Cassie. "We'll get them back."

"You're right," Keyen vowed. "We will."

Chapter Sixteen

Rori and Bass jerked around when the door abruptly slid open without warning.

"This way." The Block was back with two other men Rori hadn't seen before.

Tendrils of their talent reached out to her. Instinctively, she pulled back.

"Now," the Block barked.

Steeling herself, she stepped forward. The instant she crossed the threshold, the whine started back up. She was tempted to pull back but knew they'd just haul her out, and it would be worse having their hands on her. She didn't want to risk the effect of them touching her.

Halfway down the row, just a couple doors from where they were held, the building ended and the colonnade formed a walkway to the next building. A thigh high stone balustrade fenced off the outside. Open green lawn stretched out a hundred meters before it dropped away into heavy foliage beyond.

Rori knew surveillance equipment would carpet the area, but if they could make it to the trees, they might have a chance of escaping. She glanced at Bass and saw his eyes flick toward the woods and knew he was calculating the possibility. As soon as they were by the next building, he looked to her as if asking what she thought. Not daring to make any noticeable reaction, she lowered her eyes slowly, giving him an affirmative signal.

Just ahead of them old fashioned double doors stood open, and the Block went in. Approaching the door, Rori stumbled as the surge of tainted minds hit her, some nauseatingly sick. She slowed.

"Get going." One of the men stretched out a hand to push her. Bass sidestepped between them, taking the shove that nearly knocked him to his knees, only bumping into her kept him upright.

It took all Rori's will to push back the nausea and step forward. The room was meant to be a ballroom, large and ornate, with vibrant colored moldings and murals on the ceiling, reminiscent of the past. She gave it only a cursory glance as her attention locked on the, at least, thirty men and women, mostly men, in the room. The whine in her head shot to a wail, and the pounding burst, making her vision blur. Nausea blossomed into sickness so fast it dropped her to her knees, and her body heaved to rid it of the tainted waves. But it was no use, it was all around.

Rori was barely aware of Bass yelling.

"C … an't." Gasping in air, she groaned. There was no way to get the words out through the agony. Everything started to fade. Rori welcomed the darkness, but it just never reached her. The wailing in her mind eased, and the pain lessened. Still, it took a minute to realize her internal shield was up and wrapped around her. Weakly, she fought to breathe.

"So, it's true." The words came in a deep masculine voice from above her, and Rori became aware of someone standing over her. It took all her strength to raise her head.

The man was easily over thirty, probably forty. He was more handsome than his images had shown him. He looked like a fallen celestial being, but there was a darkness in him that was so strong, she recoiled from it, though it wasn't tainted. There was no doubting he was a high talent.

Her reaction didn't seem to faze him. "You're back with us now." Drasc Creed swung the restraints that had been on her wrists in front of her face. "These can stay off if you behave yourself."

She followed as his gaze shifted to the side.

"So amazing. Part of your talent actually works with the restraints. I've never heard of that before, something to look into." He looked to Bass and Rori followed the movement.

One of the guards held onto the restraints on Bass's hands while his other hand held a laser gun pressed to Bass's neck with such force it tilted his head to the side.

"Even you can't put a shield in a place so tight between, so, if you want him to live, you will not try anything. I would hate to lose him, but he is expendable." That said Drasc turned away.

Hands grabbed her from behind, hauling her up. Rori was aware of the skewed talents of the two men, but at least, they didn't make her sick. Still unsteady, she didn't truly make it to her feet as she was dragged along behind Drasc. He walked to the front of the room where he took several steps up to a chair on its own raised platform. Rori was halted at the bottom, and Bass was brought up to stand beside her, the weapon still pressed firmly against his neck.

Drasc Creed dropped into the chair and took up a lounging position with one leg hooked over the arm. But for all his nonchalant demeanor, Rori felt the tension in him. It was all warped in with his megalomaniac personality.

She shivered when he looked her over.

"Aurora Straye." He seemed to take too much pleasure in saying her name. "I guess I really should introduce myself."

His pompousness got to her. "I know who you are. You were once a Guardian. A protector of the people, and now you are nothing but a power hungry, murdering villain in the worst sense." She didn't try to censure in the venom behind her words. She knew it wouldn't make any difference.

His bottom lip twitched slightly but otherwise he didn't move. Then he bowed his head in recognition of her outburst. "Very good. Well then, I suppose you are wondering why you have been brought here. You have been chosen to be my wife and the mother of my dynasty."

The breath caught in her lungs on hearing the declaration. Even after what she'd heard earlier it hadn't prepared her for the shock. It took her a second to find her voice. "I emphatically decline."

"Oh, I'm afraid that will not be allowed. You see we are a perfect match."

Rori wanted to yell *"No, Keyen was her perfect match,"* but didn't dare, and Creed was already going on. His next sentence shocked her more.

"All your testing proves you are far more compatible than any other female talent I've found. Any child produced by us should be a highly intelligent, strongly talented, surely the strongest talent ever. Physically, they should be extremely attractive."

Rori fought for calm. "You are inflating yourself. And what testing?" Rori locked on that to hide her revulsion.

"All the information in your file," he said simply, confirming her fears.

"You have my file?"

"I have every file of any notable talent. Edda has been most useful. So helpful it is really too bad her talent is so unstable. She showed such strength and potential at first. She has been able to direct me to a number of available talents that suited my needs. She alerted me to you. She knew something was up when Hiymm came to Areathea so excited. But she has served her purpose."

Rori felt sick again, but it had nothing to do with drug enhanced talents.

He took no notice, shifting back to his own superiority. "You see, I know everything that happens at Guardian headquarters," he sneered. "They thought they could push me aside, that their ideals were better. Guardians of the people. It is all lies to keep us who are truly superior from reaching our full potential and being recognized for what we really are. Gods."

A cheer went up in the room. Rori glanced at Bass. Even with a weapon pressed to his head, there was no disguising the loathing in his eyes for the man who would rule the world if he could. And Rori feared, with his insane bunch of talents, he would if they didn't stop him.

"If you have it all planned out, why do you need me?" She pressed for more information and got it.

"Every God needs a Goddess at his side, one worthy to be there."

"I will never be at your side."

"Oh, but you will." He glanced at the woman, Faen. "Even strong minds bend after time. You and Mr. Morus will eventually take your places at my side and any other worthy talents that survive."

Rori felt Bass shift at his name and spoke up to keep attention from her. "Do you really think your artificial creations can stand against true talents?"

"Oh yes, Faen is one of my greatest." He paused and looked again at Rori. "You are the only person ever to defy her. It was most distressful to her, but it was then that I knew for certain you were the one. Unfortunately, it will take time, and I'm afraid that is one thing we don't have much of right now. So much to do in taking over the world. The council convenes in the morning. I don't want to miss it. It's such a prodigious occasion," he gloated.

"So you really are going to kill the council." Rori stepped forward, only to be grabbed and hauled back. Beside her, the laser was pressed tighter against Bass, making him gasp as it cut into his air.

"They are just a bunch of self-important, no talent fools. Who do they think they are to tell their betters what to do?"

"Meaning you."

"And you," he said smoothly, leaning forward. "Think of what you can do."

"You are not doing this for me or anyone else." Rori glared in challenge.

"Why should we spend our lives serving them?" He stood, aggravation poured off him. "They should serve us." His voice rose with the words and a cheer went up from the people in the room.

Rori felt his emotions swell and, with it, the insane power of lust. She shook her head, standing straight and proud. "No, you are talking enslavement. I will not be part of it. I choose to serve the people."

Creed surged to his feet and paced across the platform then stopped to stare down at her. When he spoke, his words were menacing. "Unfortunately, you don't have a choice as you will soon learn."

A smattering of snickers followed his words this time, but Creed ignored it turning his attention to the rat man. "Take them to their new quarters." He looked back at Rori and Bass. "At least, until they have had a change in thinking."

Rori let her talent swell, but a glance at Bass had her settling it back down. Not that she could do much. After all, her talent was good only for defense and swaying emotions.

With a jerk of Drasc Creed's hand, their guards turned them, forcing them from the room. As she walked Rori's thoughts went back to what Creed had said, 'Even she couldn't shield that tight'. But how did she know. She'd never tried.

Slowing her pace so she lagged behind, she studied Bass. The guard still had the weapon tight to his neck, but as she focused out calming waves, the guard relaxed his hold slightly.

Taking that as a good sign, Rori decided to try

something else. "*Bass can you hear me.*"

Rori caught the reaction from him but no answer came. She tried to refine and strengthen the shield between his wrists and the binder and felt him trying to access his talent. "*How?*"

"*I'm shielding around you. We've got to get out of here.*" There was a tug on her senses but no answer came. Again, she tried to fine-tune the shield. "*Can you access your talent to break the binders?*" Rori felt him pull for his talent and the blockage. After several attempts at trying to fix the shield it became obvious it was a no go.

Frustration radiated from Bass, but he gave a slight negative movement of his head.

"*Okay. We still need to try.*" Her thoughts went to making a plan. It didn't take long to see their best chance. "*When we get to the balustrade, you'll just have to dive over and make a run for it.*"

There was another negative shake.

"*You'll have to. If we can make it to the woods, we can lose them. Don't worry, I'll be with you all the way, but you're going to have to run with your hands behind your back. We'll worry about getting the restraints off after we're free.*"

Rori caught a quick look of questioned concern as the lines around his eyes tightened. "*I plan on being right with you. But, if it comes between you and me getting away, you go. Creed won't hurt me, but I have no doubt he will retaliate against you.*"

Bass kept his attention straight ahead, but Rori could almost feel his glare. Still he made a slight nod.

Rori pushed more relaxation out to the guards and noticed the effect on the men. The balustrade was just up six meters ahead. "*Five, four,*" she counted off in her mind, "*three, two…*"

A man came running toward them. "Creed doesn't want them in the holding cell. Take them directly to the labs. They are preparing rooms for them there."

As soon as Rori heard the words, she knew they couldn't let themselves be taken down below and certainly couldn't be split up. They had to go now. She related her thoughts to Bass and saw him shift and knew it was in preparation to act on her signal.

"Go, now," Rori yelled the words into his head at the same time as clasping her hands together and slamming them into the closest man to her. The man dropped to the ground. Beside her, Bass jerked his head back away from the weapon and rammed his body into the Block.

Out of the corner of her eye, Rori saw the man with the weapon move it back to Bass and threw up a shield. The explosion off the shield burst back on the weapon. The man dropped it, clutching his hand, not that it mattered as Bass was already free. In two steps, he dove over the balustrade. He tucked and rolled to his feet.

Rori followed. Clearing the railing, a hand struck her foot. She ripped free, but it knocked off her dive. Rori slammed to the ground, twisting at the last second, taking the impact with her shoulder and side. She shifted to stand, but before she could push up, something plowed into her back, smashing her into the ground. Rori swung an arm back and tried to twist away but didn't connect with anything and couldn't break free as the rodent man settled more firmly on her back.

A thud landed beside her, and she turned her head in time to see the pyro send a ball of fire toward Bass. Fire burst against the shield she got up, followed by pops and sparks from laser pistols. Bass turned and staggered a step as he started to change direction back to her.

"Go," Rori roared in his head as more fire balls burst just short of him. *"You have to go."*

The indecision was strong from Bass, but at another volley of sparks flaring off the shield in front of him, he turned and broke for the foliage. Behind Rori, iron hands clamped down on the back of her head. She struggled to keep her focus on Bass. He was almost to the trees. A man, realizing his laser was useless, bolted after him. Rori shifted the shield, shrinking it down to a stumbling block that caught the man just below the shin, sending him tumbling as Bass disappeared from view.

Rori was moving the shield back behind him when a sharp blow hit the back of her head followed by her face being shoved into the grass, breaking her line of sight. The shield dissolved and things faded. For a moment, Rori felt herself losing consciousness and welcomed it but at the last second, was jerked back by a rough shake.

"Creed's not going to be happy with you," the voice growled in her ear. "And I wouldn't get any hopes up. Even if he avoids our security, it's almost dark, and there are a lot of animals that will be comin' out to hunt. He won't be seein' mornin'."

Chapter Seventeen

The instant the restraints were clicked down on Rori's wrists, the tainted waves washed over her so strong it dropped her to the ground. Once more her body heaved as if it could rid itself of the unsavory touches. It eased slightly as the man on her back stood but returned when he reached down, grabbing her arm to pull her up. It was agony being drawn over the balustrade. To give herself strength, she focused on the thick foliage that swallowed the light like it had Bass.

Fortunately, the lift they led her to was only a couple dozen meters away, and only two men followed her inside. Once the doors closed, they released her arm. Weakly, Rori slumped against the wall and fought the nauseating effects.

"How hard did you hit her?"

"Not that hard."

"Creed's going to go ballistic if she's injured."

The words filtered into Rori's mind just as the doors slid open. Rori groaned when the man gripped her arm to haul her upright.

"Maybe we better have her checked out to be safe." The other man, though larger in stature, seemed nervous.

"It wasn't that hard," the man defended himself, though the way he shifted his body, his nervousness was as plain as if she was reading it.

It wasn't hard for Rori to pull off a groan and stagger her steps since her legs really didn't want to hold her.

"You might be right," the one holding her said. "Let's put her in her room and find Phallip."

It took all Rori's concentration on the route to memorize it. Fortunately, there were only two turns and fourteen steps down the next hall before they halted long enough for the guard to deactivate the lock. As soon as the door opened, she was pushed into a small room where she was dropped on a small bed.

To her relief the restraints were removed. Immediately, her head began to clear and her senses eased. She didn't let on, slumping back in mock unconsciousness.

Rori remained still even after the door closed, cutting off all light. She heard the lock sound, but didn't mind. She just wanted to drink in the calm across her senses and take time to think.

Her thoughts went immediately to Bass. She wondered if he'd made it free, and how he would handle the night predators. She didn't doubt they were there, though they were close to town. As a seeker, she'd been on enough searches to know a lot could happen, even close to civilization. If his hands were free there would be no problem, but they weren't. And beside the restraints on his talent, his hands were trapped behind his back, impeding his movements. Still, Bass was well trained in survival. He was quick, agile and smart.

Rori repeated the thought in her mind, but it didn't alleviate her worry. Knowing there wasn't any more she could do, she moved on to her own dilemma. She wasn't any more certain of her own fate. One thing she did know, she was not going to be Drasc Creed's empress. That meant she had to be smart, too.

Overplaying and using her reaction to the tainted talents was useful. She was free from restraints. And, if she could get out of the room, there might be things she could do to escape. The most important was reaching Keyen. She tried not to think of it as impossible. She'd done the impossible before when it was called for, and it was called for now. Her life, Bass's, the council's, and possibly the world all relied on stopping Drasc and his crew.

Rori was so locked in thought she jumped when the door swooshed open. Light spilled into the room, back lighting the figures standing in the doorway making them look like demons. Fear shot through her before she could tamp it down.

"Come on."

The words reached her, bringing with it the recognition of the voice. The Block was back. She could now make out the outline.

"Get up," he ordered as she'd failed to move.

Shakily, she stood. Her unsteadiness, only partly necessary must have been convincing because the tall, thinner shadow stepped into the room and caught her arm to steady her. Rori started to pull away, but his words halted her.

"I told you we needed to have her checked out."

"Just get her going. We leave in a couple hours," the Block grumbled.

"It's not my fault Phallip was tied up until now."

Rori let herself be led from the room, wondering how much time had passed. If going by the fatigue of her body, she figured it was late. Just two portals down she was taken into a room not much different from the med-lab at Guardian headquarters, but instead of an Areathea type medic, there was a small bald man, with beady eyes and a twitchy nose. She couldn't help wonder what it was with all the rodent types around there.

"Sit down," the rodent, who she guessed must be Medic Phallip wheezed.

When she failed to move, the guard gave her a push toward the exam table. Another shove had her bumping into it. Before Rori could even get the protest out, she was boosted up, and Phallip came to stand before her. Rori got a taste of tainted talent as he studied her and realized two things. One, the room wasn't shielded, and two, he'd been experimenting on himself, though he wasn't as off as others. Still, she had to suppress a shiver as his senses ran over her. Rori pressed for a blank feel around herself.

His nose twitched and his talent crested then receded. "Impressive. You are hard to read. So strong. You are everything they said, aren't you? I can't wait to study you." He rubbed his hands together in anticipation.

Rori shivered again as she watched the action.

He pursed his lips, nodded, and started to move around her. Rori followed him with her eyes but stopped when she noticed the woman step out of the adjoining room. The hypno, Rori felt a flash of fear that exploded when she felt the mental numbing attack.

Immediately, she blocked it, and too late, realized it was just a diversion. From behind her, a dark cloth dropped over her head, cutting off her vision. Rori spun, striking out with her hand. She caught Phallip in a glancing blow before he could move away. The next instant, hands grabbed her from behind, pinning her arms to her sides. The mental attack surged. Rori felt the woman's glee and strengthened her shield.

"Get her strapped down." Phallip wheezed. "It's obvious she's fine. But, I'd like to have her ready to do the exam in the morning while you're all gone. Creed is anxious to know when he can plan his wedding night."

At the words, Rori almost lost focus on her shield as she doubled her struggling. It was the snicker Phallip added on the end that made her fury burst. She directed the extra energy into the shield, breaking the attack.

Rori heard a satisfying shriek from the woman as she was forced down on the table. She tried to pull free and claw at the men, but her arm was pinned down and a restraint was clicked into place. The pressure was double on her other arm. Rori made a grabbed for the hood but before she could come close her free hand was locked down with a final sickening click.

"Now dear, don't worry." She heard Phallip coo. At first, she thought he was talking to her until his next words. "She's the top of the range. It will just take a little more adjusting, but over time, you'll win out."

Rori's objection was cut off when she felt straps being clamped down over her legs.

"There that should hold her," one of the guards spoke.

Someone tugged on the bands. "Excellent." The wheezing came again. "Now, I suggest we get some rest. Tomorrow is a most auspicious day."

Rori heard the Medic rub his hands together again and pulled at her bonds.

"What about her?" the Hypno asked.

Rori felt the venom behind the words and realized again her talent was still not blocked.

"As they said, that will hold her. Her talent will be of no use in helping her get free," Phallip answered.

"You're certain?" Doubt came from the woman.

"Positive, I have a copy of all her testing. Her empathy and shielding abilities can do nothing against those straps, especially, without her eyesight to focus."

Rori was again left alone in darkness but this time it was due to the hood over her head. She tried thrashing her head from side to side but couldn't dislodge it. She turned her attention to the restraints, pulling first at them, then trying to slide her hands out until her wrists were raw and started to bleed. Even with the added slickness of her blood, she couldn't break free. Exhausted, she fell still. Her mind drifted in fear and frustration until fatigue took over, and she fell asleep.

☙

Keyen pushed a leaf the size of his torso aside and held it for Cassie and Sansa to follow. They moved almost silently through the thick foliage. He knew Tankin and

Ultin were about a hundred meters to his left, not far from the cliff trail.

Keyen paused to focus on the IPI's image, checking their progress. They were just outside the perimeter of Creed's complex. It had taken them two hours, working their way around security and through the foliage to reach that point but they were finally in position.

Soon it would be time to move. He felt no relief in the thought. Rori and Bass had been taken over twelve hours ago. The knowledge ate at him. Not much longer he promised to himself.

At least the council had agreed to meet early to start the debate about if there was enough proof to sanction them going in. And, if they didn't, well, they were going anyway. That had already been decided between them.

"Keyen," Cassie's voice was barely a whisper but he heard it plainly.

"What is it?" He turned to her.

"I'm picking up something," she said.

"Visual." He studied his own screen, logging movements of different large sources that could be animals or humans.

"No, it's a feeling. Like…" she broke off, and Keyen knew she was reaching out with her talent. "I'm not reaching Bass, but I feel like … I'm feeling him."

"Where?" He glanced at Cassie, getting the direction she indicated then back to the image on the IPI. It didn't take long to detect a large body in the trees only about twenty meters to the right and ahead of them. He couldn't make out what it was because it was hunched against a cluster of trees. Keyen weighed the option of shifting closer to the estate.

"Let's check it out, carefully." Keyen studied the grid for any alarms, picked a path and moved forward with Cassie and Sansa fanned out on either side of him. He was only two meters away before he could make out the shadowed form visually in the near darkness. He held up a hand for the women to stop and crept forward. He was almost on him when the figure dropped on his back and kicked out. Ready for an attack, Keyen block it easily. Coming down, he pinned the man, pulling his arm back for a punch. He caught himself barely in time.

"Bass," he let out, relaxing his hold.

On the ground, his friend sagged in relief. "What took you so long? I was starting to attract a lot of attention from unwelcome neighbors. I don't know how much longer I could have evaded them."

"Bass." Cassie popped through the undergrowth and dove at him.

Bass groaned as he rolled back on the ground with her hugging him.

"Binders," Bass whispered and sat up with her aiding him.

"Let's see." Keyen shifted behind him and focused a small light, then his talent. When he got no reaction, he pushed for more power. A full minute passed before they popped open and fell away.

"Thanks." Bass brought his hands in front of him and started rubbing his wrists then his arms.

"Where's Rori?" Keyen couldn't hold back the question.

"They still have her. We tried to make a break for it, but Rori didn't get free. I didn't want to leave her." Self-recrimination came strong in the darkness.

Keyen felt his own heart burn with wanting her, but kept it from his voice. "It's all right."

"I stayed around the area in case I could help her. But with the binders on, I've just been playing hide and seek with them."

"I know you did your best. Tell us what happened." Keyen placed a hand on his shoulder, squeezing down in reassurance.

Bass just started to give an outline when Ultin and Tankin joined them.

"Rori was right," Keyen said, "there was no choice."

"I know. Creed would have used me against her," Bass continued. "The man's crazy. He plans to take over the world, and he wants Rori for his empress. His word."

"Raebent hues," Keyen let out.

"Thought you'd feel that way," Bass said. "It looks like he did kidnap others. He's been looking for his perfect mate, but he's decided Rori's the one. He has Edda, one of the med-techs, feeding him info."

"Tank," Keyen barked.

"I'm on it." He was already establishing a link to Hiymm. After reporting the new events, he told him about Edda. Hiymm joined in, listening to what else Bass had to report.

"I think they were too busy to spend much time looking for me because they are planning on hitting the council soon. It sounded like first thing in the morning." Bass glanced to where the sky was beginning to lighten. The others followed his gaze.

As if reading their thoughts, Hiymm answered. "He knows we're meeting early. I was just headed over there now." Whatever he was going to say next was lost in a low rumble that echoed through the trees, sending all the wildlife into nervous chatter then dead silence.

"What's that?" Sansa asked, as they all shifted to look around.

"If I don't miss my guess, I'd say a very large hanger opening," Ultin said in hushed tones.

"Hiymm," Keyen said, "they're leaving." A cluster of hoversleds, large and small, rose in the air above them.

"I heard," he answered.

"Do you want us back?" Keyen asked the words, though the thought of leaving without Rori tore at him.

There was silence for a second. "Negative. Go after

Rori. I'm giving you full clearance for whatever force is needed."

"You don't think he took her with him?" Fear added a quiver to Cassie's voice.

This time there was no pause over the link. "No, she'd be no use to him yet because he can't control her. He'd want her kept where he thinks she'd be safe. That's his fortress. You'll have to be careful but get her and back here as soon as you can. We'll hold them off until you do," Hiymm said with conviction.

CRED

Rori came awake at the quiet swoosh of the door. She strained to see through the hood, but no light permeated the material, just the sounds of someone moving around the room. Again, she wondered how much time had passed.

"Good, you're awake." Phallip's wheezy voice came out of the darkness. "Not that it matters." A hand locked down on her arm. "You've been fighting with the bonds. So useless, there is no way you'll get free."

Despite his words, Rori tried to pull back from his grip, making the bindings bite into her arm.

"Now none of that, there's no need. This won't hurt. With all the noise of the preparation to leave, I couldn't sleep, so I thought I'd get started on some tests."

"What are you doing to me?" Rori twisted her head, not that she could dislodge the hood, but she couldn't help trying.

"This is just a simple blood test. Edda has been sending me all your results, but I'm afraid she's not reliable anymore, and Areathea isn't looking for exactly the same things I am."

"And what's that?" Rori forced the words out over the fear rising in her.

"You wouldn't understand."

"I understand that what you're doing is making these talents unstable."

Anger flared in the room, assaulting her senses. The hand on her arm tightened painfully. Rori knew she'd hit a sore spot with the man, though, in an instant it was gone, replaced with what she could term only as a wave of pure justification.

His words confirmed it. "Some were less than suitable candidates. And it takes time to perfect greatness."

Rori wanted to scoff at his 'greatness' but held it in. "Isn't Creed worried you'll create someone as or more powerful than him?"

"I only use lower-med levels. There is no risk. You would have been a candidate in your previous state, though I wouldn't have bothered with your type. Who would have guessed you held such power, most intriguing, especially that you could suppress it for so long. It makes you wonder how many others might be suppressing the strength of their true latent talents. It is something I must study."

There was a pause as Rori guessed he thought about it.

"But for now," Phallip said abruptly, and the pressure on her arm tightened again.

Rori flinched and tried to tug away.

"Hold still," Phallip ordered and she felt a jab of pain. "This will only take a minute. I want to start checking your blood to see what information is locked there that they missed."

The hands were gone, and the words started to drift away as if he was already lost in another thought. A second later, she heard the door slide open and shut. But Rori didn't relax. She tightened her muscles pulling on the bonds. Nothing happened. She wanted to scream out loud but settled for in her mind.

"*Keyen!*" she cried, knowing she couldn't reach him, just taking solace in his name.

"*Rori.*" When her name trickled back to her she thought it was her imagination until it was repeated stronger. "*Rori.*"

"Keyen."

"I'm here. Where are you? Are you safe?" Need, desperation and love fueled the words.

"I'm fine." Tears filled her eyes, dampening the hood, but she didn't care. *"Where are you?"*

"Just outside the estate. We're coming for you."

Her relief was overwhelming. *"Bass."*

"We have him. He's all right. Can you tell us where you are?"

"Lift, Bass can show you. Middle level, right, second hall." She tried to remember and send him the visual. She felt him understand and hoped it really did work.

"We're on our way."

"Be careful. I don't know how many are here, at least thirty enhanced talents then some plain guards."

"Most have left."

"The council." Dread rose in her.

"It's okay, we'll get you first."

Rori knew she should object, but her relief was too great, and she could feel Keyen already moving and knew he needed his concentration.

CB80

Keyen felt Rori's touch pull back from his mind to just a feather-light contact and turned his attention to the fortress in front of him. He brought up the schematics on the IPI, refreshing his memory before turning to the others.

"Rori's okay." He looked to Bass. "Lift to middle level."

Bass nodded. "I can find it. It's halfway down the courtyard." He looked at the IPI image Keyen projected and pointed to the location. "There."

"Okay, we don't know how many we'll be facing. It's safe to say the strongest talents left with Creed and the attack force, but he wouldn't have left this place unprotected."

"What makes you think Creed's left with them?" Sansa

212

asked.

"He'd have to be there. This is his big moment," Keyen said.

"I'll buy that," Ultin agreed. "The man's a megalomaniac."

There were nods around of confirmation.

"Okay, first thing is, we want to take out the communication." Keyen pointed to the spot on the projection. "Tank, do you think you can take that out from here?"

The big man looked to the top of the hill where the communication tower could just be seen over the foliage, silhouetted by the lightening sky, and grinned. "No problem, they'll be hearing humming for a week."

"Good. Simultaneously, we take out the guards and auto-weapon fields along here. Sansa and Ultin go left. Bass, you up to it?"

"Oh, yeah." There was no hesitation.

"Okay, you and Cassie go right. Tank and I will take the middle. These two here," he pointed to the image, "have got to be guards, and we have two in towers, here and here. Watch them, we don't know if they're talents, but we can be certain they're armed."

It only took them a minute to spread out. On Keyen's signal, Tankin focused his talent into a sound wave directing it at the tower. Sparks and a squeal burst in the air.

"I guess a bit much."

Keyen heard him whisper but knew the man had no remorse. Keyen broke into a run, using the distraction of the guard looking up to take him by surprise. Stunned, the man dropped. Not far away, the other guard did the same as Sansa and Ultin emerged from the trees. A burst from Ultin's laser struck the guard on the tower overlooking the water. While, with less subtlety, the guard on the other tower was raised in the air, lowered over the edge then dropped ten feet from the ground.

"Nice," Tankin said over the comm.

"What can I say, I owed them," Bass returned.

A burst of energy erupted near Sansa, who dropped, rolled and came up returning fire at the top of the tower. Keyen spun, picking off the second guard on the tower. To his right, a laser activated, but in the second it took to turn his direction, it exploded thanks to Ultin, who already was shifting to take out another gun. Cassie and Bass demolished another guard, dropping an ornamental figure from the garden on him, and Tankin took out the last.

The way clear, they all ran for the balustrade. The touch of arrogant showing off ended as they took up positions along the rail, now they were entering their enemy's stronghold, and they knew they needed to be more cautious. Keyen and Ultin took the leads rolling over the railing and dropping into a crouch. Keyen's laser blast caught the guard just as he fired. The guard dropped, his shot going wide. Behind Keyen, lasers scorched the floor, but Ultin returned the volley, drawing the fire as Sansa leaned forward catching the man by surprise.

A second passed and at no other movement, the others dropped over the rail. Bass indicated down the hall, and the others followed the way to the lift.

Keyen motioned to Ultin and Tankin, who took up positions on either side of the lift while the others stepped inside.

⋘⋙

Rori flinched as the wail of an alarm cut through the air. *Keyen*, relief coursed through her. They were coming. She was tempted to reach out for him, but the possibility of distracting him stayed her. *Patience*, she told herself, *it won't be long now*. The thought hardly crossed her mind when she heard the door slide open.

"Keyen," she cried out just before picking up the rush of panic and rage.

"No, No, No," Phallip whined. "This can't happen. My research. The perfect specimen."

There was a shuffling around the room. Rori tried to follow the movements and cringed as he came near her. "We have to go." The words were mumbled.

A hand clamped around her wrist, and she heard a clank of metal bump the side of the table. Instinctively, she knew it was binders. "No," she screamed aloud and mentally, trying to put up a shield around her wrist. Not being able to see made it difficult, but from his reaction it must've worked.

"Stop that," he yelled.

Rori was unprepared for the blow that hit the side of her head and, for a second, she lost focus on the shield. It winked out. There was the sickening click of the binders locking down, followed by a nauseating wave of tainted talent.

Only being one person, it wasn't so intense but it was heightened by his rage. By the time Rori managed to settle her nerves, he had her unstrapped, the other binder locked on her other wrist with her hands behind her back, and was tugging her off the table.

For a rodent, he was surprisingly strong. Hampered by being hooded and her hands bound, she was dragged across the room. She stumbled, half on purpose, going down. She crashed into what she guessed was a counter, not that she cared. She was just trying to slow him down. Pain flared in her knee. She felt damp warmth soak the material of her pants.

"Get up."

She was dragged to her feet by the back of her shirt. The door swooshed open. Rori used it as a hopeful distraction and threw her body back against the medic. There was a grunt, and they both started to go down, only to come in contact and be held up by the wall. Another blow caught her, this time across the back of her head.

"Don't hurt her." Phallip barked, his breath coming in pants. "Just get us out of here."

"The sled's ready." A voice she didn't recognize reached her as a large powerful hand clamped on her arm.

She detected no signs of talent but there was no relief from the hand that was like a metal band. Rori was propelled across the floor. No amount of dragging her feet seemed to make a difference. When she tried to drop to her knees, she was dragged back up and thrown over a shoulder without the man hardly breaking his stride.

"No," Rori tried to scream but the air was knocked from her lungs.

"Come on," the man under her rumbled out.

"I'm coming." The medic wheezed, running to keep up.

Chapter Eighteen

"*No,*" Rori's shout echoed in Keyen's mind as the lift doors slid closed. He tried to reach her but the link was cut off. Like a caged animal, he struck out at the door of the small space.

"What's wrong?" Sansa asked, studying the smooth walls looking for possible danger.

"I lost contact with Rori."

"Binders." Bass supplied the answer.

Keyen nodded as the doors slid open. Cassie touched his arm. He looked down and understood what she was saying.

He drew in a deep breath and let it out slowly. "I'm okay." He forced steadiness.

"Let's go get Rori then." Bass took up a position against the wall, and Keyen followed suit. With a nod from him, they both swung out into the hall, each facing a different direction, dropping low. A laser blast scorched the wall above their heads. Bass took out the first man. Keyen spun, taking out the second before he could get off another shot.

"Clear," Keyen called and Sansa and Cassie came around the door, weapons ready. They made it down the hall without further contact, but as they peeked around the corner they met a wall of resistance.

Bass pulled back in time to dodge a laser burst that took out a chunk of the wall behind them. The shock wave was so strong it almost knocked them from their feet.

"Whoa. If Ultin was here, he'd say that wasn't being very nice," Bass exclaimed.

"What do you say we return the favor then," Sansa said, shifting closer to the corner.

"My thoughts exactly." Keyen fingered the control on his weapon strengthening the power. "On two." He looked around making sure everyone was ready. "One, two."

He and Sansa spun halfway around the corner, each firing at the same time. The explosion rocked the tunnel, throwing the five men at the end to the ground. Bass and Cassie were already around, locking on the single man trying to rise. The gun was ripped from his hands, flying a safe distance down the hall. A laser shot from Cassie dropped him to the floor unconscious like the rest.

They paused long enough to put on restraints before stepping over the men into the next hall, moving quickly but cautiously. Around the next bend, they found the hallway empty. Sansa covered the corner while the others trotted the half dozen steps to the door. This time it was Keyen and Cassie who took up position on either side of the door while Bass continued down to the next bend.

Keyen took up a firing position while Cassie activated the door. At a glance, the room looked empty. Cautiously, Keyen stepped forward as Cassie covered him. He registered the overturned table and a smear of what looked like blood on the floor but continued around the room, checking a small storage room off to one side.

"Empty," he said, coming back to the door.

His communicator clicked and Ultin's voice came over it. "It's clear up here. Everyone's fled."

"Acknowledged. Head down to the cliffs. See if you can pick anyone up there." Dread started to fill him. They were too late. She was gone. They'd taken her. He tried not to think of the blood smear on the floor, but it was there just a meter away.

"Keyen," Sansa called his attention. "I heard something. It sounded like Rori."

It only took a second to retrace his steps to her.

"Down the hall, that way." She motioned with the tip of her weapon.

"That'd be toward the cliffs. A hanger opening," Bass suggested, reaching them.

It made sense, and no one had to say they were trying to get Rori out that way.

"Let's go." Keyen took off at a ground-covering lope, slowing only briefly at each intersection to make sure it was clear and listen for any sound. Ahead, the hall ended at a set of double doors. They reached it as a faint whine penetrated.

"Hoversled," Keyen yelled, activating the opening mechanism. Nothing happened.

"Locked." Sansa supplied but Keyen was already concentrating his talent, gathering up energy. He sent it out in a large push and the doors blew back.

"Whoa," Bass let out.

Keyen ran through the opening not waiting for the others. In front of him, morning sun poured through the open hangar doors, glinting off the hoversled just starting to lift off. Power again crested in Keyen. This time, he reached out and caught the sled, locking on and pulling it back. Engines whined then cut out as Keyen dropped the hoversled on the deck.

The side panel slid open and two men stumbled out, hands held high. Keyen and Sansa strode toward the vehicle while Cassie and Bass covered them. Sansa motioned the men down. Keyen was focused inside.

"No, no, no." A gaunt, sharp-faced man rocked back and forth inside. "This can't happen. No."

Keyen turned his attention to a figure that sat in the chair in front of him. Even with a hood covering her head and shoulders, Keyen knew who it was. "Rori," he let out, and she turned his direction as he climbed aboard.

"Keyen," she gasped out as he reached her. Pulling off the hood, she blinked against the light then propelled herself up into his arms. Keyen was only too happy to catch her to him.

"You're okay?" He turned his head, pressing his face into her hair, then pulling back to kiss her.

"Yes." She edged back, tears trickled down her face but she beamed up at him. "Everyone all right?"

"All's fine." He steadied himself. Now that he had her, he could think again. Glancing back outside, he saw the others had the men in restraints. He turned back to her. "Let's get these binders off you."

"No," screeched the man in the seat behind them, leaping on Keyen.

Keyen slammed him back into the wall, and the man dropped to the ground.

"No, she's mine." The man clawed at Keyen's leg.

"Wrong," Keyen declared. "She's mine." His hand flexed, and for a minute, he thought of hitting him, but looking at the cowering man, he reached down instead. The man threw his hands up as if to protect himself. Keyen pulled a set of restraints from his pocket, grasped one wrist, locked it on, then did the same to the other before turning his attention back to Rori. "Now, let's get you free."

Rori turned. A second later the binding fell away.

"You're getting better at those." Bass came up to stand in the doorway.

"I have them figured out now." Keyen smiled as Rori moved past him.

"You made it." She hugged Bass.

"Did you doubt me?" He winked.

"Let's just say, I was worried."

"I guess that's acceptable." He looked at Keyen. "I've never seen you pull a hoversled out of the air before. I didn't know we could."

"We probably can't." Cassie came up to them.

"True." Bass looked thoughtful. "Don't ever get you mad."

"You mean," Sansa joined them, "don't ever get between him and Rori."

Keyen felt his face heat as Rori looked up at him but was saved from any further comments as the comm-links came to life. "The council hall is under attack," Tankin announced.

Keyen was relieved for the subject change, except that it meant people were in trouble. "Let's go."

"Think this will still fly?" Bass asked.

Keyen understood what he meant. "I didn't do anything to the engines."

A second later, Bass was at the controls and brought all functions on line. "We're good," he said over his shoulder. Sansa and Cassie finished moving the medic against the wall next to the other men and boarded.

"Tank, have you made it to the cove yet?" Keyen asked.

"Affirmative."

"Good, we'll pick you up."

Bass was already nosing the sled out of the hangar. The two men were waiting, jumping on board before it touched down. They were off.

Keyen took the seat next to Rori. "Let me see your leg."

"It's okay. I just fell on something sharp."

"And we don't know what so we sterilized it." Keyen cut her off, already removing the utensil from his pocket to slice through the material at the knee of her pants.

The cut was small, only the width of his thumb, but he took great care in tending it. Aware of the soft skin under his hands, Keyen forced his thoughts to a professional level, but it was hard. He'd almost lost her. He wanted to take her in his arms and keep her safe.

Her hand settled over his. He raised his eyes to meet her gaze.

"I love you," she said softly.

He interlocked their fingers and raised his hand to cup her cheek. He leaned in to kiss her, long and deep.

Ahead, a throat cleared. "I'm all for you two being in love," Ultin said. "But we're approaching the city."

Keyen dropped Rori's hand and called up information from the IPI. Images of explosions and laser bursts filled the screen in what looked like a full-fledged war. Orn's team and the security force were heavily outnumbered.

"Oh, my." Cassie gasped as a corner of the council building collapsed as they watched.

"Bass, bring us in on the left. See if we can't trap Creed's forces between us and the others. Let's stop this maniac. Formation two." He looked to Rori. "You up to this?"

"I'm good to go. Believe me."

Bass brought the sled down hard and fast just around the corner across from the council building, giving them some protection.

Rori was the last one off the shuttle, fastening on the equipment belt Sansa had brought for her as she went. The others were already fanning out, Sansa, Bass, Cassie, and Ultin going to the left, Tankin and Keyen heading right. She took up her position just to the left of Keyen, so she was centered to shield the group. She could hear Keyen's conversation with Orn as the two worked out a strategy.

The second they came around the corner, they were immersed in chaos. Fires burned in dozens of locations, set off by the pyro and explosives. Sansa focused her attention on extinguishing the ones that endangered people while Ultin located the pyro. Rori found the pyro first.

"Behind the Unity statue," she said to Ultin, feeling a touch of panic as she watched the pyro pulling in energy for another blast.

"Got him," Ultin answered back.

Rori watched long enough to see the pyro's fireball burst apart as it was intersected by Ultin's.

"Anous is down." Orn's voice came over the link ripping Rori's attention away.

She brought up the man's location. He was behind a destroyed slider directly in front of the council building. There were so many laser strikes across the area there was no way anyone could get to him. Rori got up the shield just as Keyen called her name.

"I've got it. It's safe to get him," she said into her link then almost faltered when she saw a gray-haired man dash from the front council doors and down the steps to Anous. There was no mistaking her grandfather. Jattin Straye still moved well for an older man. Rori felt a twinge of panic as a burst of laser fire blew against her shield directly in front of her grandfather.

Jattin reached Anous's location, stopped to return some shots of his own before disappearing down behind cover. A second later, her grandfather's voice came over the link. "I have him, ready to go."

"Ready," Rori acknowledged and Jattin came into view, Anous slung over his shoulder. His pace back up the stairs was slower but still steady. The instant they disappeared inside, Rori shifted her shield to Tankin who was pinned down behind a small pile of debris just to her right.

"Thanks," he said when the first blocked blast fell short.

"Wouldn't you like to get somewhere a little bigger?"

"Sure would. About seven meters right was where I was headed," he said back.

"Go." He was already moving. A hail of fire bursts flared against her shield so intense it almost blinded her, but a second later, he was under cover.

"Tank, why don't you give some of these guys a

headache?" Keyen came over the link.

"My thoughts exactly," Tankin answered. "Just making sure I had some space.

Rori had heard of Tankin's ability to produce sound waves that could actually render someone unconscious but had never seen him do it because the sound waves affected anyone in their path. She felt his talent build, but her attention shifted to the left, giving cover to Sansa. Sansa's acknowledgment was cut off by a large boom that shook the ground.

"Way to go, Tank!" Ultin called out. There was no more sign of the pyro. Ultin was now in a fire fight, along with Keyen, against several groups of Creed's men.

Rori felt energy shift as Keyen pulled in a large amount of it and locked on to a hoversled from which Creed's men fired. The sled lifted in the air tipped on its side and crashed down. For a second, silence filled the air.

Rori picked up waves of fear and panic from the attackers then, through it all, a burst of immense rage. She had no trouble tracing it back to its origin. Drasc Creed stood off to the side, back behind a group of his men, waiting to walk in as conqueror. Anger burned from the man as the tide against his forces began to turn.

Rori saw him point at Keyen and felt fear of her own. A shower of laser blasts rained down on Keyen's position. She barely got up a shield in time to cover him. The decorative wall he was behind shattered and to Rori's horror started to tip. Before she could shift her shield, the wall halted and tumbled back the other way as Keyen applied force of his own.

"Bombs," Cassie yelled. A multitude of small objects floated out over the square in all directions, some thrown, some controlled by telekinesis. A rush of power surged around Rori as Cassie, Bass and Keyen reached out with their minds to redirect them to safer areas. Ultin and Tankin ignited some in mid-air using fire and sound but more followed. There was no way to counter them as explosions began to shake the area.

Rori stumbled, gripping the wall beside her to keep from falling. The bombs were coming from so many different directions there was no way to shield everyone. Screams of pain, panic and fear came from everywhere.

"No," Rori cried out as she saw Keyen knocked to the ground by an explosion detonated near him before he could push it away. She couldn't see Cassie or Bass for the dust and smoke in the air.

Another hail of bombs filled the air.

"No." This time, it was a whisper from her as subconsciously she reached for the detestable things. Rori stretched an arm out as if to grab them with her hand as did her mind, wrapping her shield around them like a cocoon.

The first few went off in minor explosions, held harmless in her shield. Then, a massive explosion ripped through the air. The ground shook. Buildings quaked as if in fear. Sound rolled out in thunderous waves. Smoke bellowed and churned over the square. Fragments burst out, only to freeze in midair. Trapped in the web Rori wove around them.

"Astounding," Ultin cried out over the comm.

"Grand. You've been holding out on us." Tankin's comment teased, though there was a lot of awe behind the words.

Rori wasn't sure what to say in return. She didn't know she could do it. She hadn't even thought of doing it. She more just did.

"Rori," Keyen called her name. "You okay?"

"Yes."

"Good move." Keyen said over the comm and his words echoed it in her mind along with his love.

"I…" Rori started to answer when a wave of mind numbing confusion hit her so intimately it took a second to realize it wasn't directed at her but Keyen. She felt pain so intense build within him, that it took her breath away.

Keyen stumbled out from behind his protection, staggering as he tried to fight the compulsion that pulled him into the open almost before Rori could get a shield around him.

"Destroy him," Drasc yelled from his position, and again, the air filled with fire from lasers.

Rori stepped from behind her barrier.

"No! Don't shoot," Drasc's cry echoed over the square. Several more blasts erupted, bursting short of her as they intersected with objects thrown up by Cassie, Bass, and a member of Orn's team. Rori hardly flinched, her attention was locked on Keyen. He'd dropped to one knee, his hand locked on his head as he tried to fight off the mental attack.

Rori ran across the space and dropped to her knees beside him, placing her hands over his. The mental confusion in her intensified, but Rori met it. Letting her mind shield flow through her to Keyen, she pushed back, countering the hypno. Rage, envy, and the desire to destroy them flared in the hypno as she fed more power into her attack.

The blast of the woman's hatred hit against Rori's shield, flaring back at her. Across the square there was an agonized scream that shifted into a wail of despair as the hypno's talent crashed in on her.

Rori felt a wave of empathy for the woman, but it disappeared as the hypno burst from behind a vehicle. The laser weapon in her hand was set on the highest setting and locked in continuous fire. The beam cut across the square scorching everything in its path. A slider exploded and a statue toppled as the beam drew near.

Keyen tackled Rori to the ground as the laser burned a trail only a foot above them. When the beam shifted back toward them, he linked onto a section of the damaged statue, flinging it back in the laser's path. Sparks and fragments flew as it burst apart.

A sharp, ear-ringing whine pierced the air.

"It's going to blow." Keyen's words barely reached Rori though he yelled them in her ear. The explosion of the overheated laser cut off anything she might have said. The ground shook, and Rori felt a wave of sadness for the young woman made unstable by the promise of making her talent stronger.

Rori didn't get to contemplate it long though, as the momentary silence that had settled over the square was ripped apart by the explosion of another string of bombs. Keyen pulled Rori up and behind the slider, using it as shelter while he sent a myriad of the explosives back at their senders.

"We have to end this now," he yelled over his comm.

Rori knew he was right, and felt a sense of pain as the fire fight picked up once more. She could taste how unstable Drasc's forces were as adrenaline fed their tainted talent and pushed them over the edge of self-control.

Tears ran down her face at the waste. True, they had elected to join Drasc, drawn by power and greed. Still, it brought her pain and her thoughts locked on the man that caused it all for his selfish hunger of power and glory.

She brought the image of him up in her mind, first of him across the square waiting to declare himself emperor. The image shifted to him standing over her, declaring she would be his, gloating and using a threat against Bass to hold her. 'Even you can't', the words filtered back through her mind, and again, how did she know if she hadn't tried. She just knew she had to stop it before anyone else was hurt or killed.

Keyen's attention was on blocking explosives and laser bursts sent toward them and buildings where groups of people took refuge. Rori straightened and, once again, stepped from behind the cover.

"Rori," Sansa yelled, followed by her name being

called by Keyen and others.

She ignored them all. Her shield up, laser fire burst harmlessly around her as she walked across the square. Inside her, she drew from the pain and fears, letting it fuel her. Power flowed through her as she kept walking, expanding her shield as Keyen and Tankin followed her. They were joined by Bass, Cassie, Sansa and Ultin. Unified, they reached the center of the square.

Drasc's people, who had ceased fire in stunned reaction to such a bold move, finally recovered and opened up fire. Keyen locked on one man, fling him to the side where he crumbled to the ground. Bass and Cassie followed suit on the other side picking off attackers one by one. Steadily they continued toward Drasc's position, countering everything thrown at them.

"Kill them! Kill them all!" Drasc yelled. Using his own talent to send one of the massive artworks that had been shorn off by the hypno's laser at them. Keyen intercept it in midair and send it back at him.

Drasc locked on another piece, but before he could send it at them, Keyen also locked on, and it became a power play of strength which Keyen quickly won, sending the curved metal structure hurtling out of their path.

A howl cut the air. "Kill them, now!"

A rain of explosives filled the air again. This time there was no panic or doubt in Rori. She wrapped her shield around them, holding them off where they exploded well out of range. The Guardians continued forward, never breaking their pace, as most of Creed's troops were knocked to the ground or thrown back.

"Drasc Creed," Keyen called out. "You are under arrest for crimes against society. Cease your actions and turn yourself in."

Rori felt a surge of power fueled by scorn and supremacy. Around them, debris shifted as Drasc's talent reached out to smash everything down on them. Cassie and

Bass joined with Keyen to force it all down as Rori focused on Drasc, weaving a thin shield all round him, tightening it down.

"What are you doing?" Drasc yelled as he encountered the first constricting band.

"Not allowing you to hurt anyone," Rori answered calmly, tightening the shield so that it forced his arms to his body.

"No, you can't. No one can," he cried, trying to struggle, no longer able to move.

"Evidently, I can."

"No, I was going to make you my empress," he wailed now, as if unable to fathom her actions.

"And I told you, I don't want to be your empress or any part of you ruling the world."

"No, it's him." He shifted his gaze to Keyen. "You chose him?"

"I love him."

A howl went up from the man. "He should have died at the festival."

Rori felt her own anger flare, but before she could do anything, Drasc's power surged in a killing wave that rolled out toward them. Keyen's own surge of power reached Drasc's. Talent slammed together in a force so strong it knocked everyone from their feet. A boom rumbled over the area, dampened by Tankin, who kept it from breaking everyone's eardrums.

Dust filled the air. When it settled, Drasc Creed was on the ground like everyone else, but he wasn't moving. Rori shifted, glancing around quickly to take stock of the team. All seemed shaken but fine.

"Tank?" Keyen's attention followed hers.

"We're all right." The big man made it to his feet, reaching out to help Ultin and Sansa up.

Rori turned back to Keyen as he raised a hand to her cheek. "Are you all right?"

She nodded, reaching for him.

He drew her in and kissed her lightly before easing back slightly. He rested his forehead against hers. "Have I told you, you are totally amazing?"

"I think you did that." She smiled at his words then sobered as she turned toward where Drasc lay. Where before there had been rage and power lust, Rori felt nothing. She didn't need to use a life scan to know Drasc Creed was dead, killed by his own power's backlash against him when it was overwhelmed by Keyen's talent.

Keyen's hand on her chin turned her back to face him. "It's better this way." He brushed his thumb over her cheek.

"I know." Rori swallowed. "It's just such a waste. He could have done so much good."

"Everyone has to make choices as to how they live their lives and use the talents given them. We can do good, or we can let power and egotism control us."

"That is very profound."

"Hey." He smiled. "I'm not just a pretty face. Actually, I can't take credit for it. Your grandfather told me that when I was an angry boy with too much power for his own good. Speaking of which." He nodded to where Jattin Straye hurried toward them from the council building.

"Rori," her grandfather called.

She barely made it to her feet with Keyen's help when her grandfather reached her, wrapping her in a big hug that lifted her off the ground.

"My little girl."

"I'm fine." She hugged him back, answering before he could ask the question.

He held her at arm's length. "When you walked out there, I swear you scared ten years off my old life." Love softened the sternness in his voice.

"Just doing what you'd have done."

"Yes, well, next time do it from a safer spot. Boy," he

turned his attention to Keyen, "you're going to have to do a better job taking care of her if I'm to let you marry her."

"I did the best I could," Keyen defended himself, a grin came to his face as his arm found its way around Rori's waist, drawing her near him. She took pleasure from Keyen's nearness as, suddenly, she felt very tired.

"What are you doing here?" she asked her grandfather.

"I headed here as soon as Hiymm told me you were taken and got finagled into giving a hand, which I better start doing, though now it looks like it's mostly clean up now. The last of the attackers seemed to have given up or slunk away." He gave her one more hug before hurrying off.

Rori looked around again, this time taking in the fact that her grandfather was right. Most of Creed's forces had fallen. There were only a handful left, and they were placidly being rounded up by the security force from the council building.

Rori, Keyen and their team and were joined by Orn's team.

"That was quite a move," Orn commented as he drew near.

"I don't know if we'll add it to regular defense training, but it worked," Keyen said, not bothering to release his hold on Rori.

"That it did. But I'd suggest you don't try that again, or if you do, give us some warning." Orn shook his head in amazement. "Anyway, I'd guess after the night you've had, your team could use a good meal and some rest."

"You can say that again," Bass spoke up with a yawn to which Orn just grinned.

"Why don't you go? We'll stay around just in case, though I don't expect problems. The fight has pretty much gone out of them."

Rori was relieved when Keyen agreed to the offer. Now that her adrenaline had burned out, exhaustion filled her body, and she realized she was starving, not having eaten since the restaurant on the beach the day before.

There was a lot of handshaking and backslaps as the other team split off.

"Are we ready to go run the gauntlet?" Keyen asked the group.

"What?" Rori raised her head from his shoulder, not realizing she'd even rested it there.

Keyen tilted his head to the side and Rori saw the mass of reporters that filled the area between them and their sled.

"How'd they get here so fast?" She couldn't believe the sight.

"They were here all along," Cassie answered.

"Just hiding back and waiting for the fireworks to end," Bass picked up for his sister. "I'd say we gave them a pretty good show." He yawned again. "I'm all for getting this over with."

"I don't think we're going to get out of here very easy," Ultin spoke up.

"At least, some of us won't," Tankin added.

Rori became aware of the gazes locked on her. "What? Because of what I did?"

"You could say that." Ultin broke into a big smile. "But I'd say it's more what you said."

"What?" Rori looked to each face for answers, but they all just grinned back at her. She shifted her gaze up to Keyen. "What?" she asked again.

He actually chuckled softly and leaned down and brushed his lips over hers. "You announced to the world we were in love."

"I did...n't." She broke off when Keyen arched an eyebrow, and she remembered what she'd said to Creed. "But, surely they couldn't have heard that."

"Oh, I'm sure they got every word." Sansa smiled almost sympathetically, but there was too much mirth behind it.

"But…," Rori couldn't get any more out. She shifted her gaze around the team and back up to Keyen.

"You two may be bigger news than the attack on the council." Ultin laughed.

"What, why?" They were walking away before Rori got the words out. She stared at their backs a minute before looking again to Keyen for help.

He shrugged. "It's a big deal when two Guardians get married," he said casually.

"There have never been two Guardians get married before." Rori felt overwhelmed and wasn't sure how to handle it. "And I never said…"

"So, we'll be the first." He kissed her, wrapping her tight to him. "Like I said, a big deal."

"But," she paused, "are you proposing to me?"

"Yes. Are you saying yes?"

Warmth and love flowed over her as did his gaze over her face. "Yes." This time, she stretched up to kiss him. They parted to hoots and whistling from the team.

"You know, they probably got all that, too," Ultin called back.

As to prove that, a volley of shouts reached them. "Commander Saegun, Keyen, Aurora Straye. Are you really engaged? Are you getting married? When's the wedding?" The crowd called for their attention.

Keyen laughed and tightened his hold on her. "You know, you declared you love me to the world. Do you think you'd mind telling me again? I kind of like hearing it."

"I love you, with all my heart," she whispered, letting her talent carry it over him while repeating the words in his mind.

"I love you," echoed back to her as he sealed it with a kiss.

About the Author

I grew up in a small town in Wyoming loving the outdoors, sports, art, and reading Hardy Boys books. After reading them all at least a half dozen times, I started writing my own stories.

Thirty years ago I married a wonderful, honorable man. I'm mother of five children and grandmother of six boys. I love traveling. Through my husband's work and vacations, I have visited much of the United States, all over Eastern Europe, Canada, Mexico, China, Thailand, Cambodia and Australia, giving me many intriguing locations and experiences for my stories.

I am a storyteller. I write the classic hero story because I think there's a need for more heroes, love, and adventure in our lives. I'm not out to change the world with my writing; I'm just hoping to make your day a little better.

Hope you enjoy.
Alysia S. Knight

Please feel free to visit me through my website:

WWW.ALYSIASKNIGHT.COM

www.ingramcontent.com/pod-product-compliance
Lightning Source LLC
Chambersburg PA
CBHW031724170626
46808CB00005B/1878